J.P. CHOQUETTE

Let the Dead Rest

scared E cat

First published by Scared E Cat Books 2018

This novel is entirely a work of fiction. The names, characters and incidents portrayed in it are the work of the author's imagination. Any resemblance to actual persons, living or dead, events or localities is entirely coincidental.

First edition

ISBN: 978-1-950976-08-9

This book was professionally typeset on Reedsy. Find out more at reedsy.com

For Jess: I'll always be the peas to your carrots.

Acknowledgement

A writer is nothing without readers. I'm very grateful to my dedicated troupe of early birds: Erin Chagnon, Pam Irish, Ann Kalinoski, and Angela Lavery. Thank you for your insights, feedback, and enthusiasm. And for catching all those little, weird things that I missed.

Thanks too, to my developmental editor, Kendra Olson, whose insights helped me not only tighten the plot but put more thought into the "why" of just about everything. Thanks to editor, Elizabeth "Shay" VanZwoll. I appreciate all the hard work you put into this book. I take responsibility for any leftover typos.

And of course, thank YOU, dear reader, for your interest in my work. I hope you'll enjoy this story and that it will be a deliciously creepy journey.

As always, my deepest gratitude to Serge for being my stabilizing rock, and to Pascal, who makes me see things in an entirely different light. I love you both more than you can imagine.

~Dios Amore~

Chapter One

Present Day, Bakersfield, Vermont
Isabel Joven

T he doorbell pealed, a tumbling chime of notes that finished several long minutes before I opened the heavy old door. A small box lay on the mat, covered in brown paper. It was addressed to me in beautiful cursive. There was no return address. I looked up to wave at the delivery driver, to thank him for his trip up the treacherous drive, but his truck was already gone.

Cold air tangled in my hair and twined around my ankles. Shadows of the leaves overhead danced across the surface of the package. The box was about twelve inches long and half as wide. I turned it over in my hands, but there were no other markings on it. I went back inside and closed the door before Sampson escaped.

I carried the box to the kitchen counter. The wide pine boards were warm under my bare feet and sunlight fell in slanted beams across the old room. With scissors, I cut away the paper and then slit the tape that held the cardboard box closed. The paper fell away. Inside the box lay a note, in the same beautiful cursive, on top of a mound of packing peanuts.

"To Isabel."

Odd.

I didn't recognize the handwriting and there was no other information on the creamy note card, not even on the back indicating where it had come from. I rummaged through the white peanuts and pulled the packing paper away. Beneath it lay a small bundle, about ten inches long. The plastic bubbles were soft against my fingers, but whatever was underneath was dense. With a final flourish, the bubble wrap revealed a small, gray-looking doll. An antique, she had to be. Her face and hands were porcelain—or maybe china—and webbed with capillary-type cracks. The body was soft cloth; a peek under her skirt told me. Her eyes were blue, or had once been and had since faded to a sort of stormy gray. The whites were also tinged yellowish and her hair was the color of dishwater. Her dress was an old calico print, simple with no embroidery or beading. She wasn't beautiful in the traditional sense, but something about her spoke to me. When I reached a finger into the paper she was nestled in and ran it along the side of her face, something shifted inside of me. A sort of shiver of happiness.

But where had she come from? I set the doll to the side and dumped out the rest of the packing peanuts, even ran my hands along all the interior flaps of the box, but there was nothing else. No other note, no tags that had fallen off, no other explanation.

I carried her into my studio, her body stiff and heavy in my hands. I'd been here at the high worktable before the doorbell had interrupted. Lots of big windows let in daylight, not only along the wall but also from the skylights tucked in the high ceiling above. Here, I created art dolls that were

2

sold around the country and the world. The right light was essential to my work. In the studio, the doll looked smaller, more diminutive somehow, but more ethereal, too. I placed her on the worktable next to me.

"Where did you come from?" I asked her. But she only looked back at me blankly. A bank of clouds passed over the sun, and all the golden light faded then. I shivered and glanced out the window. Dry leaves blew together in an unseen breeze and branches overhead shook. I left the doll where she lay and went to find slippers and a sweater. I was curious about the gift, but I was also on a deadline. The work for the upcoming exhibit was non-negotiable. Many professional artists spent their whole lives dreaming of a solo exhibit at the Metropolitan Museum of Art. I couldn't let anything distract me, with my own solo show only weeks away.

The dolls I made from clay, wood, and fabric-lined the shelves in the studio. Most of these were under eighteen inches in height, made from a variety of materials. A journalist had once referred to my dolls as "eerily fantastical," and I think it was the best description they'd ever received. They were more sculpture than doll, and many were based on folklore and literature from hundreds of years ago. There were dolls depicting the saints and sinners in Dante's *Inferno,* while others memorialized characters in tragic English literature, like Kafka's Grete Samsa in *The Metamorphosis.* Some were just creatures or characters that came to me in dreams or poked at my subconscious while I wandered in the woods on one of my daily walks. I never lacked ideas, only hours in which to produce all the dolls that lived in my head. The dolls in the studio were creations that were between shows or awaiting collectors. In the art world, there are few things

3

more exhilarating than finding a patron of your work.

On the table before me lay a large block of clay wrapped in plastic and a Mason jar packed with carving tools. The wall above the worktable was a kaleidoscope of color, texture, and inspiration. Packed with scraps of fabric, sketches of dark, shadowy creatures, Gothic-inspired memorabilia, and bits of fern, bark, and other minutia collected on my walks, the bulletin board was like a projector view of my mind. Interspersed with this melee were framed copies of certifications and awards I'd won over the years. "Isabel Joven, National Institute of American Doll Artists, Master Instructor," and "Gold Winner for the 2015 Professional Doll Makers Art Guild," along with others dotted the wall.

I had just started to form the basics of the face—the nose, the brow, and the chin—when the phone rang. The trill was jolting in the quiet and I nearly jumped. I'd let the answering machine get it. But then, it could be my agent, Helen.

I crossed the studio in three steps and grabbed the cordless phone from the small table near the doorway.

"Hello?"

"It's me," my brother said, not bothering with a greeting. He never did.

"Oh, hey," I said and pinched the bridge of my nose. "I just have a minute. I'm in the studio—"

"Yeah, that's fine." He sounded distracted. "I'll get right to the point. Look, Isa, I know that you have your heart set on staying at the house. But I've been in touch with a realtor in St. Albans and he thinks that now is a great time to put it on the market. In fact, he has a family moving from out of state and they're interested in something just like the farmhouse. Isn't that great? They want land and something with history."

He cleared his throat. "I have his number. You can call—"

"No," I said, surprised at just how forceful my voice was. "I'm not calling a realtor. And I'm not moving. Nigel, we've had this conversation a dozen times, and every time it's like it doesn't sink in. I'm. Not. Moving. Please, just stop. This is my home—"

"It was our home, Isa. Do you really think that Mom and Dad wanted this for you? Living out in the boondocks on your own, like a hermit? When's the last time you went to town? Had any contact with another human being?" He stopped for a moment. I could nearly hear him telling himself to breathe.

"Look," he said finally, his voice quieter. "It wouldn't hurt to just call the realtor. Let him take a look at the place. I'm going to be up that way again in a week or so. The attorney's got a little more paperwork for me to sign. If it's something you want to proceed with—"

I started to tell him it wasn't, but he plowed on, made his voice a little louder. "If it's something that you want to proceed with, then we'll meet with him while I'm there. Just think about it, okay?"

I grunted in response, the hand that pinched the bridge of my nose sliding down to cover my face. "Fine," I said, moving my hand away. "I'll call him. But I'm not moving, so this is just going to be a waste of his time."

"Sounds good," Nigel said, ignoring the part of the conversation he didn't like. "Let me give you his name and number."

I pulled a felt-tip pen from my pocket and wrote the information down on my hand.

For several long minutes, after I hung up, I stood at the worktable. First, I felt anger—hot and raw—in my chest. How dare he pull this with me? But that morphed into something more familiar. Fear. The fact was that Nigel was the executor of our parents' will. And while my original intent had been to use my half of the inheritance to keep the house, medical bills and estate fees had eaten up most of what we'd been left with. Nigel saw selling the house as the opportunity to get something—anything—from my parents' estate. Whereas I saw the farmhouse as home, he saw it only as a financial burden. But it was the only place I'd truly ever felt safe.

I shook myself mentally. I had to focus right now on the show. Maybe it would be the turning point in my career that I'd been waiting for such a long time. Feeling eyes on me, I turned. I expected to see the lumbering, feline frame of Sampson, but nothing was there. Goosebumps popped up on my arms and I pulled my sweater tighter.

As I moved to extract a carving tool from the big Mason jar on the shelf at the back of the worktable, I saw the antique doll. Her gray eyes studied me, her mouth a dull, pink smile. I reached up and ran a hand over her dress, smoothing it down. Feeling more peaceful and centered, I went to work on the ball of clay in front of me.

Chapter Two

I stood on the train platform, my heartbeat tap dancing in my wrists. The big clock above said that the train was a minute behind schedule. *Please, please hurry.* A thin line of sweat dampened my forehead where hat met skin. He was almost here. I'd tried counting it out while lying in bed last night—how many days Will had been gone—but sleep had pulled me under before I'd finished. It felt like a million; like an eternity.

I peered down the track again and then stepped back. It wasn't ladylike, my mother's voice reminded me in my mind. There was a crowd on the platform—men and women, a few children darting in and out like honeybees. Thinking of my mother reminded me of Will's, who'd died during childbirth. Even though my four younger siblings were too much sometimes—too much chaos and noise, too much work—I couldn't imagine growing up like Will.

"Wasn't it lonely?" I'd asked him once when we were enjoying a picnic near the river. "Didn't you miss having brothers and sisters?"

7

He'd laughed, chucking me under the chin. "You can't miss what you don't know, Etta."

"I think I want two children," I'd said without thinking, then blushed.

"Two is a good number," Will had said. "A boy and a girl, maybe? Or two girls, as pretty as you."

The train whistled now, and I jumped, startled.

"Here it comes," a man further down the platform shouted.

Time slowed then and everything around me—the smell of fresh loaves of bread from the nearby bakery, the coolness of the air, the warmth of the sun on my cheeks—fell away. Will had come home.

* * *

"Two years, four months, and twenty-two days," I said, sitting across from him at the table of the cozy Italian restaurant.

"What's that?" Will asked, squeezing my fingers. He sipped the last of the red wine in his glass, and his dark eyes shone in the candlelight.

"That's how long you've been away. It feels like a lifetime."

"Heck, that is a long time, isn't it?" He drained the last of the wine and refilled his glass, then tipped the bottle toward mine. I shook my head and covered it. Already my head felt slightly thick and fuzzy.

"It's strange," Will said. "A lifetime, but in some ways, it feels like everything that happened over there was just a bad dream. Like you feel when you come out of a picture show, you know? And you can't quite get your head back into the real world." He looked around the room.

"Was it awful?" I knew I shouldn't pry, but my curiosity was greater than any sense of decorum.

"Yeah," he said, looking back at me. "Yeah, it was."

I waited for him to say more, but he didn't. He just squeezed my fingers again and took out a packet of cigarettes. He offered me one first, which I accepted. We sat at the table drinking each other in between the light haze of smoke that swirled. He looked so much the same, yet in some ways so much different. There were lines around his eyes that hadn't been there before. And then, of course, there was his leg…. The cane rested on the corner of the table, an unspoken reminder that no matter how hard we tried, nothing would ever really be quite the same again.

After dinner, we walked around the city at a slow pace. Will's right leg gave him a somewhat jerky gait, his cane tapping with every step. My arm was linked through his though, and we talked not about the time he was away, but the time ahead.

"Let's get married in the autumn," he said abruptly, stopping under a blossoming tree on the corner. The petals were lit from behind by the moonlight and the tree appeared to be glowing around its edges. "Once I've had a chance to find work…get myself established. You'll need time to make your dress and invite your family. I don't have many to invite." We started walking again.

I nodded and snuggled closer to his arm, my chest filled with warm light. I was surprised that I wasn't glowing like the streetlamps above.

"I've been saving money from the mill," I said. "And I'd like to keep working. Just till the children come along."

Will stopped abruptly. I glanced over, surprised to see his eyebrows pulled down tightly in a frown.

"We've talked about this before and I haven't changed my

mind. I can provide for my family, the same as your father provided for yours."

I sighed, the little bubble of happiness leaking just a bit.

"I know how you feel about it. But work—even though it's not glamorous—makes me feel like I have a purpose, you know? Besides, like you said, it will just be until you get established. Not forever." I tugged on his arm and he reluctantly started walking again. True, my job was dirty and monotonous, but it was satisfying to get my paycheck every week. I felt industrious and useful. And it was nice to have Lily, the closest friend I'd ever had, to commiserate with. Once I was a housewife and mother, would I lose her friendship? I pushed the thought away.

"Once we've enjoyed married life for a while"—I pinched his arm and batted my eyes at him with a wide smile. He smiled back slowly in response—"and decide to start our little family, I'll have all I can do to wait on you and roll myself around with my big, pregnant belly." I laughed, but Will didn't join me.

"It'll all work out," I said. "You'll see." But inside, I felt a little tendril of dread. Would Mama be all right without another set of hands? And what about the half of my paycheck that I gave her now? She'd told me over and over again that I should keep all the money, but of course, I couldn't. Perhaps if Will's father was less of a miser...but what was the good of wishing that?

"No son of mine is going to squander what I've worked so hard to build," Will had said once in an uncanny impersonation. "You've got to make your own way in this world, kid."

"Small wonder some lucky woman hasn't snatched him up," I'd joked, but Will's face had gone dark. Though he was a joker, and some would say a dreamer, there was a darkness to Will, too. We all had our dark sides though, didn't we? Once we were married and had our own place, Will wouldn't have to deal with his father so much, anyway.

"I wish I had more," he said. "The Army wants you to sacrifice your life and pays you fifty dollars a month to do it." The frown was back.

I squeezed his arm and smiled at him.

"I don't care about the money," I said. "Better to be poor and happy than wealthy and miserable. Besides, we don't need a big place to start. I'll be happy to have more than one room and, most of all, that we're together."

"I know," he said. "I just want to prove to my old man that he's not the only one who can be a success. Show the old bastard that I've got a mind for business, too. I've got so many ideas, you know? There are so many possibilities out there. I just wish…." He sighed and ran a hand through his hair, then tugged on it. Thinking about his father seemed to open some hole inside of him and sucked out everything else.

"I'm sorry, Etta. I'm spoiling the night, aren't I? Forget about my father. And forget everything else. In fact, that's enough talking, don't you think, Miss Hayes?" Will asked and pulled me under a large oak tree with drooping branches. His breath was warm on my face, and then my neck, his lips caressing softly.

"Oh, Will," I said when our lips finally broke apart. "I've missed you so much."

* * *

Later, we lay under blankets in the back of his rusted Chevy. Lily would laugh at the speed of our "knowing" each other.

I turned and propped myself on an elbow. Will was looking out the window at the bright pinpricks of stars in the sky. He turned and exhaled loudly. His face had looked dark and shadowed, but when he looked at me, the shadows were gone. He was his same self again, handsome and sweet.

"Etta," he said, a smile turning up one corner of his mouth.

I smiled back.

"I have something for you."

"You do?" I asked. I tried to keep my voice neutral. There was no money for a ring right now. I'd told him over and over that, it didn't matter, that we should continue to save the money we were making for the future. We would want a house for the kids. To have a real lawn to mow, and space to hold backyard barbecues with the neighbors, wouldn't we? A ring was a luxury—unnecessary. So then why did my heart hammer so hard in my chest? Why had my fingers begun to shake?

I sat up, pulled my dress quickly back over my head, and smoothed the skirt. He eyed me, his lips twisting into that half-smile that made my stomach drop. He tossed both of our cigarettes out of the window and left it cracked so that more of the fresh night air washed into the car. I breathed deeply.

"Hold out your hands and close your eyes," Will said. I heard him rummaging around in the front. There was a rustling of paper, then a grunt as he strained to reach something. He swore softly under his breath, then settled back beside me. I couldn't keep the smile from my lips. My hands were cupped, prepared for the small box that would nestle perfectly there. Perhaps his father had come around, after all, giving him the ring that had been his mother's. A fluttering hope tickled my belly. But instead, I felt the outline of a larger package—heavy, with scratchy paper.

"All right," Will said. "Open your eyes."

I opened them. A rectangular box, wrapped in brown paper and tied with red and white string sat in my hands. A cold wash of disappointment drenched me, but I smiled brightly.

"Should I open it now?"

"Sure," Will said. "Just know something before you do. This gift is special, Etta." His face was serious. "Go ahead," he said, "open it."

Carefully, I slipped the string from the box and removed the paper. The box inside was familiar, and as I looked more closely in the moonlight, I saw that it was a cracker box. I glanced at Will.

"It gets better," he said with a chuckle.

I opened the box. Will had cut down the length of one side so that it opened like a small treasure chest or coffin. I cracked open the lid and stared. Inside was a doll—a blonde-haired, china-or-porcelain doll, about ten inches tall. She wore a simple, calico dress and her face, pale in the moonlight, smiled up at me. Her mouth was a sly bow and her eyes were blue. Something about her face was fox-like. She was strangely heavy for her small size, and her body was soft in my hands.

I smiled and tried to hide the disappointment that had crept its way up the back of my throat.

"Thank you," I said, and smoothed a hand over the dress. "She's lovely."

"She's more than that," Will said, and I glanced at him. He watched me, dark shadows hiding his eyes.

"She is?" I asked. "Why?"

"Trust me," Will said. "This doll is going to be an important part of our future."

I smiled and hoped it looked authentic. "Where did she come from?"

"I brought her back with me from overseas. I thought of you when I saw her. And about the little Etta we'll have someday."

I nodded but didn't trust myself to speak without crying. Why had he given me this? Even as a child, I'd never been fond of dolls. Their staring, dead eyes. Their frozen faces and stiff hands. My head had started to pound. The wine we'd sipped earlier had made my stomach sour.

"I want you to promise me that you'll keep her safe, Etta."

I glanced up at him, surprised by the tone in his voice.

"Of course," I said, and patted the doll in what I hoped looked like a nurturing manner. "Of course I will."

"Good." Will smiled that crooked half-smile again and ran a finger down my neck and over my collarbone. My heartbeat quickened, and my breath caught in my chest.

"Thank you," I said, and placed a hand on his cheek. "She's beautiful."

Chapter Three

Present Day

"Marianne, do you know anything about this?" I held the vintage doll out toward her. After she took it, I tugged the sleeves down on my sweater without thinking. I did it so often I wasn't even aware I was doing it most of the time. Under the hem of the sweater's sleeves, my skin sported large, reddened patches. Marianne caught my eye and smiled. In all the time I'd known her, she'd never said anything about my skin. I was grateful for it.

We were sitting at the kitchen table; she, on a rare occurrence, was home in the afternoon because she'd forgotten her cell phone. We'd just finished lunch, a quick meal of reheated soup, and some of the fresh bread she'd picked up at the local bakery. Marianne wiped her hands on the cloth napkin spread over her lap and held them out to take the doll.

"I don't. She's heavy, though, isn't she? For such a small thing. Old too, by the looks of her."

"You didn't give her to me?" I asked, and watched her inspect the doll.

Her smile remained perfectly intact and she shook her head.

"No offense, but she's not very cute," she said in a conspira-

15

torial whisper.

I smiled.

"You don't know where it came from?" she asked.

"No. She arrived this morning on the front step in a box with no return address. There was a note...I think it's in the studio. It just said, 'To Isabel.' You're sure you didn't get her for me, as a surprise?"

Marianne laughed and handed the doll back to me. "If I were going to surprise you with a gift, I'd choose something much prettier. Maybe your brother sent her. Or an art friend?"

I frowned. I couldn't remember the last time Nigel had sent me anything from sunny California, and I doubted that any of my "art friends" as Marianne liked to call them—just acquaintances, really—would do so, either.

I hated research. And because I wasn't tech-savvy, I chose not to have the internet at the house. Satellite internet rates were steep, anyway. My sales rep, agent, and web guru all knew to just call me directly with questions. When I needed to, I went to use one of the computers in the library. Right now, though, that didn't seem a very good use of my time. Still, I was curious about the doll.

"You don't happen to have any contacts who might know anything about old dolls?" I asked Marianne. She was a human Rolodex. Whether someone was looking for an acupuncturist or a book recommendation, she could help them find the perfect match.

"Hmm?" She pushed her mug away and stretched her arms over her head. "Let me think about it for a bit."

We sat in companionable silence. She broke it finally by snapping her fingers. "Oh, I know!" She retrieved a scrap of paper and pen from the desk in the corner. "You should get in touch with Partridge Lee. She's a fixture at the Fairfield Historical Society. She's been there as long as I can remember. And if memory serves me correctly—and it may not at this point"—she laughed—"I think her passion is old toys. She'd probably love to learn more about the doll. In fact, she might be able to track down where she was made."

"That'd be wonderful," I said. "Her name is Partridge? Like the bird?"

"Well, it's a nickname. Her real name is Patricia, but don't make the mistake of calling her that," Marianne said. "I think the place is only open a couple half-days a week, but if you call, it should give you the hours. Partridge spends a lot of time there, even if the place isn't officially open. Chances are good you could get in to see her this week sometime."

I thanked Marianne. Inside, though, my stomach tightened. Even after all these years, it was hard for me to meet new people, to endure the curious looks and sidelong glances. But I'd have to meet her eventually if I wanted to find out more about the doll.

"It would probably be easier if I brought the doll to her?"

"Probably." Marianne smiled. "I love having a reason to get you out of that house, and socializing."

I laughed. My sixty-four-year-old roommate was forever trying to get me to go out. Nigel would be impressed. Eventually, talk turned to the exhibit at the Met.

"I was able to find someone to cover my hospital shift, so I'll be flying to New York for the opening," she said. "Or I could go earlier if you need help transporting things or taking care of anything during that week. Isabel Joven's personal assistant." She winked at me. I smiled and felt heat creep up my neck and into my cheeks. It was still hard to get used to having someone do things for me, rather than the other way around. Agreeing to have Marianne as my roommate in the rambling old farmhouse had been a smart decision. She was part mother hen, part older sister.

"It will be expensive—the plane and the hotel. Are you sure you want to come?" I asked.

She brushed my objections away like flies and I felt my shoulders lower slightly in relief. The show, while exciting, also terrified me. Every time I thought of it—of the actual event—my hands started to tremble and I felt nauseous. All those people—strangers—looking at me, at my work. Inspecting both with a critical eye. It would feel good to have a friend in my corner, but it wouldn't cancel out all the discomfort.

"Of course I'll go. I wouldn't miss it for anything," Marianne said and began to clear the dishes. Before she left, she wrote down the address and phone number for the historical society, which I tucked into my pocket.

* * *

I waited until three o'clock to drive to Fairfield. I'd called the historical society and gotten the hours. It was too early to quit work in the studio for the day. I'd finish up when I returned. My shoulders and back were tight, and my mind swarmed with niggling worries about the exhibit. And Nigel. It wasn't a good place to create from.

The car bounced over the potholes and dips in the long driveway. At the end, the mailbox leaned precariously to the left. A small thatch of overgrown grass grew up around it, a testament to the fact that it hadn't been trimmed rigorously enough. I cracked my window open, letting the cool, fresh air fill the car. Leaves swirled and tumbled around the car, and a fine mist had begun to fall. I had read somewhere that windy weather means a change in temperature is coming. Unlike many people who craved the summer sun, I preferred the cooler weather. Hopefully, the wind would blow in chillier air, not hotter. It was easier to cover my skin when the weather grew colder, too, and hide it against unwanted looks. I tugged my jacket sleeves down further over the backs of my hands. The patches were more vivid in the outdoor light.

I took back roads from my house to Fairfield; the car crunched over gravel and dirt surfaces. The trees above provided an arbor over the road and in some places the boughs dipped so that I expected them to hit my car, but none did. I slowed down at curves, careful not to take up more than my side of the narrow road.

The town of Fairfield was small, with only a bakery, gas station, post office, and a couple of other businesses lining its main street. An elementary school stood near the four-way stop and children ran and screamed, playing on the brightly colored playground equipment. A girl with dark hair stood alone by a tree, her hair tangled in the wind under an ugly beige hat. A memory suddenly surfaced. First grade. I'd been so proud and excited, standing in my new dress on the playground. I'd looked around me: other girls talked in little groups or ran, squealing to the swing set. Finally, three pretty girls approached, their arms linked. I turned toward them from studying my shoes, hope no doubt was evident on my face.

"What's wrong with your skin?" the prettiest one in the middle had asked. She'd wrinkled her perfect button nose as if she'd smelled something stinky. "Are you catching?" The blonde girl on her left with thick braids had laughed at this and then all three had turned and ran off. Their giggles followed me all the way under the slide, where I hid until the whistle was blown.

"No one played with me, Mommy," I'd cried that afternoon. "They thought I was ugly because of my skin." My mother's arms had been strong around me and she'd run a hand over my head, murmuring, "Shh," but I couldn't stop. My heart had snapped in two.

I shook myself mentally, readjusted my hands on the steering wheel. I saw the doll from the corner of my eye and glanced over. It was a relief to push the memories away, to focus on something tangible. She lay flat on her back on a soft scrap of flannel that had been in the studio. Who had owned her? Had she been well-loved by a little girl, or put high up on a shelf to look at, but not touch? Her pale skin and gray eyes were almost translucent in the bright daylight. A beam of sunlight fell across her and I felt a warmth in my chest. It was strange—I'd barely had the doll a day, but something about her made me feel happy. Content. Peaceful, even.

A few minutes later, I arrived at a white clapboard church. I pulled into the sparsely graveled driveway and found a sign on the door which told me that the historical society was located on the third floor. Inside the building, the air was cold and slightly musty. The stairs creaked and groaned under my feet. I smelled candle wax and the leftover fragrance of incense, making me think of Sunday masses when I was little, attended with my very Catholic grandmother. I'd loved the smell of the candles and watching the tiny votive lights glow and flicker. I was slightly terrified of the priest, though, who said most of the mass in Latin.

I reached the third floor. A sign on the door assured me that I was in the right place, and light from the room created a glow behind the frosted glass. I pushed my way through. A stooped woman stood behind a long table, covered in books, black and white photographs, and a card catalog in an army-green metal box. She turned when I came in, a smile perched on her bright, wrinkled face.

"Are you Ms. Lee?" I asked, suddenly realizing I didn't know if she was married or single.

"I am," she said, "but call me Partridge." Her voice was deep and gravely, a pack-a-day voice.

I smiled back. "My name is Isabel," I said. "My friend, Marianne Fletcher, said that you might be able to help me."

Her eyes, which had traced over my face and neck, returned to mine and her smile broadened. "Marianne," she said with obvious admiration. "How is that woman? I haven't seen her in ages."

"She's well," I said. "As busy as ever."

Partridge set down the book she'd been holding gently on the table. "And what about you? What do you do for a living?"

"I'm an artist," I said. This was met with a clicking sound from the old woman. "I make art dolls."

Her eyebrows rose but she only said, "And you make a living doing that?"

"I do," I replied. There were two common reactions to my career choice: disbelief or envy.

"Back in my day, women had one of two jobs," said Partridge, as though reading my thoughts. "Motherhood or sisterhood. But I guess that's one of the ways the world's changed. For the good, really. I certainly never wanted to be a nun. And motherhood?" She made a noise with her throat that could have been a laugh or a strangled cough. "Well, I do love my kids. But sometimes they tend to smother, you know?"

She shook her head, "But you didn't come here to listen to me ramble. You're looking for some information. On your family history?"

I shook my head. "No, I received a doll yesterday"—I nodded to the bundle tucked under my arm—"and wanted to find out more about it. Marianne said that you did this type of research. I'm happy to pay you," I hurried on, "I just want to find out more about where it came from. I'm not much of a history buff myself."

"Sounds like an interesting project," she said. "And I do love vintage toys. I'll be busy here for the next several hours, but if you don't mind leaving it with me, I can do some research and get back to you with anything I find."

The flannel blanket suddenly felt slippery in my hands. I didn't want to let it go. Some protective instinct told me to hold tight to the doll, not to let it out of my sight. But that was ridiculous. What was the harm in Partridge keeping the doll for a while?

"Of course," I said. "How long do you think you'll need to keep her?"

She smiled. "Well now, let's see. I'll measure it and do a brief inspection, try to find the maker's mark—it's not always where you might think it would be—and start a little file on her. Shouldn't take more than a day. Two at the most."

"Thank you so much," I said. "I really appreciate your help. And please keep track of your hours and I'll send you a check."

Partridge nodded. "If it were family you were looking for, that'd be free, you understand? But since this is a little outside of my normal research parameters, I wouldn't say no to a small stipend. My social security check doesn't go as far as you'd imagine."

Chapter Four

1944

"Claudette Elizabeth Hayes, I will not call you again." My mother's voice echoed up the staircase along with other familiar sounds—voices murmured, china clinked, and chairs scraped across the dining room floor.

"One day you'll miss all of this," I told my reflection over my dressing table. It seemed impossible. What I longed for was to board a bus or a train, one that was empty, where I could think thoughts in quiet and where I wouldn't have to do anything. I longed to go somewhere, anywhere other than the factory. Mostly, I longed to be with Will.

I smoothed my hands over my hair after inserting the last pin. They smelled of wool. The scent had soaked into my pores and the crevices of my fingers. No matter how hard I scrubbed, it remained. The din from the kitchen had risen another octave. I snatched my handbag and a jacket from the hook and closed the door behind me. A variety of familiar smells assaulted me on the steep staircase: the scent of fried bacon, rotting vegetables—someone had left a bucket of peelings in the hallway—and blessedly, of coffee. I pushed the door open and saw the same scene which greeted me every morning.

A long table lined with adults and children, where everyone gathered over steaming plates and inhaled their breakfast.

"Sorry, Mama," I said, putting a hand on my mother's back as she strode past. She held a plate piled with Johnnycakes. "Should I get out the apples?"

She grunted in response and bent to add the towering plate of food to the table. Jimmy, my second-to-youngest brother, reached out with both hands. She slapped them away.

"Guests first. You know the rules." Jimmy looked about to cry until Mama put a hand on his shoulder and dropped a kiss on his head. He leaned against her and she gave him a quick squeeze, and then walked back toward the kitchen. I followed.

"There's no fruit left, except one apple I left out for your lunch," she said quietly once the door had swung shut. "We'll have to make do with what we've got until Friday."

The boarders' rent was due at the end of each week, so Friday had also morphed into Mama's market day. Our house, a large Victorian in downtown Winooski, had been beautiful and spacious before the war. Now, it was filled with a mixture of young working couples and older singles, most of whom worked either in one of the mills or factories in the area. My father would have turned in his grave to see what had become of our beautiful home. If that was, he even had a grave.

My mother had taken the news of his death as she had any of life's challenges: with a no-nonsense attitude. Not at first, though. First had come the shock, the reality that he would never again walk through the front door, never again toss my little brothers and sisters high, never again wrap his arms around my mother from behind, resting his chin on the top of her head.

I'd found her in their bedroom, curled on her side, one

overly hot afternoon, salty streaks on dry cheeks, her eyes staring at the far wall. The room had smelled of dust and heat, and her hand had curled so hard around the thin telegram that I couldn't make out the words at first. "On behalf of the Department of the Navy, it is my sad duty to inform you…." But she'd quickly rallied and figured out a way to keep me and my brothers and sisters in our family home. Even if that meant we shared it with a lot of strangers.

"Anything else I can help with?" I asked, snagging a piece of cold toast that was blackened on the edges and smearing it with jam. I glanced at the clock. I had two minutes if I were to make it to work on time. I sipped coffee and wished I had time to finish the cup.

Mama shook her head. "Is your lunch packed?"

"Not yet," I said, and reached for the tin box on the high shelf near the pantry.

My job was another thing that would have caused my father to roll in his grave. A traditionalist, Papa had been a good Protestant who believed in the importance of family and a wife who stayed home to tend children, not one who punched a time clock every day. I smiled. I'd felt so much excitement when I'd gotten the mill job. But being a "working woman," it turned out, had been more glamorous in my mind than in real life. The mill was hot and the machines that towered over us were loud and dangerous. The owner liked to employ girls younger than me even, as they could dart their hands and sometimes their whole bodies into the tightest places when needed. Since I'd been there, there had already been five accidents, one of them which left a little boy without his left arm.

I hurriedly put a lunch together—a slice of Spam between

26

two slices of bread, and the treasured last apple—kissed Mama, and grabbed my purse and jacket. I pushed through the kitchen door and nearly collided with Mrs. Gregor, the oldest resident in the current cycle of boarders.

"Good morning, Mrs. Gregor," I said dutifully. The door swung shut behind me, nearly hitting me in the rear end.

"That your dolly?" Mrs. Gregor said, pointing to the doll lying on the empty chair in the corner. She never bothered with a preamble.

"Yes, ma'am," I said.

"I told her it was," said Mary from the far side of the table. "I said it was yours, but she didn't believe me."

"Hush," I told Mary. "Is it in your way?" I asked Mrs. Gregor. "I can move—"

"Not in my way. Just wondered where it came from, that's all. Girl said it was yours." She jerked her head toward Mary, who was staring back indignantly at the old woman. "Plain little thing, isn't it?" She frowned toward the doll. It lay on its side and stared toward us. Resentment solidly pushed against my ribs.

"It was a gift," I said and moved toward the doll. Retrieving her, I sat her up on the sideboard on the far side of the room. She leaned against the stack of extra plates, her little, heavy body stiff. "And I think she's perfectly lovely," I lied.

Mrs. Gregor made a noise that I could only describe as a snort. It appeared that with age, Mrs. Gregor had let go of the constrictions of etiquette along with a girdle.

"Lovely, my foot," she mumbled, as she moved toward the hallway.

"Have a good day, Mrs. Gregor," I said as she retreated. The only reply was the quick, hard close of the door after she'd passed through it.

"I don't like her, either," Tommy said. I glanced down. He stood at my elbow but looked not toward the closed door, but the sideboard.

"Why ever not, Tommy?" I put a hand on his shoulder. Tommy was the third eldest and had apparently grown two inches in a month. He was nearly to my chin and had a nature that frustrated my mother and made life harder for himself. He'd saved frogs from certain death by the older children and even scooped up worms after the rain and found new homes for them in the garden. Once, he'd placed himself in front of the toy swords of the village bullies when they'd been tormenting a skinny stray cat. He'd come home with both eyes blackened, grinning because the cat had gotten away.

"She's not a nice doll. Looking at her makes my insides feel all twisted up. I don't mean it as an offense to Will, Etta," Tommy said, looking up at me again. His dark eyes were pleading. "I just don't like her." Tommy adored Will, and Will in turn treated him as he might have a younger brother. "Don't say anything to him, please."

"I won't say a word," I said. I dropped a kiss on his head and he glanced up at me in surprise. "That's because I love you," I said. "And this"—I pushed him toward the hallway"—is because you need to empty out the scraps before school."

Sally started to wail. Her three-year-old fist was raised over her head in frustration. She was the youngest and a fussy child, much to my mother's dismay. Every one of the rest of us, Mama insisted, had been congenial and easy to soothe. Not Sally. Maybe in some unconscious way she missed our father, though she'd known him for only a few months before he went overseas.

I moved to comfort her, but my mother appeared at my side and gave me my own small shove toward the door.

"Go, Claudette. You'll be late."

"See you this afternoon, Mama." But my mother was already distracted by the whining Sally and the boarders around the table.

Outside, the air smelled fresh and green. New leaves and grass and a hint of lilacs made the best perfume in the world. I breathed deeply. The sun was two fingers' width above the horizon now, and the air glowed slightly as the morning fog burned away. Down the short walk, through the gate, and unto the street, I walked, before I heard a voice call from down the street.

"Etta," I heard. "Wait up!"

I turned and smiled. Lily jogged to catch up with me, her tin pail banged against her hip, and she held her hat on with one hand.

"I thought you must have already left," I said after we'd fallen into step. "I'm a couple of minutes late."

"My mother made me feed the twins," Lily said and rolled her eyes. "You know how that goes."

I laughed and linked arms with her. Though we'd grown up in the same town, we'd met at the mill. Not so strange, as she lived blocks away and had attended St. Mary's—a private, Catholic school in Downtown Burlington. I'd gone to the public school right here in Winooski. Our shared place as eldest daughter and second mother to a brood of children—Lily's mother had nine—had made us into fast friends. We commiserated about work, too; both of us had planned our exit strategies for the past few months.

"Here," she said and flipped open a cigarette case. She

extracted two and handed one to me. The other she put between her lips. We paused on the corner and shielded the match with cupped hands. The taste and smell reminded me immediately of Will.

"So, how was it?" Lily asked, as though she'd read my thoughts. She had an unnerving sixth sense. She could always tell when I was leaving something she deemed important out of a story. And she had a knack for weaseling information out of me, even when I wanted to keep it for myself.

I blew out a stream of smoke and felt my shoulders relax.

"Why, Lily Dawson, a lady never tells." She pinched my arm then and I laughed and turned fast on the street corner, my skirt swinging. "I can't believe he's really home. It was so, just surreal. Seeing him, talking with him, it was—"

"I'll be he couldn't wait to see you." Lily took a drag on her cigarette. "In your birthday suit," she said and smiled hugely.

I slapped her lightly on the arm.

"What was it like?" she asked as we fell in step again. Traffic was loud this time of the morning. Maybe I could pretend I didn't hear the question.

"Etta. Earth to Etta, do you read me?"

My cheeks warmed and I couldn't keep the smile off my face.

"You did it. I knew you would. Oh, it's so romantic," Lily said and held her cigarette as though it were a microphone beneath her mouth. "Boy goes off to war and returns to his loving girlfriend. They make passionate love, and he tells her all the tragedy that he's seen while she clutches him lovingly to her breast." Lily fanned herself with her free hand. Her cigarette dropped ashes onto the pavement.

"Oh, all right." I laughed. "It was lovely and that's all that I'm going to say."

"That's all?" Lily said. "You must give me all the details, Miss Hayes, to use in my next story."

"Lily!" I hissed, but she just laughed.

"I'm joking," she said.

Lily would quiz me mercilessly for more details without redirection. But the night before had been special, precious to me. Plus, it felt like I was betraying Will by talking about it.

"What are you working on these days?" I asked. Normally when I attempted to move Lily on to another topic—particularly when we were discussing my love life—it would be futile. But I knew her as well as she knew me. Lily loved writing. I dreamed of picket fences and chubby babies with Will. Lily dreamed of becoming a famous female novelist…after she'd won a Pulitzer Prize for her hard-nosed journalism.

"It's something new," she said demurely and blew a stream of smoke up toward the sky. "A love story about a little feral girl found in the forest in the early 1800s, and the psychologist who takes her case."

"Oh. Isn't that a little odd? The age difference, I mean."

"Well, he isn't in the picture until she's older. You know, late teens or early 20s. She's found in the woods and then, tragically, ends up in the looney bin for several years until this handsome psychologist makes it his life's mission to help her."

"Ah," I said. "How do you come up with your ideas?"

Lily explained the intricacies of her writing process and inspiration as we finished our walk to the mill. Honestly, I wasn't listening well. My mind had returned to Will. His handsome face with the strong jaw, his dark hair, and the way it waved in the back, his delicious, woodsy smell. And the warmth of his skin…

We stubbed out our cigarettes by the sidewalk in front of the Winooski Woolen Mill and walked up the short drive. It was a huge brick building that butted up against the Winooski River. Today, the river was a torrent of dark, churning water. Ice from the winter had fully melted and the edges of the riverbank were plump and swollen.

We walked into the building and were immediately met with the smell of lanolin, the oil that sheep naturally produce. It lay thick in the air. Huge machines clanked and whirred, and the pounding of hundreds of footsteps sounded on the creaking wooden floors. We stowed our jackets, handbags, hats, and lunchboxes, and punched in on the big time clock.

Chapter Five

Present Day

I felt the warm and furry body of a cat pressed against my face, followed by a fish-scented lick to my nose. I groaned and burrowed deeper into my duvet. Sampson was not to be ignored, however. Sunlight poked its fingers above the curtains. The air under the blankets was warm and lulling, though. Maybe he'd go away, figure out the can opener himself. But no, his big paws kneaded my shoulder, his meows growing more plaintive.

I'd slept badly, tossing and turning with fragments of dreams still winding their way through my mind. The doll was in them, but then later a little girl who looked like the doll, and she was running, the hem of her white dress muddied. There had been something else, something in the shadows that I couldn't quite see...

Sampson meowed again, plaintively and I emerged from the cocoon of tangled sheets and blankets and pulled on my robe and slippers. The room was chilly and looked much as it had before I'd collapsed into bed last night: a pile of clothes strewn over the wide oak floorboards, a half-full glass of water on the nightstand, a pile of toppled books in a pile by the door. I groaned. Sampson purred loudly in response and butted me with his head.

"I'm going," I said and stumbled downstairs to the kitchen. I filled the cat's bowl with wet food. He purred around my ankles incessantly until the bowl was set on the floor. I rinsed the can out in the kitchen sink and saw the trees. The sky was lit from the mid-morning sun and it made all the colorful leaves glow. Amber, deep crimson, and vibrant orange leaves shimmied and shook on the dark branches. I stared for several minutes, mesmerized. Eventually, I started the coffee pot, leaned on the counter, and tried to untangle the knots in my brain. It was useless though until I'd had my first cup.

I pulled on my paint-stained overalls after breakfast and worked in the studio. The phone ringing finally interrupted me at just after two o'clock.

"Hello?"

"Hello, is this Ms. Joven?" The voice on the other end of the line was unfamiliar, hesitant, and female.

"Yes," I said simply, half-ready to hang up if it was a telemarketer.

"I'm Kim Everett. My mom is Patricia Lee…Partridge?"

"Oh yes, hello."

"Hi. I just wanted to tell you that there has been an accident. She asked me to call you and tell you that—she said you'd know what this means—that your doll is okay but that it will be a while before she's able to find out more about it."

"Oh no," I said. "I'm sorry to hear that."

The other woman sighed through her nose and I pictured her pinching the bridge of it between her fingers.

"Thanks. I've told her a million times that she needs to get the Trustees to do something about moving the historical society office to a better location. She said that there's no money, but I knew something like this would happen. She fell down the stairs and broke her wrist, bruised a few ribs."

"She got hurt at the historical society?" I asked.

"Yes. She's there all the time and, well, you know those upper stairs are a rattletrap. She's at Northwest Medical Center now. They're keeping her overnight because of her age…but don't tell her I said that. She refused to go to the rehab place, so I'm going to look into a visiting nurse for her at home. Anyway, she wanted me to pass the message on to you about your doll. It must be old?" She continued without waiting for a response, "She said that if you're in a hurry to get it back, you can collect it at the historical society anytime today. The door isn't locked until the church people leave tonight at seven—they've got a meeting or something going on. She said to tell you that she'll be happy to research it further when she's feeling better but had a feeling that you were anxious to have it returned. Oh, and she left the few notes she found in the file that's right with the doll. So you can just take both if you want."

"I…thank you," I said. "I'll take care of it. Thanks for the call and please tell your mom that I hope she'll make a quick recovery. Listen," I lowered my voice slightly. "I wanted to give her something for her time. Could you give me her home address?"

Kim rattled it off and I scrambled to find a piece of paper. I scrawled the address and her mother's home phone number on the back of an envelope. After we'd hung up, I called the flower shop in St. Albans and ordered an arrangement to be delivered to the hospital that afternoon. Then I wrote a check for Partridge and tucked it in an envelope in the outgoing mail.

* * *

I felt better after I collected the doll—she really should have a name—and put her back into her original box. It was balanced on the passenger seat of my car. The file folder where Partridge had started taking notes was in my bag. I pulled it out and balanced it on my knees in the driveway of the church. I tried to decipher Partridge's scrawls. It wasn't easy.

I got, "1941?" along with a term I wasn't familiar with: "Parian." Then there were a few lines of script that sloped badly to the left. "No maker's mark found. Initial search on hairstyles: best determination, doll made in the early 1940s. Germany, most likely. Possible Switzerland? Doesn't fit any mass-produced re: time period." I turned the paper over, but there weren't any other notes. Disappointment washed over me. I'd hoped for more concrete information. Then I immediately felt guilty. Poor Partridge. How long had she lain where she'd fallen before help had come? Had it been only minutes until someone else in the building heard her, or hours? I tucked the paper back into the folder, which felt empty and slid it under the doll's box. I had a stop to make before I headed home.

Downtown St. Albans greeted me with cheerful flags encouraging me to "stay, play, shop, dine," and more. Big urns of mums in autumn colors dotted the corners, and tall dried cornstalks wound with white twinkle lights framed each of the old-fashioned-looking black streetlights.

I found a parking spot on Main Street two blocks from The Art Shoppe, a gallery of three artists. The front windows were freshly cleaned and showcased oil paintings and watercolors of landscapes. A little bell tinkled when I walked through the door.

"Good morning," a voice called from the back room. "I'll be right out. Please feel free to look around."

"Thanks," I called, and strolled around the small space, the cardboard box in my arms. It was silly, but I didn't want to leave her alone in the car. It was cold out there and yes, okay, I realized that she was a doll and not my pet or another human, but still. I looked around me. The walls were covered in canvases and the floor held black display racks with prints of some of the originals.

"Sorry about that," a male voice said behind me. "I was just unpacking something. How are you today?"

"I'm well, thanks. How are you, Josef?" I turned.

"Isabel," he said and reached out toward me, then saw the box and stopped. I felt a mixture of disappointment that he'd been prevented, and relief that he couldn't enter my bubble. It was no less strange seeing him now than it had been all those months before. Time heals all wounds...unless you're faced with them up close and personally. His dark eyes surveyed me and I pulled at my scarf, tried to cover more of my neck. Not that he hadn't seen that part of me and much more before.

"Congratulations on your latest success." His face bore a wide smile. I tried not to notice the perfect, white square teeth, or the way that smiling made the wrinkles around his eyes appear. Tried not to notice the smell of him: a mix of cloves and the sharp notes of his aftershave.

"Success?" My mind blanked for a moment. I'd told only three people about the show: Nigel, Marianne, and my artist friend, Julia. How had Josef...?

"My agent and your agent bumped into each other last week at an event," Josef said smoothly, his eyes on mine. "It's wonderful to hear. Congratulations." He held out a hand. My gut twisted but I smiled back, set the box on the floor, and shook his outstretched hand. He covered it with his other hand, both warm and soft with callouses along the first finger where he rested his paintbrush. I felt the same electrical current run through me that I always did when he was near. Is that why I'd wanted to come here, to see him again? Or, subconsciously, did I want to gloat about the Met?

"Thanks," I said. "I'm still a bit in shock."

He nodded. "You're looking well," he said. He had a way of drinking you in that made you feel like the most delicious beverage he'd ever sampled. His dark eyes roamed my face now, and I thought like a stupid schoolgirl how glad I was that I'd applied some lip gloss in the car and run a comb through my hair. Shivers ran up my backbone and I released his hand. Instantly, I felt colder.

"You're looking well, too," I said, then glanced at the wall nearest me. "I was just in town, running some errands, and thought that I'd stop by to see the new pieces." I swept a hand over the walls of the gallery. What I wanted to say was, "Are you still seeing Clarice?" but I kept the words tucked behind my teeth. Instead, I turned to look at the back third of the room. It was always changing; new pieces hung every month or so. The artists knew the importance of keeping things fresh while featuring their larger, more expensive pieces at the front.

"Of course," he said.

He turned and walked to the far wall, telling me about the way that he'd captured the lighting in a painting that featured a waterfall in Fairfax. I nodded and made appropriate noises, but I wasn't really listening. As he talked animatedly, my eyes traced his high cheekbones, his tumble of dark curls, and the way that they fell over his collar. His shoulders were broad and—my cheeks burned now—I remembered the muscle well that lay underneath his shirt. I looked back at the painting as he gestured, my tongue dry and my heart hammering in my chest. *It's over, it's over, it's over,* my brain reminded me. If only the rest of me would remember.

Realization emerged as I half-listened to him describe the brush strokes he'd used for the waterfall—for the first time ever, I was in the place of power in our relationship. Or would have been, if we'd still been together. When we'd first started seeing each other, I hadn't really believed he could want me. But my skin—he'd assured me more than once—was not as bad as I thought. I was too sensitive about it... And besides, hadn't Degas preferred women with real bodies, flawed and imperfect, for models? The longer we were together though, the harder Josef pushed me to try other mediums, convinced that doll making would never garner the merit of true art critics and clientele.

"Painting, Isabel, that's what you should do. You have a good eye. Even sculpture—it's more hands-on, like the dolls," he'd told me over coffee one morning. "You have so much promise, but I don't see doll making," he might as well have said taxidermy, "as an up and coming art trend."

When he'd left me for Clarice—a popular water colorist who lived part-time between Shelburne and Boston—I'd been devastated. He'd insisted it was because we'd grown apart. I couldn't help but wonder if it was because of her connections in the art world were much more enticing than mine.

I'd thrown myself into my work as never before when we stopped seeing each other. My parents had been gone only a year, and I was finally, truly alone for the first time in my life. Maybe it was the pain that drove me. Probably it was. It certainly changed the direction of my work. Whereas before my dolls had been brighter, more literal, they morphed into what they are now—Gothic, darker versions of their former selves.

While my career never "took off" in the traditional sense, success did happen slowly. I began to be featured in some mid-grade galleries around the country. Articles were written about my dolls, first nationally and later internationally. Those led to more prestigious galleries, and eventually inclusion in modern art museums. Collectors began to seek out my dolls rather than my working to find buyers for my dolls. Still, to Josef, I remained a doll maker, a craftsman, not a true artist.

"It's not that your dolls aren't interesting or that they don't have a message," Josef had said. "It's just that they're, well, *dolls*."

Was that why I'd come today? To prove my work was important, to insist that I, too, was a "real" artist? I suddenly felt itchy with embarrassment. I wanted to leave, but Josef had just started to tell me about the last of his paintings, a sunset over Lake Champlain. I pulled at the scarf around my neck, murmuring "mm" and "oh, yes, I can see that," as he pointed out the intricacies of his technique—the shadows the clouds made on the water, the curl of the whitecaps.

"It was great to see you," he said finally and kissed both my cheeks in turn after we'd walked back to the front. I smiled back. "Let's get together Friday night for a glass of wine." I stopped in the middle of pulling the ends of my scarf back together.

"I, uh…" My words lodged in my throat like a hunk of dry bread. "I'm not sure—"

"Come, Isa, it will be nice to properly catch up. This week is the Friday Art Walk." He put a hand on my elbow and I felt the familiar tingle. "Join me, why don't you? We'll discuss your show and"—he shrugged—"everything."

Josef was an old friend. Yes, we had a history together, but old friends did things like get a glass of wine together in a public place, didn't they? So, what did it matter about Clarice?

"I'd love to," I said.

"Meet me here at eight and we'll walk over to *Chantal's*. Sound good?"

I nodded a strange buzz of pleasure in my brain. "Sure," I said. "See you then."

* * *

It had started to rain. The wipers screeched across the windshield. There was not quite enough moisture for them to effectively dispatch, but too much not to use them. The air from the heater was lukewarm and I glanced at the knob to make sure it was on hot. That's when I realized I'd left the doll, safely tucked in her box, on the floor of the gallery. I had to get her back. A strange feeling that I didn't recognize sat at the top of my belly, a cold clench. Fear? But why? Josef, even if he opened the box, wouldn't do anything to the doll.

I drove too fast back toward St. Albans, my head beginning to ache between the center of my eyes. I glanced at the clock. It was after four o'clock. This time, I found a spot directly outside of the gallery and jogged up the few steps. I nearly tripped over the top one in my haste. When I pulled the door open, I saw a mother with two young kids playing on the floor near the high counter.

"...can't wait to get it wrapped up," the woman was saying. "It is going to be such a wonderful surprise."

"Mommy, Jake took it," a little boy with blond curls whined, pulling at his mother's coat hem from the floor beneath her.

"What, hon?" his mother replied as she searched the depths of her handbag.

"He won't let me have a turn," the little boy whined again. I glanced toward the other boy, whose back was toward me. The box lay before him upside down, like a squat table. It bounced as he moved something across it. I couldn't see what it was because of the angle of his back and head. Without thinking, I launched myself across the room and reached toward the top of the box. I'd moved so quickly that my brain hadn't known what I was doing until I towered over him, my hands outstretched.

"Don't touch it," I said in a hoarse voice. My hands grabbed at the doll.

"Hey!" the boy, Jake, yelled. He pulled the small figure toward him. My hands scrabbled after it, closed around the soft body, but he immediately jerked it back away from me.

"What in the world...?" I saw his mother turn from the corner of my eye just as I lost my balance and tumbled onto the floor near the boy. My hands kept scrambling, searching for the doll which he held just out of reach.

"That's mine," I said. "Give it back."

"Excuse me," the woman's voice was high-pitched now and she was moving toward me. "Get away from my son."

"I—"

"Isabel?" I glanced up and saw Josef coming from the back room with a flat, long package in his hands. "What is going on?"

I glanced toward the little boy in front of me. He was cowering, hunched forward toward the box, his body protecting the toy from my grasping hands. I righted myself, the pain between my eyes more intense.

"I'm sorry," I said and moved into a crouch. I pulled my hands close to my body. I tried to make my voice sound more normal and less like a lunatic's. "It's just that the doll you're holding is very old. She's fragile and I don't want her to get broken. Can you please give her back to me?"

The boy's shoulders were shaking. Was he crying?

"Please move," the woman said angrily and pushed her way between me and Jake. "Are you alright sweetie?" she asked in a quiet voice, smoothing a hand—perfectly manicured with smooth skin—over the back of his head. He mumbled something I couldn't hear and then they both stood.

Josef stood behind the counter, his mouth agape. I would have laughed normally but was too focused on the boy's hands. I rose to my feet. A corner of the overturned box poked out to the left of the woman's legs. She glared at me, her mouth turned tightly down at the corners.

"I'm sorry," I said. "I just—"

"Please, Angelique, excuse us," Josef said, coming around the counter. He must have put the package down on the counter because with his free hands he grabbed my arms and pushed me gently away. "What is going on?" he hissed under his breath. His breath smelled of old coffee, but not in an unpleasant way. "What is wrong with you?"

"I—"

The question was rhetorical because he immediately turned me back toward the mother and sons, his grip around my shoulders firm.

"Your canvas is right here, Angelique," he said, giving me a little push toward the counter. I stood to its side, watching as he retrieved the flat package and handed it over the counter to the woman. She stared at him a moment, then reached out to retrieve the package. I looked toward Jake. In his hands was a soft, plush lion. It was well worn, threadbare on the front paws with a messy, snarled blond mane.

"My doll?" I whispered to Josef.

"Is safely in the back room. This is an extra box that some frames came in. The boys were making a fort for their friend Leon, weren't you, fellas?" Josef smiled at the two boys who stared back at him glumly.

"Would you like to take it home?" Josef continued, motioning toward the box. "I'd be happy to carry it out to your car—"

"No. Thank you," Angelique responded, holding out her free hand toward the younger boy. He clutched it and the trio walked toward the door, the woman murmuring something to Jake who looked over his shoulder at me. The younger one did, too, tears still visible through his wild curls. He stuck out his tongue and I looked away. A wave of heat washed over my face and down my neck.

"I'm sorry," I said after the tinkling of the bells on the door stopped. "I thought that he had my doll and I didn't want anything to happen to it."

Josef didn't respond, just walked to the back room. He emerged a few seconds later with the box in his arms. A cooling wave of relief washed over me.

"Thank you," I said, and took the box from him. "I really am sorry, Josef. I hope that I didn't—"

"You should probably leave now," he said and nodded tightly toward the door. "I can't believe that this old doll is worth that much of a fuss. Oh, and I'm sorry, Isabel, but something has come up. I won't be able to make it Friday night after all."

My stomach lurched but I only nodded. What was the use of trying to explain myself further? I clutched the box to my chest and pushed myself out the front door backward, careful not to let it slam shut after me. The mother was still strapping her boys into a shiny SUV near mine.

Should I say something? She glanced toward me, her face still tight and furious. I turned, walked to my car, and closed the door. The sound of my breath filled the space. My hands shook on the wheel as I backed out onto Main Street. As I started home again, my right hand rested protectively on the box beside me.

Chapter Six

1944

"Etta, Etta!" Jimmy danced up and down on the street corner as I waited to cross. My feet ached from standing on the hard, wooden floor all day. Ahead of me, though, lay not a bath or a chance to rest, but a pile of potatoes to be scrubbed or the dining room table to be set. A large, blue car moved slowly through the intersection. I glanced up and down the street one more time and then jogged across the road.

"What is it?" I asked. Jimmy pulled at my arm. My lunchbox slid to the end of my fingertips and nearly fell to the ground, but he caught it and held it for me.

"It's Mrs. Gregor. She's had an accident," he said and swung my lunch pail. "She fell down the stairs and broke her leg. It snapped just like this!" He slapped his hands together and made a disgusting noise with his mouth. "The bone was sticking straight out of her leg, Etta. It was all white and there was blood everywhere. Puddles and puddles of it," he said gleefully and pulled me along the sidewalk.

"Oh no," I said. "Poor woman. Did it just happen?"

Jimmy didn't answer, he just skipped and pulled me along.

46

"Hurry, Etta. Wait till you see."

I pictured poor Mrs. Gregor lying in a pool of blood on the staircase and broke into a run. Jimmy grinned at my haste and pumped his little arms and legs to keep up.

We burst through the front door to find nothing out of order. The front staircase was swept clean, as it always was. No people milling about, no woman moaned feebly on the stairs. The only thing on the staircase, in fact, was Will's doll, tucked between the fifth and sixth rungs of the banister.

"James Michael Hayes, did you tell me a lie?" I swung around and grabbed his skinny arm.

"Ow!" he yelled and pushed at my fingers. "I didn't tell no lie, Etta. Go and ask Mama if you don't believe me."

"What's all the commotion?" my mother called from the dining room. I walked through the door and found her setting the table.

"Jimmy said that Mrs. Gregor had an accident on the staircase?"

My mother paused and straightened up, then put a hand to the small of her back and rubbed. "Oh yes, poor thing. She's at the hospital now."

"Told you so," Jimmy crowed and dodged when I moved to swat him. He grinned and sauntered into the kitchen.

"Out of there, Jimmy," my mother said, her voice firm. "I found your hand in the cookie jar once already this afternoon. If I see it again, I'll send you outside to find a switch."

"But I'm hungry, Mama," Jimmy whined, and slouched against the doorframe.

"Dinner will be served soon." My mother glanced at the clock. "Now, off with you. Start your chores if your homework is all finished."

47

"Jimmy said it was a bad break," I said and pulled off my jacket. "That the bone was coming out of the skin and there was blood everywhere."

My mother glared at Jimmy, who had the good sense to scamper from the room.

She sighed. "No, it was just a regular break, no bones or blood. I do feel bad for her, poor thing. I wasn't here when it happened...I'd taken Sally to the cobblers. She must have lain on the steps a good thirty minutes before we got back."

"Did she say what happened?"

My mother shrugged. "Just lost her balance. She said she was upright one minute and flat on her back the next." Mama smoothed a hand over her apron. "I'm not sure what will happen. She'll have to stay at the hospital for a day or two, likely, but after that...well, she won't be able to manage the stairs. Perhaps Mr. Jones will take her room temporarily and she could take his. Easier access to everything." She sighed again and dusted her hands together. "I need to punch down the bread dough. Can you start the potatoes?"

I nodded.

"I've got Mary peeling carrots and Tommy is emptying the ashes. He can help you when he's done."

* * *

The accident was just the start of the bad things that happened that week. The following morning, the milkman inadvertently left us spoiled milk, then my father's photo fell from the wall, the glass shattered into a thousand pieces.

"Well, that's over," Mary stated as she swept up the glass shards. "Bad things come in threes, don't they?"

"Hush, Mary," Mama said as she walked by with Sally on her hip. "That's just a silly superstition."

"Peggy Olms said that bad things always happen in threes and that you should never cross in front of a black cat. She said that her grandmother died, her father lost his job, and she got a failing grade on her math test all in the same week. And math's her best subject."

"Mary," Mama said, "Peggy's grandmother was sick for a long time. Her father might have lost his job because of his penchant for drinking on his lunch break. And maybe she was so worried about her grandmother and her father that she forgot to study properly for her test. Now," she said and pointed toward the door, "don't forget that I need the kale from the garden."

Sally, who had been pulling at the neck of my mother's dress, suddenly looked at me and smiled.

"Pree-dol?" she queried.

She'd taken to calling Will's doll "pree-dol," meaning that she, at least, found the doll pretty.

"It's upstairs, Sally," I said. "I'll get her for you later."

Sally's little face crumpled, and my mother jiggled her on her hip.

"Come, Sally. We'll go check the pantry, shall we?"

Helping Mama in the pantry was one of Sally's favorite things to do. She thought it was our very own store and would pretend to be Mrs. Schneider at the local market. She loved to hand Mama things and crow, "ten cent," or stack the canned goods into wobbly towers.

"I want pree-dol," Sally said and yanked harder at my mother's dress. "Pree-dol, Etta."

"I can go up and get her," I told my mother, but she shook

her head. "Sally has to learn that she can't have everything she wants exactly when she wants it. Now," she said more sternly to Sally, whose voice had risen to a fevered wail. "We're going to go tidy up the pantry. You can play with the dolly later if Etta says you can."

Sally's cries followed her and my mother out of the room. I stood in the living room alone for a few minutes until I heard the clock chime five.

A feeling of dread squeezed my insides. What if I ended up not with two chubby, happy little children, but two Sallys? Immediately, guilt bloomed in my gut. I loved my little sister. Sometimes I just didn't like her much.

Chapter Seven

Present Day

I t was early in the morning—two o'clock? Three?—and I stood at my worktable, a jumble of cloth and beads, fiber and ephemera in front of me. It looked like a creative bomb had gone off, leaving a detritus of colorful scraps, rusted keys, and drips of paint.

Finally, I'd heard from Helen. The good news? Everything was going as planned for the Met. However—that word always meant bad news was on its way—the exhibit was going to open sooner than either of us had anticipated. It turned out—and I tried not to let this hurt too much—that the artist originally selected for the honor had a family emergency and wasn't able to follow through. It would be death to his or her career, but it had opened a spot for me, albeit earlier than we'd anticipated. Apparently—I read between the lines of Helen's carefully worded call—I was the least important of the other artists with solo shows in the next several months. I wished Helen hadn't told me, even though of course she'd had to. Feeling second best had made me start to question myself. And my skills.

"Isabel," Helen had said, her voice chiding after she'd told me and sensed my despondency over the phone. "Don't let this bother you. It's still just as great an honor, just as meaningful an accomplishment as before. I needed to be totally honest with you. And I also knew that you could take it." She'd paused and cleared her throat "You're strong and resilient. And your work is just as valuable and just as important now as it was before."

"I know," I'd said. But I didn't, not really. It felt as though she'd punched me in the gut through the phone line, but I'd worked to keep my voice even and light. "I'm still just as pleased," I'd lied. Instead, everything felt tainted and off-color, skewed.

I rubbed my eyes and looked at the sculpture-in-progress on the worktable. She was a Gothic sprite and one of the most intricate in the collection. Her dress alone had taken me weeks of work, every layer hand stitched, every bead hand applied. She was larger than the others, too, measuring twenty inches. Her clay skin was brown, her hair made from human hair that I'd purchased from a wig shop in Burlington, and braided into intricate plaits threaded with bone fragments. Those I'd found on one of my walks and bleached and dried until they were pure white.

I let her rest against the table, her gray and black dress billowing out. The antique doll sat on the table, propped against the low shelf that ran along the back of it, and watched me as I worked.

"You still need a name, don't you?" I asked and smoothed a hand over the old doll's head. As expected, I felt a little loosening, a little warmth in my chest.

"What do you think about Gretchen or Martha?"

She eyed me blankly.

"No? What about Vivian or Marietta? Emily?"

I smiled, then rubbed my eyes and ran my hands through my hair.

"Well, I'll see you both in a few hours." I yawned.

* * *

The house was chilly when I wandered down to the kitchen just after nine that morning. I turned up the thermostat and rubbed my hands over goose-bump-covered arms. I'd start a fire later. There were only a few sticks of kindling left, which meant a trip to the covered back porch for a fresh load of logs.

Marianne had left a note—she wouldn't be home till late in the evening. I grabbed an ugly, moss green sweater from a hook in the hall and pulled it on while I waited for the coffee to brew. The sun was out and made warm and cozy patterns on the old floorboards. They creaked as I walked back and forth from the cabinet to the fridge, then to the drawer holding the spoons. Sampson sat in front of his food dish, enjoying breakfast, his purr, and the burble of the coffee pot the only other sounds.

As I walked down the hall to my studio a strange feeling came over me, like tiny pinpricks along the back of my neck. I rubbed a hand there absently and sipped from the mug in my other hand. The studio door opened with a soft creak and I turned on the light.

My breath stuck in my throat, all the air gone from my lungs. The mug of coffee slipped from my stiff fingers and smashed to the floor. Hot liquid splashed up onto the hem of my jeans and soaked through my socks. Then I heard my breath, ragged and too fast in my throat, and a strangled moan.

Before me lay the Gothic sprite doll I'd worked on only hours before. She lay on her side, her skull crushed in on one side. A single eye stared at me below a crater-sized hole. Her dress was shredded—there was no other way to describe it. Small bits of black gauzy film and thicker gray pieces covered the floor underneath like confetti. Parts of her hair were spread over the table, too, mixing in with the fabric and loose beads.

My stomach roiled, and I ran to the bathroom and vomited.

How? How could this have happened? I splashed water on my face, which was hot. My cheeks were cherry red, as though someone had slapped me. I dried my face and took three deep breaths, but my heartbeat raced on.

"Sampson!" I yelled as I walked back down the hallway. It had to have been him. Him and his big, clumsy feet. It wasn't the first time that he'd caused a disaster in my studio or elsewhere in the house. I knew I should keep the studio door shut, but he would only sit outside it and meow plaintively until I gave in. Even with the CD player set at high volume, when I worked and left him outside the room he cried and scratched at the door to get in, to be wherever I was. Now he was nowhere to be seen. Probably curled in the bed upstairs, tired from his mess-making.

When I returned to the studio, the same scene greeted me. I looked away from the wrecked doll and saw the antique one still on the shelf over the worktable. Her face was—odd. Her skin looked lighter and less webbed; her eyes looked bluer. I shook my head and tried to think. What did this mean for the show? The show—oh, God—what was I going to do? I sank down on the stool at the worktable. I traced a finger over the hole in the sprite's head. Pain—physical pain, as though someone had struck me—filled my chest.

When I created a doll—I'd once told a journalist—a bit of myself is left inside it. On two occasions in my career, I'd refused to sell to certain clients because of this. In one case, a man was demanding and rude, insisting that I make changes to customize the doll for his wife whom he was buying it for. I'd refused both the changes and to sell it to him. The second time was a young, professional woman who had made offhand critical comments as she perused my booth at a posh art sale. She'd acted as though I were putting her out by charging what were fair prices for my work. I'd refused to sell her anything and she'd left my booth, furious.

It took a half-hour to clean up the remains of the ruined sprite. I should have thrown her away, disposed of everything related to her, but I couldn't. Instead, I bagged everything up and left it in the closet in my studio.

Sampson trotted across the room toward me as I laid a fire in the stove in the living room afterward. He meowed and pressed his side into my leg, but I ignored him. After the fire was snapping and crackling, I pulled on outdoor clothes. I needed a walk to clear my head. Sampson darted back and forth in front of me in the hallway, but I pushed him aside with my foot.

"No," I said, as I slipped out the door. "You've gotten into enough trouble for one day."

A misty rain fell as I stepped outside and I pulled the scarf around my neck tighter and the hat on my head lower. A cold wind blew through the trees and made the branches sway. Leaves tumbled down in cascades toward the ground.

My thoughts were jumping in my head like popcorn. The ruined doll. The cat. The show. Nigel and his threat to sell the house.

I stopped suddenly as a new thought emerged: what if it hadn't been the cat in my studio? What if someone had been there—inside the house—while Marianne and I slept? The thought made me shiver more than the cold air creeping up my jacket's sleeves. I never locked the house doors—not out here where it was so private and remote. There was never a need. It would have been easy for whoever it was to get into the house. But why? If someone was going to break in, then surely they'd have more sinister intentions than breaking a doll.

I blew the air out of my chest and shrugged the thought away. I needed to center myself. To stop the thoughts, I had to concentrate on what was around me now in the woods. The sounds and smells. My breathing. I took deep breaths in and out until a little of the tension in my shoulders eased.

I walked nearly every day, no matter the season. I liked the way that the landscape was constantly changing, never exactly the same. Sometimes the signs of that were hard to find, other times they were obvious. A bird called overhead and another answered it, and far off I could see the faint "V" of Canadian Geese migrating south. They were too far away for me to hear their strange, honking voices. A gust of wind shook the branches of a maple tree to my right, and cold rain built up in the leaves showered over my shoulders and head.

An hour later, shivering and wet, I returned to the house, anxious to get to the fireplace. There, a wall of heat saturated me. After a couple of minutes, I stretched my arms above my head and rolled my head from side to side. It had been weeks since I'd taken my yoga mat out.

Returning to the house had opened the floodgate of worries. What was I going to do about a replacement for the Gothic sprite in the exhibit? Even if I worked day and night, there was no way I could finish one just like her in time. Perhaps an older doll of the same general size in the back stock could be reworked…? I turned to let the fire warm the other side of my body and when I did, my heart tripped in my chest.

"How did you get out here?" My voice was a hoarse whisper.

The antique doll lay on her side on the couch, her face smiling at the wall on the far side of the room. I hadn't brought her out here. Or had I? Maybe I'd carried her out afterward after the studio had been cleaned.

I walked to her and crouched down in front of the sofa. Warmth washed over me along with a feeling I couldn't immediately place as I smoothed a hand over her head. The feeling grew stronger. It was protectiveness, I realized. And something else that I couldn't put my finger on. Sampson trotted to my side but I ignored him. I was too angry to forgive him yet. He sniffed my knee delicately, then looked up at me with his strange, tawny eyes. He followed my hand to the little doll. Then he backed up a step, two, and pinned his ears back.

"What's the matter, Sampson?" I asked. He made a strange sound at the back of his throat and hissed toward the little doll. Then, his tail a thick plume behind him, he ran from the room.

I frowned at his reaction—strange—and smoothed my hand over the small doll again. "Don't worry," I whispered to her. "I won't let anything happen to you."

Chapter Eight

1944

"It's wonderful news, darling. I'm so happy for you. For us," I said. Will sat across from me on the bank of the Winooski River. We'd just finished a celebration picnic. He'd gotten a job at a service station downtown. The weather was beautiful, a perfect mix of balmy, lilac-scented air and puffy white clouds.

I lay back on the blanket that we'd spread over the new grass, breathing in the smells. Will moved to lay beside me, but the motion obviously caused his right leg pain. He grimaced slightly, but then positioned himself on his side and stroked my cheek with his fingers. I smiled, rolled my head to the side, and looked at him. "Are you all right?" was what I wanted to ask, but he would hate that. Hated any mention of his injury. Instead, I asked, "Do you know any of the other men you'll be working with?"

He shook his head. "Nah. But there aren't too many, it's a small place. I'm sure I'll get to know them sooner. Soon," he corrected a wide, sloppy smile on his face. He'd pocketed a bottle of his father's scotch and had drunk a bit too much of it. I'd tried not to let it show—that I felt hurt he'd gone there

58

first and told his father before me—because this should have been a happy time.

"It was just so I could get this," he'd said, wagging the bottle at me with a laugh. I'd laughed back, but inside, worry gnawed. He drank a lot these days, more than I remembered from our time together before. But what did I know of what men drank? My father had been a teetotaler, never touching a drop of liquor.

I'd mentioned my concern to Will once, but he'd brushed my comment aside like a mosquito that was pestering him. His face had darkened. "Everyone in Europe drinks. It's just the way it is there, Etta. Besides, it helps with this." He'd waved a hand toward his leg. "You're not going to start harping on me, are you?" I'd assured him that I wouldn't. And today, he'd had a bit too much again, but I'd been true to my word and not said a thing. Besides, what did it matter? If he wanted to overindulge and treat himself, was it right for me to say that he shouldn't?

I pushed back a lock of his hair that had fallen over his forehead, and he smiled. Then he leaned back on the blanket and pulled me over on top of him.

"Will!" I squealed and slapped my hands feebly against his chest. "People will see."

"Well, let them," he said. "Let them see me loving my future wife."

I laughed again as he buried his face in my neck. I loved him. I loved this. His touch, the smell of him, the feel of his weight against me, of his strength. His lips found the tender skin and brushed over it. Goosebumps raced up and down my arms. I ducked my head down and found his lips with my own. The world above and around us melted into oblivion.

Suddenly, his body stiffened under mine and became rigid like a corpse. I pulled back and looked at his face. It was pale, and his eyes were wide. His breath came out in short, jerky gasps.

"Will?" I said and pushed myself off him. I placed a hand on his chest. "Will, what's wrong?"

I followed his line of sight. A soldier walked past, his uniform neatly pressed, the starched collar digging into the skin of his neck. Where there was supposed to be a right hand, an empty sleeve was pinned. Will continued to stare; his breath came in strange little huffs. The sun ducked behind the clouds. Instantly the air felt cool and damp. I shivered.

"Will?" I moved my hand on his cheek. His hand grasped my arm and I smiled. Now he would turn toward me and shake his head, laugh at some joke I'd missed. He sat up but didn't turn toward me, and he didn't laugh. Instead, his hand bit into the flesh of my arm and squeezed hard. Still, he stared after the soldier, and Will's face...it was as though another man's face had crept up behind it. Pushed against it from the inside.

"Please, Will, you're hurting my arm." His fingers continued to dig into my skin and I twisted against them. But they felt made of metal, of steel.

"Will!" I yelled. A fluttery feeling had risen in my chest. "Will stop, please." I pulled at his fingers with my other hand, and then dug my nails into the back of his hand.

His grip loosened and I pushed his hand away, rubbed the spot on my arm where an imprint of his fingers had left a mark. He shook his head in slow motion, like someone who'd just come out of a deep sleep. He turned toward me then and once again his face was just him, just my handsome, sweet fiancé.

"Etta?" His voice was soft and low. "Are you all right? I'm

sorry, sweetheart. Did I hurt you?" He looked at me as I rubbed my arm. I tugged the sleeve of my dress down over the area and ignored his questions.

"What happened?" I asked.

His response didn't come immediately. Instead, he dropped his head into his hands.

"I'm sorry," he said again. "I didn't mean..."

"It's fine. I'm fine."

Of course, it wasn't fine. My arm ached and burned, but telling him that wouldn't help. He hadn't meant to hurt me. He just hadn't been himself, hadn't been there, mentally.

"What—what did you see?"

Will acted as though I hadn't spoken.

"I didn't mean to...I shouldn't have grabbed you like that. I thought you were someone else. Please forgive me, Etta."

"Of course," I said, and scooted closer. I wrapped my arms around him. His entire body shook, trembling like Jimmy or one of my sisters after they'd had a nightmare. "I'm fine, Will. It's all right." I soothed him, whispered it over and over in his ear until finally, finally, the shaking stopped.

The sun had snuck out from behind the clouds. Its warmth caressed my face and danced across the planes of Will's.

"It was like I was back there," Will said finally, quietly, a few minutes later. "Like I was back in the ditch. I could hear—" His voice broke and I rubbed his back for a moment. He continued, "I could hear the men shouting, screaming. I could hear the bombs. They were deafening, Etta. Once one went off, all you could hear was this siren of noise in your ears. It flattened out all the other sounds, you know?" He paused and looked at me. I nodded.

"It was worse then because you couldn't hear if someone

was coming. Couldn't hear your commanding officer or the guy standing next to you. It was like you were a rat in a maze all sealed up in a box. You couldn't see where you should go, and you couldn't hear anything because your eardrums felt blown to bits. And the blood and mud and shit everywhere..."

His voice broke off again. Then he got awkwardly to his feet and bent to retrieve his cane. "I need to walk," he said.

"Will," I called. I got up and realized I'd taken my shoes off. The grass was cool and damp under my feet. "Will, wait."

He moved faster than his usual halting pace. When I finally caught up, he was slightly out of breath, a thin sheen of sweat shining along his temples. I grabbed his arm.

"Will?"

He turned so suddenly that I nearly lost my balance. His eyes were wet, and he grabbed both of my arms, the skin of his palms hot through the thin fabric of my dress's sleeves.

"I'm sorry," he said. He pulled me to him, crushed me against his chest. His arms were tight around me and his body shook once again. "I'm making a mess of everything, aren't I?"

"Shh," I said, "It's all right. Everything is going to be all right. You're home now—safe. You never have to go back to that place again." I rubbed my hands over his back and held him until the trembling stopped.

* * *

"Mine. Mine!" Sally's voice had reached a fevered pitch as she hugged the doll, Will's doll, to her chest. She'd been in my room again, a bad habit that only I seemed bothered by.

"It's not yours, Sally," I repeated, my voice firm. "That's Etta's doll. It was a gift and it's very fragile. Give it back, please." I held out my hands.

"No!" She wailed and held the doll in a death grip. Her plump fingers bit into the doll's soft body.

"Claudette?" my mother's voice called from downstairs. "What's the matter up there?"

"Nothing," I called back and forced my voice to sound cheerful. "Be right down."

An idea formed. "Sally," I said, my voice calmer. "Do you want to take care of my doll while I'm at work?"

Her blonde curls nodded, and her sobs changed to hiccuping breaths.

"All right," I said, and smoothed a hand over her head. "Will you be very, very gentle with her?"

Another nod.

"Will gave me that doll and he must love it a lot, don't you think? He asked me to promise I'd keep it safe. So if you're going to take care of it, you'll need to be very gentle and careful with her. Can you do that?"

"I'm careful," Sally said and clutched the doll close. "I'm careful with pree-dol." She looked up at me, her face teary and earnest.

"Good." I wiped my sister's face clean with a handkerchief. "And do you know that babies need lots and lots of rest?"

Sally nodded again.

"So, she'll need to take lots of naps before I get home from work."

"I'll be a good mama," Sally said.

I sighed and dropped a kiss on her head.

"I suppose we'll have to give her a proper name, won't we," I said, going back to the mirror and adjusting the scarf I'd put on.

"Her name's Gerda," Sally said. "Pree name," she crooned to the doll and rocked it in her chubby arms.

"That's a nice name," I said. "How did you think of it?"

Sally looked up at me her robin's-egg blue eyes.

"She told me."

"Ah," I replied. "Well, now it's time for us to have our breakfast. You can take Gerda to your room and play with her after that."

"And I'll be very gentle," Sally said and patted the doll's back with only her fingertips. "Mamas should always be gentle, huh, Etta?"

"Yes, Sally," I said. "Mamas always should."

"I don't know how what you did," Mama said, pulling me aside later. "But that's the first time in the past two weeks that she hasn't bawled during breakfast."

I smiled. "She's taking my doll under her wing; maybe Sally needed a job."

My mother chuckled and handed me a thick oatmeal cookie. "For your lunch," she said.

Chapter Nine

Present Day

Marianne and I sat with two mugs of tea and a hideously painted teapot between us.

"I like to support local artists," I'd said when she mentioned the ugly teapot soon after moving in.

"Me too," she'd responded, "but I don't have that level of dedication." We'd laughed.

"This one's my favorite," she said now as she admired the mug that she sipped out of. It was a beautiful shade of mauve, with a cacophony of flower petals etched into the surface of the clay.

"I know," I said with a smile. "Remember the show where I bought it? I almost left it there, but you convinced me it was meant to come home with me."

"And you're grateful you listened to me, aren't you?"

"Of course," I said and laughed. The sound surprised me, but just being around Marianne had a lightening effect.

"So, what are you going to do?" she asked, and I knew she meant the ruined doll. I had mentioned it when she first sat down but refused to show her the remains. I sipped from my cup and the tea burned the tip of my tongue. I cradled the mug in my hands and let the steam heat my face.

"It's too late now to start another doll, at least anything of that size and with that level of complexity. I thought I'd go through some of my old inventory, pull something from there. There's a gypsy doll that might work, or another, a sort of mime. Either of them could be updated, changed for the exhibit. It'll be better than starting from scratch."

Marianne nodded, swirled a spoon through her tea.

"Still no idea how it happened?" she asked gently.

"It must have been Sampson," I said and sipped from my own cup, but an uneasy feeling tickled my backbone. "I'm sure it wasn't an intruder, but it might be a good idea to start locking the door. You still have that spare key?"

Marianne nodded. We sat in quiet for several minutes and sipped and chewed without talking. I appreciated that about Marianne. Her ability to just be in silence. It was exhausting spending time with someone who constantly felt the need to fill in every gap in the conversation with chatter.

"I see you've bonded with this one," Marianne said finally and nodded toward the old doll that was sitting on the sideboard next to us. The doll stared back at us with empty gray eyes.

"She was lonely," I joked.

"Has Partridge gotten back to you with any information?"

"I didn't tell you? She had an accident. Broke her wrist and hurt her ribs. Her daughter, Kim, called me, but I guess I haven't talked to you since then. She was at the hospital but was going home."

Marianne made a sad clicking sound. "Poor old dear. What happened?"

"She fell on the staircase at the church."

We sat in silence for a few minutes and then Marianne tucked a radiant shock of indigo hair behind her ear. "There's something a little strange about her, isn't there?"

At first, I thought she meant Partridge, but then realized she was referring to the antique doll.

"What?" I asked. I felt a little press of resentment in my chest. First Sampson, now Marianne?

"I don't know. She's pretty—in her own way, I guess. But a little creepy, too. I'm not sure how to explain it, really. Just that there's a sort of darkness there, almost like a bad aura."

"Can objects have auras?"

She shook her head, then nodded, distracted.

"I'm not sure." She glanced at her wristwatch, a small, gold piece that her late husband had given her. "Oh no, I'm late," she said and rose from the table.

I followed her to the entryway where she slipped into her jacket.

"I'm sorry I don't have time to help you clean up—"

"Don't worry about it," I said. "I'll see you later."

She smiled and waved her fingers as she walked to the car.

"You'll figure it out—for the show I mean," she called over her shoulder. "You're creative. It's your gift."

I watched until her silver Audi was out of sight down the long driveway. My morning walk had been cut short when the rain had started, but now—typical Vermont—the sun had peeked out, the air was crisp and delicious. Maybe I'd go out again, try to sort out the tangle of thoughts in my head. I left the tea things where they were. I'd clean up when I got back. Sampson regarded me with one eye open, his form comfortably draped on a big, old wingback close to the fireplace. I walked to him, rubbed a hand over the top of his head, and down over his neck the way that he liked it. He purred more loudly and closed both eyes.

"Keep an eye on things," I said and dropped a kiss on the top of his head. "Doll killer."

The air smelled of dying leaves and a hint of wood smoke as I pulled the door closed behind me. I breathed in deeply and filled my lungs with the wonderful smell. My feet slogged through piles of heavy, wet leaves and a breeze caressed my cheeks, teasing strands of hair out from under my hat.

I followed the bumpy, dirt road first, then cut through the neighbor's field toward the woods beyond. They let me walk here year-round. The property was posted, so hunting wasn't allowed except by the owners themselves, and I knew the areas to stay away from during hunting season. I followed the clearing, stayed along the tree line, but didn't go into the woods today. I wanted the openness around me, the lightness of the sky. Birds called in the crisp air, and far off a dog barking, the sound echoing. The sun was starting to dip low in the sky when I tripped. I went down on my left knee with a little gasp of surprise. My right foot tangled in a thorny vine. I kicked at it, but it was snarled firmly around my ankle.

"Stupid thing," I muttered. I crouched and used my gloved fingers to extract my boot from the vine. As I did, something white caught my eye. A rounded white form protruding from the ground, just under the pine trees where the field met the woods. I moved closer and pushed the overgrown grass away. I pulled more of the vine back. Beneath it was a very old, very worn headstone. It was small, and the letters were too faded to read.

I sat back on my heels. Did the neighbors know this was here? I looked around the area for another stone. There were none. It wasn't unusual to find old gravestones in the woods or in deserted clearings. Often entire families had been buried together on the family farm. It was strange, though, to find a single stone. Why would it be all by itself? I'd have to ask Mr. Bartlett sometime. I made a mental note of the position of the stone and stood up.

The sun had faded, and I still had a long walk to get back home. As I turned to leave, I heard the loud *caw-caw-caw* of a crow. Twigs crunched under my feet as I headed back toward the well-worn path my feet had made on my long walks. There was a loud rustle behind me and I glanced back.

Caw-caw-caw the crow screeched again and settled itself on the stone. It glared, its dark eyes fixed on me. A shiver ran down my spine, like a hundred ants marched up and down. I turned back and pushed through the overgrown grass toward the road. Faintly, through the breeze that carried the wonderful fall smells, the bird's croaking call followed me.

* * *

I arrived back home refreshed, ready to head to the studio, and start sorting through my older inventory. First, though, I'd clean up the tea things. I walked into the dining room and moaned. The table looked like a bulldozer had been through. The teapot was overturned, and tea had run from it all over the table and puddled on the floor underneath. The saucers were askew, one of them turned over, and Marianne's mug—the beautiful handmade one—was broken. I ran to grab a pile of rags to clean up and tossed the fragments of the mug in the trash.

"Sampson!" I swore under my breath as I mopped up the

now-cold tea, then sat back on my heels. Everything was relatively dry now. The cat must have been after some of the lemon curd left on our plates. The floor still felt sticky, though at least it was dry. I'd have to get the mop out later. Sighing, I brought the handful of rags to the laundry room, then washed my hands and retreated to the studio.

"Speak of the devil," I said. Sampson regarded me from the tall filing cabinet in the corner. "Been busy?" His tail swished from side to side. Strange, he usually only climbed or jumped to a high perch when something frightened him. Lightning in summer or the wind when it howled around the eaves.

Let him be scared. It was his own fault he'd made such a racket.

I pulled out the boxes of wrapped dolls. I chose two—the gypsy doll and the mime—and set them on the worktable along with a pile of fabrics and a jar that held some tiny found objects. I spent a long time inspecting them. It was hard to change the idea in my mind from that of the doll I'd worked so hard on to one of these older dolls. The mime, I finally decided, would be the better choice of the two. She had nearly the same proportions as the ruined sprite, and if I took her down to her bones and repainted her face…it could work. It would have to.

As I worked, I tried to keep my mind on what I was doing. But worries about everything else pressed in. This was the time—the only time—that I wished for shared studio space. A place where I'd be distracted enough by other artists' chatter or music or people wandering in and out as we had at college, to get out of my head.

Would this really work? What if my idea to replace the doll was a dismal failure? What if I couldn't get her finished in time? What if…? I stopped for a late supper, reheated soup in a small blue enamel pot, and fixed myself toast. Classical music played on the little radio I kept on a shelf by the sink. The strains of a Mozart piece had begun as I brought the food to the dining room table. A scattering of crumbs from the bread lay on the far side. I hadn't noticed them before and eyed them as I took the first sip of my soup. Then I sighed, got up, and retrieved the dishcloth to wipe them up. If I didn't do it now I'd likely forget, and then Sampson might try to "help" again. Who knew what he'd break the next time?

I bent over the table. How had crumbs gotten all the way over here, anyway? I stooped over and froze. I couldn't have seen what I did. I blinked several times, then reopened my eyes. It was still there. There were letters spelled out of the crumbs. A "g" followed by an "e" then an "r" a "d," and lastly an "a."

"Gerda." My voice was loud in the quiet kitchen. At that moment, the radio turned to static. I jumped. I looked back toward the window over the sink and as I did, I caught a glimpse of the old doll. She sat on the counter. Her gray eyes looked directly at me. Had I left her there? It was a precarious position. I crossed through to the kitchen and picked her up. I felt the same familiar sense of peacefulness wash over me.

"Gerda," I repeated. "Is that your name?"

I felt foolish when she just stared back at me. What had I expected? For her to nod?

"It's a beautiful name," I said. "Gerda."

I blinked. Had her eyes shifted slightly toward me? I laughed. The stress really was getting to me. I set the doll on the sideboard and returned to my dinner. Marianne must have written that name on the table when I wasn't looking. It was the only plausible explanation. But why? As a joke?

Unless…I looked back toward the doll. Had her head had turned slightly? She seemed to stare past me now, her gaze on the thin curl of crumbs at the far end of the table.

Chapter Ten

1944

"Stop it, Sally. Put it away," Jimmy's voice was stern as I trudged up the long, steep staircase. It had been a bad day. The supervisor had marked me tardy coming back from lunch break, even though it was less than two minutes after the whistle. I'd gouged my finger on one of the looms and then bled all over the wool I had been working with. That, he'd informed me, should cost me a day's wages, but he'd let it slide "this time." He made sure to point out my mistake to every worker standing in the area. *Ho-ho-ho. Let's all stand around and jeer at stupid, clumsy Etta.* My cheeks burned again when I thought about it.

"I don't like it!" Jimmy's voice reached a fevered pitch.

I stomped to the room that Sally shared with Mary. "What is going on?" I said and crossed my arms.

Sally had Will's doll—Gerda—on the floor with her in the middle of the room. She was holding her toward Jimmy, who was backed into the corner nearest the door.

"I won't play with you ever again," Jimmy said. He held his hands out in front of his face as though he was warding off birds or bugs.

"What in the world is the matter?" I asked him.

Sally crowed and grinned at me. She shook the doll a little and whispered in its ear, then giggled as she held the doll's face to her own ear.

"Gerda says she don't like you, Jimmy," Sally interpreted. "She said you're a naughty boy. Naughty boy. Naughty boy!" she said in an annoying singsong voice.

"Sally, stop," I said firmly. She looked at me and grinned.

"Jimmy," I said, and put my hand on his thin shoulders. He jumped. His eyes had been clenched shut, and he opened them and looked at me. "What's wrong?" I asked.

"I hate that doll," he said and peeked over me toward Gerda. "She isn't nice. She says bad things and I don't like her."

I squatted down so that I was at eye-level with my little brother. "She says bad things? She's just a doll, Jimmy."

He shook his head frantically from side to side. "Nuh-uh. She says that I'm naughty and that she's going to punish me."

"What, you?" I said with mock horror. "But you're the man of the house. Isn't that what you're always telling us?" Jimmy had announced this role soon after my father left, puffing his thin chest out with pride and saying, "Don't worry, Mama. I'm the man here now," whenever my mother or I discussed some new concern. Now the boy who handled snakes like they were party streamers and gutted the squirrels he shot with his slingshot shook and cried.

"That doll says that—"

"Enough," I said and rose to my feet. "That's enough. Dolls don't talk, Jimmy. And anyway, why are you playing in here if you don't like her? And you," I swung around and fixed my gaze on my littlest sister. "You are supposed to be careful with the doll. Hold her gently. And if Jimmy doesn't like her, then

74

for pity's sake, just put her away if you're playing together. It's time to put her away now, anyway," I said and sighed. "Time to start your chores, both of you."

Sally began to cry then; big round tears fell down her plump cheeks. I left the room. Holding my tongue had become a nearly overwhelming challenge.

"Etta, I really do hear her—" Jimmy started as he trailed after me into the hallway.

"Stop…please," I said. "Go get changed out of your school clothes and see what Mama wants you to do first."

I watched him for a minute. His thin shoulder drooped as he made his way to the bedroom he shared with Tommy. He glanced back before he entered the room. I smiled, grimly, and went to my own room to change clothes.

* * *

Three weeks later, Will and I walked again along the banks of the Winooski River. This time there was no sun. In fact, it was unseasonably cool for June. Thick clouds covered the sky like a dark, gray sweater. I pulled my jacket closer, then linked my arm through Will's. We walked following the water that tumbled and talked loudly over it.

"It wasn't my fault. I swear to you, Etta," Will said. "McLane had it out for me, from the minute I started there."

"I know," I said.

"Stupid mick," he said. I winced but said nothing. It was because of this man, after all, that Will had lost his job—his new job—and he had every right to be angry.

"You know what it was, Etta? He didn't want me there because I'm young because I have new ideas about how things should be done. Better ideas. Ideas that his stupid, slow brain would never dream up. He wanted to do things the old way. Well, I told him, 'times are changing, the world is changing. You've got to catch up.' But he didn't want to hear that." Will swore under his breath and looked out at the churning river.

A fissure of frustration built in my chest. When I'd imagined Will coming back home, it had been images of us strolling along the riverbank and planning our future. Sitting with mugs of coffee and scratching out our budget as we prepared for life as a newly married couple. I'd pictured the drives we'd take. Ice cream cones shared at the beach on a hot summer day. But rather than these happy outings and times dreaming and planning together, it felt as if everything was about Will. He'd come back more dependent than before. And instead of talking about his big dreams of success and our lives together, he just wanted to blame everyone around him for what went wrong. It wore on me. I pushed against the anger, though. Pushed against it and tried to focus on the positives.

"You'll get a new job, something even better," I said. "Didn't you say Bobby knew of a place?"

"Yeah," Will said, and the frown on his handsome face eased. "I'm going over later today to meet with the boss."

"That's wonderful," I said and squeezed his arm. "And in the meantime, I still have my job and…." As soon as the words were out of my mouth, I wanted to snatch them back. Will's frown deepened again, and he turned toward me and stepped closer.

"I don't need your help," he said, and his voice sounded hard, bitter. But then he cupped a hand gently over my face. I leaned into it, felt the warmth and strength center me. "I'm sorry, sweetheart. I just—"

"I know," I said. "You don't have to explain."

I knew what it meant for a man to have a job, an income to be proud of. I knew what it meant for Will in particular. That he could make it on his own.

"It'll all be fine," I said. "You'll see."

* * *

The scream that woke me that night felt like a thousand ants running up my spine. I threw back the covers and ran from my room without even bothering to light the lamp. The floor was cool under my bare feet and I cried out when I collided with something soft in the hallway.

"Claudette?" my mother whispered. Unlike me, she'd thought to take a lamp with her, though the flame was small. She was still dressed, and I felt momentarily confused. Was it night or day? But no, the light shining through the hall window was moonlight. The scream sounded again. From the boys' room. We headed that way without a word.

"It's all right, Jimmy," Tommy said, standing by the edge of our younger brother's bed. "It was just a bad dream."

"What happened?" my mother asked as she moved to the bed and sat on the edge of it. Jimmy, in the lamplight, was shiny with sweat. His small chest heaved up and down, and his eyes bulged slightly. I stood by the door but could swear I heard the gallop of his heartbeat.

"Please, Mama, please make her go away," Jimmy gasped, as though he'd been running for miles.

"Who, your sister?" Mama glanced at me, but Jimmy shook his head frantically from side to side.

"Gerda."

"Who is that?" Mama said, and reached to put a hand on his head. He flinched, then relaxed slightly under her touch.

"It's my doll," I said. "The one from Will. Sally named her Gerda."

My mother used his sheet to wipe away the sweat from Jimmy's forehead. His thin frame continued to shake as the lamplight cast shadows over the room.

"She was here, in this room, Mama. She tried to climb into my bed and I threw her..." He pointed to the far corner of the boys' small bedroom. "I threw her over there. She was saying awful things to me. She said—"

"Hush now," Mama said firmly. "Like your sister said, it was just a bad dream. They can seem very real when you're sleeping, but they are nothing more than your imagination working away while your body is resting. Now"—she stood and squeezed his shoulder—"would you like me to keep the lamp on and get you a cup of water?"

Jimmy nodded meekly, but I noticed that as soon as my mother left the room, his eyes darted again to the corner of the room.

"Let's have a look, shall we?" I said to Tommy. He yawned and collapsed back into his bed in response. I shrugged and walked to the far side of the room. A baseball glove lay on its side, a jumble of jacks nearby, and something that looked like part of a bird's nest—fragile and falling apart—had slipped off the shelf nearby and spilled its dark, dusty bits onto the wide floorboards. And there, just under the shelf and barely visible, a small, white doll's arm stuck out. I reached for it.

"Don't!" Jimmy cried near my shoulder. I jumped and so did he, then tears started to fall again. "I told you she was there," he said. "Don't take her out, I don't want to look at her!" He ran back across the room and jumped into bed. He pulled frantically at his thin blanket and turned his back to me, curled in a ball at the far edge of his bed.

"Okay, now you can get her," he said with a muffled voice. "Please, Etta, get her out of here."

I sighed and pulled the doll out from underneath the bookcase. The light was poor, but she looked whole and undamaged. Sally had probably left her in her earlier. Gerda smirked at me with her sly little mouth and I turned her face away from me and carried her back to my own room. Mama murmured to Jimmy in his room, and I yawned and stuffed the doll under my thick woolen underwear in the bottom drawer of my bureau. Maybe Sally would forget about her. Or I'd tell her that I couldn't find the doll, just for a couple of days, until Jimmy calmed down.

I fell back into my own bed and dreamed of long hallways and shadowy faces and a small, white-gray doll that followed me with her own tiny, jerking steps.

Chapter Eleven

Present Day

The next morning, I overslept, burned my tongue on my coffee, and pinched my finger in the studio door. Still, there was one plus—it was Wednesday. Every other Wednesday, Julia and I met for breakfast at Luna's, a small café in downtown St. Albans. She's an artist, too, so we spend time commiserating and celebrating each other's successes.

I brought the vintage doll with me to the studio and found her a good spot on the high shelf above the worktable. Her smile remained intact, her eyes blank as she stared over my shoulder. Sampson rubbed against my ankles, but when I brought him up to my chest and rubbed against his neck with my crooked finger the way he liked, he stiffened.

"What's the matter?" I asked. He pushed all four of his paws against me and looked frantically toward the shelf, toward the doll.

"Why don't you like the new doll?" I asked. But he'd already pushed his weight against me. I sighed and let him down on the table. He scrabbled off it and across the room, where he took over the rocking chair. On the flattened needlepoint pillow on the chair, he turned in a circle, stretched, and lay down with his face toward the wall. His tail flicked.

"Drama cat," I said and cranked up the music. An hour later, the timer went off in the kitchen. I set it to keep track of appointments because once I started working, I lost all track of time. I took a quick, military-type shower, rubbed ointment into my arms, legs, stomach, and what I could reach of my back. Then I dressed, careful to avoid looking at myself in the mirror. Erythrodermic psoriasis was the heavy-duty version of regular psoriasis. That's how a dermatologist had described it to me once. Most people were familiar with psoriasis—there were commercials about it constantly—but this form of the skin disease was more severe. Itchy, peeling red rashes covered most of my skin. An oral medication kept the worst of the itchiness at bay. But it didn't do anything for the sidelong looks and raised eyebrows when I was out. The condition flared under stress, too. During the time I cared for my parents, it was the worst it had ever been.

I sighed, gathered my coat, keys, and purse, and left. The air outside was cool but not freezing; leaves already fluttered down from the trees. Peak season—when the trees were at their most glorious with vibrant reds, yellows, and oranges—had passed two weeks ago. The sky had morphed from robin's egg blue to dull gunmetal gray, and the leaves fell in intermittent sprinkles. Autumn was my favorite time of year, maybe because it was so fleeting.

I drove into St. Albans, cresting Fairfield Hill, and saw the small city that lay before Lake Champlain like a child's play set. It took a few minutes to find a parking spot but finally, I slipped into one on Main Street. Julia waited for me, two cups of coffee on the table. She had long, auburn hair that she wore in a messy bun and cartilage piercings from the top to the bottom of her right ear. Her thin form was covered in a mishmash of flannel and flowers on top, and torn jeans on the bottom. She stood when I approached the table and gave me a quick hug.

"Good to see you," I said, and we settled at the table.

"You, too. Have you eaten breakfast yet?"

"No, and I'm starving," I said. "What are you in the mood for?"

"Not sure. I'll go up with you."

We walked to the high bar, behind which a harried barista filled cups with steaming coffee. A glass case was filled with pastries, coffee cake, and bagels. The cooler weather and overcast day had drawn a crowd. A mother sat with her two young children at a nearby table while two businessmen in suits talked and laughed with familiar ease. A group of students who looked young enough to be in high school sat around a large table nearby. I put my back to them, my heartbeat increasing. I tried to focus on the case in front of me, but listened intently to their voices, readying myself for the comments that might fly my way. None came.

When it was my turn, I ordered a chocolate-filled croissant and Julia ordered an apple-filled pastry. When we'd settled in back at the table, we chatted about an upcoming show that was going to be held in a couple of weeks. Various artists that we knew had work in it. I asked Julia if she knew which art competition she'd enter next.

She shook her head. "Not yet, but I'm working on my list."

Her list had been created on January first and was a spreadsheet that captured information on all the upcoming shows in New England and beyond, in which her work might fit. Julia created collages made entirely of butterfly wings and insect parts. Ethically, she only felt right using already-dead subjects, so she also spent a lot of her time trolling online auctions and local estate sales to find products for her creations.

I steered the conversation from my own work whenever she asked. The news about the Met had done something—caused a fissure between us that wasn't there before—and I didn't want to reopen the wound. Marianne told me to rip off the Band-Aid. Talk about the show the same way that I would any other art event I was preparing for. But I wasn't so sure. I glanced at Julia, but she flipped through the notebook she always brought along to our breakfast meetings. She was ultra-organized and always made notes to refer to the following week.

"So," she said, "last week you'd said that you were going to contact the Arts Council about that potential grant. Did you do that?"

"Not yet," I said. "But I will after…." I looked away, embarrassed. So much for avoiding the topic.

I glanced back at Julia and she smiled. Her eyes were bright behind her glasses. "How's the prep for that going anyway?" Her tone was neutral…or was there a slight edge to it?

"It's fine. Well, except for the fact that the centerpiece of the exhibit was ruined."

"What? What happened?" She pushed her plate a few inches to the side and leaned her forearms on the table, tapping her pen against the notepad. She looked like a journalist, ready to take shorthand of whatever I told her.

"I'm not sure exactly, but suspect it was the cat. I went into my studio yesterday and there she was, with a concave head and a dress that looked like it had been through a paper shredder."

"Oh, no," Julia said. *Tap, tap, tap* went the tip of the pen. "That's tragic. Can you repair her in time for the Met?"

I shook my head. "No, I'll have to figure something else out."

She nodded. The pen slowed its tapping as she gazed out the window across from our table. "That's tragic," she said again, and then smiled at me brightly. "But that's what builds our resilience, right? Something good will come out of it, I'm sure."

I nodded and we talked of other things, but throughout the rest of breakfast, I felt a little pinprick of doubt. Had she secretly been a bit pleased that the centerpiece of the show had been ruined? Then another thought came, a memory from a show we'd done together two years before. Julia, standing next to my booth as we'd struggled to right one of the curtains that had slipped from its rod. "Well, you don't have to worry about that," she'd said, responding to my hopes for a successful show. "You're the epitome of success now. An internationally known artist!" She said it in a showman's voice. "I can only dream of the day." She'd laughed, but had there been something under the words? Something darker?

"…hadn't you?"

"What?" I asked.

"I asked if you'd lined up other shows for after the exhibit. Hadn't you talked about doing some others to sort of piggyback off the Met?"

"Oh, uh, yes, but I haven't had time."

"You should really get on that," Julia said, flipping her braid back behind her head. She smiled at me, but her eyes narrowed slightly as though she were scrutinizing me. Suddenly I felt like one of the bugs she wanted to add to her next collage.

"This is probably your one shot at this kind of success. Why not capitalize on it?" She popped a stick of gum into her mouth and smiled at me.

My cheeks grew hot and I mumbled a response about trying to fit it into my schedule. We said goodbye a few minutes later with a quick hug on the sidewalk before walking to our cars.

"Hope everything works out," she said as she squeezed me goodbye. "Let me know if you need anything."

"Thanks," I said. "I will."

I turned toward my car and felt a wash of guilt that I'd suspected her of being jealous. But at the same time, angry. She'd acted as though I was goofing off rather than promoting my work. Didn't she understand the stress I was under?

As I drove away, I felt a tightness in my chest. When I glanced in my rearview mirror, I saw Julia. She stood alone on the sidewalk, watching me drive away. For some unknown reason, my eyes filled with tears.

Chapter Twelve

1944

The week that had started poorly continued to get worse.

The morning after the doll incident—Tuesday morning—the kitchen caught fire. No one noticed at first. My mother, in a completely unheard-of departure from routine, sat to eat breakfast at the long dining table. Jimmy's eyes widened as she scooted a chair close to him, taking the spot usually occupied by Mrs. Gregor.

"Pass me the flapjacks, would you please?" Mama asked, and Jimmy, his mouth agape, had done so.

"Close your mouth, Jimmy," Mama said softly, then poured a little syrup on a small stack of cakes and added a little extra to his.

He ate the rest of his meal with relish, rather than picking at it with one hand supporting his head as he had been earlier.

"These are good, Mama," he said and grinned at her.

She smiled back and nodded. "They're not bad, are they?"

Most of the boarders had already left for their various jobs when Mama looked at the clock and announced that the children would be late for school if they didn't leave right away. I hurried to grab my lunch tin from the counter in the kitchen where it sat. When I swung the door open, smoke hit me like a wall.

"Mama!" I called and flailed my arms in front of me. I tried in vain to clear a path, to see where it was coming from. My mother rushed into the room.

"Holy Moses," she said and ran across the room. She jerked open the window over the sink. Immediately, the smoke headed in that direction. Then we saw the flames. They leaped from the edges of the cookstove, a blackened shape barely visible now that the smoke had cleared somewhat.

"We need water," Mama said. I rushed to the sink and tipped the bowl holding the dredges of flapjack batter into the large ceramic sink and filled the bowl with water from the tap. Then I ran to the stove and threw the water. It hissed and popped on what was left of the fire, then ran in streams down the sides of the stove.

My mother grabbed an armful of rags from the basket under the sink and threw a handful on the floor to try to sop up the brackish water. Above the stove, the ceiling paint was discolored.

"Thank God the boarders were mostly gone," Mama said. She sighed and inspected what was left of the charred material on the stove's top.

"Where's your sister?" she said and turned toward me. Her face was calm, but I recognized the slight squint in her gaze, the firm press of her lips.

"Mary?" I asked.

Mama nodded. "Go and fetch her."

I ran up the stairs and tried to smell my dress at the same time. Now I was not only late for work but smelled like a dirty chimney.

Mary sat at the small dressing table, braiding her hair. She glanced at me when I walked in, a half-smile on her face.

"Mama wants you," I said. "In the kitchen. There was a fire."

"A fire?" She got to her feet and ran down the stairs ahead of me. "Is everyone all right?" she called over her shoulder.

"Yes," I said. "Thankfully, everyone is fine."

I stopped in the hallway to retrieve my purse and hat, then walked quickly to the kitchen to get my lunch pail.

"...told you more than once, you've got to pay attention to what you're doing. Do you know that this is?" Mama pointed toward the blackened remains of whatever it was on the stovetop.

Mary shook her head. "I didn't—"

"Hush," Mama said, and her voice said she was serious. "It's a potholder, Mary. The one I saw you using earlier this morning when you took the kettle off for tea. How many times do I need to remind you to get your head out of the clouds when you're doing your chores? Especially when you're working in the kitchen. You could have burned the house down; do you realize that? And then where would we be?"

Mary turned away from the stove and looked pleadingly to me.

"I put that potholder back in the drawer, I'm sure of it. Etta, you saw me, didn't you?"

I nodded, then shook my head.

"I can't remember," I said. "And I have to go. I'm late for work."

"But—" Mary said, but Mama interrupted her.

"No more extra reading before school, Mary. You've always got your nose in a book and it's distracting you from your chores."

I snatched my lunchbox from the counter and started to pull the door closed behind me. As I did, I noticed something. How in the world…?

There, on her side and staring at my mother and sister and the burned remains of a potholder and dripping stove, lay Gerda. Sally must have found her in my drawer. That little sneak! I'd have to talk to her when I got home from work. I left the doll where she was and ran down the hall and out the front door.

* * *

The morning had turned out better than I'd imagined. My supervisor himself had been in a meeting when I arrived tardy, so while my pay would be docked, at least I'd avoided another saliva-specked lecture. Lily and I met on our lunch break and walked across the street to the Star Bakery. Birds kept an eye on the street below and had a running commentary going between the trees outside of the brick building. We'd decided to splurge and enjoy an impromptu dessert picnic, but we'd have to hurry to get back before the whistle blew.

I pushed the door open and laughed as Lily described her latest frustration as a female novelist. The smell of warm baked things hit me. My mouth watered and my stomach growled simultaneously. A dark-haired man stood behind the counter, waiting on an elderly woman, but the rest of the place was empty.

"Must be our lucky day," I said. "We beat the lunch crowd." The glass cases were filled with napoleons and donuts, crusty loaves of bread, and rolls. Lily and I made our purchases, then brought them out to the riverbank and found a nice spot. On a napkin between us, we spread three donuts and two napoleons...

"Oh, this is the life," Lily said moments later. She leaned back with her head cradled in one bent arm.

"What, the picnic, or working at the mill?" I teased.

"No, silly. This time in our lives. It will never be like this again, you know." Lily looked up at the fat, white clouds that drifted overhead. "We'll never be this free again. Soon you'll be married and having babies, and I'll be a famous novelist and have to move to New York City to be closer to my agent. I'll likely fall in love while I'm there. After all, who could resist my success and my money?"

I swatted her and laughed.

"Don't be daft. You can't move away and leave me here all alone."

"You won't be alone. You'll have Will," she said. She elongated his name and put a hand to her forehead, then laughed.

A funny feeling arose in my gut. The thought of the days ahead, of my life being one with Will's and then adding babies into the mix...would I end up like my mother? That wasn't the life I wanted. And without Lily, my one and only friend, who would I confide in? I lay back on the grass, its soft points pricking the skin on my arms. What would life really be like in a year or two? Or ten? One of the clouds passed over the sun. Lily sat up and pulled on her sweater, which had been wound around her shoulders.

"It's so romantic, isn't it? Our lives and all that lies ahead," Lily said. "Will you come and visit me in the city? I'll probably have an apartment on Fifth Avenue, and we can walk in the park and push your babies in their pram for hours. Well, between my important publishing meetings, of course."

"Of course," I said and laughed, but it sounded hollow. The sun reappeared, and I turned my face up toward it. Was Lily right? Was this the freest we would ever be? I didn't feel especially free. I worked, helped Mama with the children, and cleaned up after guests.

"Etta!" a voice called. "Etta!"

I turned. A figure approached, running. I recognized the boy as he drew closer; it was Tommy. Why wasn't he in school?

I stood. Crumbs fell from my skirt as he approached.

"Tommy? What in the world are you—"

"Etta, you've got to come!" Tommy leaned over, his skinny arms on his knees. "It's...Sally," he gasped. "There's been an accident." I started running before he could finish but his voice called after me. "Mama needs you."

Chapter Thirteen

Present Day

"Sampson!" I called, perched on the back step, halfway out the door. "Sampson?"

Where was he? Of all the mornings, he had to choose this one to squeeze his way out of the door. At least I assumed that's where he was. He hadn't been around all morning and I had a meeting with Helen in just over an hour. She'd flown into the Burlington Airport—had arrived already, a quick glance at my watch told me—and we were meeting for coffee downtown to discuss the show. She had other clients in the area, so her appearance wasn't only for my benefit, but I was still excited.

Except now I couldn't find the cat. I hated the thought of leaving him outdoors if he had escaped the house. Who knew how far he'd wander? I didn't have a cat door, so he'd be stuck in the chilly air until I returned. Plus, I'd hoped to go to the art supply store after lunch and maybe treat myself to a book at one of the cute independent bookshops before coming home.

"Sampson?" I called again and made a sort of squeaking noise with my lips. He usually came running when he heard it, as he rightly associated it with treats that smelled like salmon. I looked all along the tree line beyond the backyard and watched for any movement. But the air was still and the trees stood like gray soldiers, straight and unmoving.

I sighed and closed the door.

Gerda sat on the counter. I'd found a tiny tea set, just her size, in a box in my studio, and set it up nearby. The sunlight at that moment slanted in through the window, making her glow. I was surprised by a wash of tenderness in my chest. She looked so fragile there, all alone.

"I'll be home before you know it," I said. "I would take you along with me, but it wouldn't be much fun for you, stuck inside my bag. You'll be more comfortable here, won't you? Though now your brother has gone missing." I glanced out the window and hoped to see a flash of orange fur. Nothing.

I headed for the door—car keys, water bottle, and a tote bag in my arms. Should I leave a dish of wet food outside for Sampson in case...? But no, it might attract a fox or raccoon or even worse, a coyote. My parents had drilled into Nigel and me the importance of letting wild animals take care of themselves. I no longer even fed the birds until mid-December, after a visit by a black bear, bulking up for winter hibernation.

I sighed and pulled the door closed, then unloaded everything in the front passenger seat. I double-checked my bag after I climbed in and closed the car door. The portfolio that featured all the dolls that I would send to the Met was in there. I couldn't wait to show Helen both the dolls and the backdrops I'd created in their final format. A little twist of fear wrenched my chest when I thought of the ruined main piece—and the doll that I was working on to take its place—but I pushed it away.

* * *

An hour later I stood outside the door of a café on Church Street. A drizzly rain had started to fall, and my heart hammered in my chest. I hated this. Being in strange places packed with people. All the glances. The murmured observations between friends as they saw my exposed skin. Even on this chilly day, my scarf and long sleeves couldn't cover my hands and wrists, or my face. I couldn't do it. I couldn't walk in there. My breath came harder. Was I going to have a panic attack? I'd had these frequently in the past—especially when my parents were ill and I was balancing their care with my work—but they'd lessened in the past several months.

I moved away from the door toward the alleyway and pressed my back against the concrete wall. I breathed in and out several times, closed my eyes, and prayed that I'd get myself under control. Finally, I felt the buzzing in my ears lessen, my breath coming more normally.

The café was crowded when I walked in. I saw Helen near the window and waved weakly. My bag slipped from my shoulder. She stood when she saw me and smiled. Helen was petite, but her manner was powerful. Always professional, she shook my hand firmly, not bothering with hugs or air kisses. Her smile was wide and genuine, though.

"It's good to see you," she said. Her eyes flicked momentarily to the patches on my face, on my neck, but she quickly brought her gaze back to my eyes.

"Have you ordered?" I asked. I could feel people at the table to the right of us staring.

Then a little girl's voice asked loudly, "Mommy, what's

wrong with that lady's face?"

I pretended not to hear anything, and Helen did the same. She took my arm and we moved toward the tall counter.

"Let's go get our drinks and then we'll dive into the details."

We placed our orders at the tall counter where a frighteningly efficient barista whipped together our drinks simultaneously, all while asking what we wanted to eat. I ordered a slice of lemon cake and Helen a slice of gluten-free gingerbread.

Settled back at the corner table near the window, we made small talk for a few minutes and watched the eclectic mix of individuals walking up and down Church Street. A man with a thick, bushy beard pushed a pink stroller in which sat an ancient-looking pug with a studded collar. Two professionals in suits hunched their shoulders against the wind coming off Lake Champlain. One nodded to the other in apparent agreement. A young woman dressed in a black tulle skirt and jeans strolled past talking loudly into her cell phone, a cigarette in the other hand.

"So," Helen said and pushed aside her half-eaten slice of bread and coffee mug moments later. "Don't keep me in suspense any longer. Where is it?"

I laughed too loudly, then feeling self-conscious, lowered my voice. "It's right here." I pulled the heavy book free from my tote bag and slid it across the table to my agent. My heartbeat thundered in my ears and my hands shook as I wrapped them around my mug and waited for her response.

No matter how long an artist creates, she will always be affected by critics on one level or another. And this was Helen. We'd worked together for—what was it?—four years now, or close to. Yet in some ways, and on a very embarrassing level, I craved her approval more than anyone else's. Why? Because

I believed in her. She represented some of the best sculptors in the country. She wasn't a hand-holder or a flatterer, but she was fair and kind. And she knew her stuff. Helen scoured the art news and stayed on top of what was happening in our corner of the art world as an aggressive dog with a very tasty bone.

"There's one thing you should know," I said as she studied the first image. "It's about the centerpiece of the exhibit, the—"

Helen held up a finger. "Just a moment. I need to really absorb what I'm seeing here."

I nodded and sat back in my seat. I'd forgotten that about Helen—her need to sit with a piece, undistracted, to take it in. I sipped my coffee and pushed aside the plate that held the lemon cake. I was too nervous to have taken more than a nibble, my stomach knotted beneath my dress shirt. I watched her face and alternately glanced out the window, waiting for her opinion. Finally, after what felt like hours, she closed the back cover, flipped the portfolio over, and rested her hands on top. She looked directly at me, her dark blue eyes giving nothing away. Did she love it? Hate it? It was close to the initial sketches we'd gone over together, and many of the dolls she'd seen in person were included in the exhibit. But the backdrop had been added in its entirety since we last met, and three of the dolls were new additions. My fingernails dug into my palms under the table and I took a shallow breath.

"I really like it," Helen said finally, and my hands unclenched a few centimeters.

"Oh good," I said, my voice breathless. "I know there is still work to be done. There's something about the backdrop in the second panel that isn't working for me..."

We bent our heads together over the portfolio and went

through each of the images. Helen made suggestions and I made notes of these. When we reached the end of the book, she looked up at me.

"What were you going to tell me about the one doll? You said it was the centerpiece." She flipped to the middle of the book, the heavy pages clicking together in a way that I loved.

I nodded and flipped forward two more pages, then tapped my finger on the close-up image of the Gothic sprite.

"This one," I said, "won't be part of the show. But I'm working on another that will be very similar."

"Why?"

"There was an accident in my studio. I think my cat knocked something off a shelf and the doll was ruined. It was…" My mind was filled with images of the sprite's crushed skull, the shredded bits of fabric on the floor, and the worktable. "It was a bad day."

"I can imagine," Helen said, and sipped her coffee. "No way it can be repaired?" Then before I answered, she waved a hand through the air. "Scratch that. I trust your judgment, Isabel, and I know that the final piece will be perfect. I'll need the new measurements though, for the Met, and photos as soon as you can get them to me. Say by Friday?"

I nodded, a warm glow spreading through my chest. "Of course."

We talked about travel arrangements for the exhibit, Helen's upcoming vacation in Greece—"after your exhibit, of course"—and the media coverage that both Helen and the museum were working on. She showed me proofs of some of the images. Seeing my name in the beautiful font along with "The Metropolitan Museum of Art," made my eyes water. Helen excused herself to the ladies' room at that moment and

I used the time to get my emotions under control. Part of me couldn't believe that this was real. Things like this just didn't happen to regular people like me, did they?

When Helen returned to the table and not so discreetly checked her watch, I gathered my things.

"Friday for the images on the new doll, okay?" Helen reminded as we shook hands again. "I'm off to see a client in Shelburne, but I'll call you that afternoon if I don't hear from you by then."

I nodded. "Sure. And Helen..." I put a hand on her jacketed arm as she'd turned to walk out the door. "Thank you."

"You're welcome. And thank you, Isabel, for your hard work. You'll see that it's all going to pay off." She smiled. "It's a great adventure, isn't it?"

Chapter Fourteen

1944

My legs burned and my lungs ached as I rounded the corner of our street. The house was like an anthill with people coming and going. An ambulance, big and gray like a waiting vulture, was parked out front. Small groups of people were crowded near the streetlights. Where was Mama? I had no air left. I stopped running. My legs felt so heavy, as though they were weighted with lead. A sick press of dread squeezed my chest closed. What had happened? Where was Sally?

Voices murmuring stopped as I passed.

"Mama?" I called, finally able to breathe. "Where is she?" I looked wildly toward the crowd of people. Blank faces stared back.

"She's inside." Our neighbor, Mrs. Razolli, appeared at my elbow. "Come, Claudette," she said and put her arm around me. "She needs you."

I wanted to shake my head, to disagree. My mother was the strongest woman I knew. She didn't need me—or anyone else—I wanted to tell Mrs. Razolli, but the words wouldn't come. She guided me, her strong arm around my shoulders.

Our steps fell in sync as we walked toward the open door of the house.

Inside, there was a strange, unfamiliar smell. The house appeared empty, but I heard voices and the thumps of footsteps on the second floor above our heads.

"What happened?" I asked, but Mrs. Razolli shook her head.

"Clear the way," a nasally male voice shouted from the top of the stairs. Mrs. Razolli grabbed me tighter and shuffled me to the side of the staircase. Her rounded hip bumped into mine and I grasped the banister. A man in uniform appeared at the top of the staircase, his back to us. Slowly he made his way down, heavy boots clunking on each of the wooden stairs. Another man stood at the end of the stretcher and they walked in unison, mirror images as they descended the stairs.

"Careful now," said the second man. "Don't jar her."

I realized then that Sally lay on the stretcher, motionless. I heard a strange sound, a strangled choking noise, and didn't realize it had come from me until Mrs. Razolli patted my arm.

"There, there," her voice murmured close to my ear. Her breath smelled of old tea and leftover lunch. I thought I might gag. Instead, I trained my attention on the gurney and the ambulance drivers.

Finally, they reached the bottom step.

"Who closed the door?" the nasally voiced man asked. He cursed under his breath and Mrs. Razolli stepped quickly to the door and opened it. The men passed through. Between them, pale as a china plate, lay Sally, tucked beneath a thin wool blanket, and strapped to the gurney. Her eyes were closed and blood oozed from several long cuts on her face. It had started to congeal, drying into her curls, which were matted on one side where the second man adjusted a compress.

"Best to find to your mother," said Mrs. Razolli, and guided me up the staircase. The air felt heavy, like a thick blanket pressing down on me. I walked up the stairs but couldn't feel my feet. Everything around me shimmered and moved, as though in slow motion. Was that really my hand on the banister? Was that whimpering sound coming from my lips?

Mrs. Razolli withdrew after she'd gotten me to the top of the stairs. There, a low murmur of voices came from the girls' room. I walked in, pushing the door further open. An officer in uniform stood by the wall closest to me. He stared as I walked in. The strange smell was magnified in the closed-in space. On the rag rug, someone had spilled ink. No, not ink, but a dark red liquid. Blood. Gray slate lay around it, jagged and broken into fragments.

I looked wildly around the room. Mama stood near the two large windows. A ray of sunlight lit her hair like a halo. Her face was crumpled, like a letter that had spent too long in the mail, and her hair, always held back in a tidy bun, was coming loose, strands of it around her face.

"Mama?" I said, my voice loud in the quiet space. "What happened?"

The man murmured something, but I couldn't hear him. There was a roar between my ears and I couldn't tell if it was in the house or my blood pounding against my skull. My mother looked at me, but there was no recognition of my voice, my face. I crossed quickly to her, and then all at once she grabbed me, folded me tightly into her strong arms.

"Claudette," she said, smoothing a hand over my back like she used to when I was small. "Oh, Claudette. There was an accident. Sally...." Her voice broke and she pushed me away from her, held me at arm's length. "The mirror fell from

101

the wall," she said and nodded toward the empty space where the large piece used to hang. "Sally must have been playing under it and the heavy frame…they don't think…." Her breath came out next in a hitching gasp. "They said there was a lot of trauma to her head. That she might be slow, backward. My beautiful little girl…." I caught her as she started to pitch toward the floor, my calm, sensible mother who never cried and was always practical. We both crumpled on the wide boards, me holding her, our tears mingled.

"You should be with her," I said. The officer cleared his throat.

"They're leaving now," he said. I nodded.

"I can't," my mother said and wiped at her eyes. "I have the guests and—"

"Mama," I said and shook her arms. "Go. Now." She sat for several long seconds, frozen on her knees. Then she nodded and stood. The officer guided her with his hand.

"I'll take care of everything," I said and stood beside her. "Go with Sally. She needs you."

Mama held a hand over her mouth; her eyes still leaked silent tears. I pressed a handkerchief into her hand. She nodded again and the officer guided her out of the room. I heard their footsteps as they descended the stairs, then the front door opened and closed. I watched from the window as my mother climbed into the back of the ambulance. A moment later, it pulled away.

I turned back to the room and stared at the mess until the officer returned.

"I'm Officer Shelton," he said. "I came when the call came in for help."

"What happened?" I said dully.

"From what I gather, your sister was playing up here. She either pushed on the mirror or it fell on its own. It was a heavy frame," he said, pointing at the back of the mirror that lay to the side of the slate. No, not slate, I realized, but the dull back of the broken mirror. I pictured her then, innocently playing, her golden curls bobbing around her face, and then that huge mirror....

"You can see here," he said, and walked to the wall where the mirror used to hang, "that it pulled the nail clean out." His finger jabbed at the hole where the nail used to be. The wallpaper around the opening was jagged, like teeth. I nodded when he looked at me.

"I should...." I said, then stopped. What should I do? The strange blanket of dullness was still so tight I could hardly breathe.

"I can help you clean up," he said, nodding toward the rug and the red smeared on the wooden floor.

"Thank you," I said. "But I'm sure you have more important things to do."

"It's no bother," he said. "I don't think it will take us long."

I nodded again. "I'll go get a bucket and some rags."

* * *

After we'd finished with the floor, I made Officer Shelton a cup of coffee and left him sipping it at the dining room table. I returned to the girls' room to collect the dirty rags and the bucket of red water. My stomach curled as I looked around and bent to retrieve a final piece of mirror that had skittered under the bed. Gerda lay under the bed on her side. She must have gotten pushed there in the chaos. I pulled her out.

There wasn't a drop of blood on her. In fact, she looked whiter somehow, almost glowing. I smoothed down her dress, and my fingers skimmed over her back, which felt oddly lumpy. I turned her over. Her dress was undone there. I looked more closely. The stitching had come undone, just a bit. Maybe Sally had picked at it, her curiosity getting the better of her.

I went to my mother's room and got a sewing needle and thread. I couldn't fix Sally, but I could repair the doll so she'd be here and ready for Sally's pudgy little arms when she came back home. *If she came back home.*

As I stitched, I noticed something odd. The doll felt warm to the touch. I set her down a minute and touched the post on the bed to see if it was my fingers that were hot, but no, that felt cool...cold even, with the light breeze coming through a crack in the window.

I picked the doll up again. Heat radiated from her. I shook my head, tried not to think, just to finish the job at hand. When I had, I turned Gerda over.

I gasped.

Her face, which had previously been white and dull, was now radiant and filled with color. Her cheeks were flushed, as though she'd been running or someone had rubbed rouge onto them. Her eyes, a pale blue, now gleamed and sparkled like sapphires. Her face and hands had changed from a pale white to bright, shimmering alabaster. I threw her down on the bed without thinking.

"What are you?" I said aloud, the sound of my voice loud in the empty space. I looked at the doll, waited for it to move, to turn toward me or cock her head, it was so lifelike. But she lay there and stared vacantly at the ceiling. Shivers ran up and down my spine and goosebumps broke out on my arms.

I stared at the doll for several long moments, but nothing changed. Finally, I picked her up and darted across the hall. In my room, I closed the door. Then I dug to the bottom of my bureau drawer. I wound a pair of thick woolen tights around her again and again until she was completely encased in a shroud. Then I stuffed her deep into the back of the drawer and closed it, hard.

My hands trembled and my knees shook as I walked down the steps to check on Officer Shelton.

Chapter Fifteen

Present Day

I hurried along the brick-paved street and glanced in shop windows, but was not compelled enough to go inside of any. The thought of the cozy art shop was replaced now with a stronger desire to return home. A knot of worry sat in my gut about Sampson. The day had turned gloomy and gray; a stiff wind laced with pelting raindrops. People bundled in colorful layers hurried from one business to another. I just wanted the warmth and coziness of the fireplace and a cup of tea and felt the physical pull of my studio.

My car was parked in a garage on Bank Street. I headed in that direction. A hearty musician was playing the accordion—the music swelled on the relatively hushed and nearly empty street. I didn't recognize the song but smiled at him as I walked past, tucking my chin further into my coat.

"Afternoon, lady," he said and nodded at me. His eyes were dark brown, even darker than his mocha-colored skin. When our gaze connected I felt something, a sort of jolt inside.

"Hello," I replied and paused just for another moment before I walked on.

"Ma'am?" he called, his voice louder than the instrument.

I turned.

"I got a message for you." His fingers continued to move over the keys, but the squeezing of his arms had slowed. The sound coming from the accordion had turned slower and mournful.

"Oh?" I said. I stopped and turned toward him fully. He was dressed in a ratty coat, his big hands extended from the too-short sleeves. They were bare and calloused and when I looked more closely, I could see fine scars all over both his hands.

"I like to give a message of hope when I can," he said, removing one hand from the instrument to adjust the knit cap on his head. "It does the soul good, doesn't it?"

I didn't have a response, so simply stood there. "What's the message," I asked.

"Well, it's a bit of an odd one. Not exactly encouraging, but I'd better share it with you anyway. It might mean something to you."

I took a step closer. His dark eyes explored my face but then his gaze returned to mine. He smiled, almost sadly.

"You've got to let the dead rest if you want to really live."

I stared. A shiver started behind my knees and ran its way up my backbone and into my scalp.

"What?" I said stupidly.

"You've got to let the dead rest if you want to really live," he repeated.

I shook my head. "I'm not sure what you mean," I said, and edged away from him. He grinned at me, then brandished the accordion and played more jauntily than before. "I don't know what it means either, ma'am," he said with a rusty laugh. "I'm just the messenger."

"Uh-huh," I said. "Well, thanks."

"You can thank me properly if you'd be so kind," he said and tapped at the open music case with his booted foot. The rain had damped the collection of bills and coins in the velvet-lined space. Drops clung from the edges, ready to plunge into the case. I sighed, reached for my bag, pulled out a five-dollar bill, and dropped it in.

"Thank you, kindly," he said and nodded at me. I turned and hurried toward the parking garage. I felt his eyes on my back but didn't turn around. The music though was trapped in my head. It revolved between my ears even when I navigated the car back onto the interstate for home.

You've got to let the dead rest if you want to really live.

What had he meant? My parents, maybe. Thoughts of them still brought the familiar ache, like the ghost of a missing limb. It also brought thoughts of Nigel. Our last visit hadn't been pleasant: he, accusing me of living with them and staying close to collect a bigger share of the inheritance; me, braying at him for his selfishness and lack of interest in them and their well-being right up to the bitter end. He'd been in California when Mom died, and out of the country when Dad had passed.

My hands dug into the steering wheel, clenched so hard that they'd turned white. I let out a shaky laugh and loosened my grip. I'd given the musician's words more weight than they deserved. He probably told everyone that same thing or similar vague phrases. A party trick that any showman knew.

But why that message?

I turned the volume up on the radio and tried to drown out the sound of accordion music.

* * *

The drive took longer than usual. The rain came down in drenching sheets and I drove slowly, tried to see through the pelting downpour. It had started just before I exited the interstate. The loud drumming on the roof drowned out the classical music station. My hands were clammy, and I moved them periodically to my trousers, one at a time, to wipe them before I returned them to their death grip on the wheel. I hunched lower and peered out of the windshield until, finally, I pulled to the side of the road on Fairfield Hill and allowed other traffic to pass by. Great, drenching rooster tails of dirty water hit my car as each one went by.

The rain lightened by the time I'd reached the center of Bakersfield and finally, I turned onto my road. I bounced along the pockmarked surface and breathed a big sigh of relief when I turned into my driveway. The fire would have gone out by now, but I'd have it roaring again in no time. I could almost feel the heat. I'd start the fire, make tea, and collapse on my favorite chair for a much-deserved rest before poking around in the studio. And hopefully, Sampson would be waiting for me by his food dish, or wet but fine near the side door.

Except it didn't happen that way. When I walked through the door, I heard water. Not dripping, but gushing somewhere. I flicked on the lights, searched all the rooms on the first floor, but there was nothing. I ran upstairs, the stairs creaking, but the bathroom was just as I'd left it that morning. None of the four bedrooms had any water leaking from a broken pipe that I could see. The sound was more muted on the second floor though, so I ran back downstairs. When I opened the basement door, I heard water pouring.

Frantically, I flipped the light switch. Nothing. I ran down the stairs and clutched onto the metal railing so that I wouldn't slip. The scent of dirt and mustiness hit me, and then the chill of the air. The sound was much louder. It was coming from the left, from the laundry area, the only modern part of the dirt-floor cellar. Had a pipe burst? I couldn't see anything, so I turned, stumbled back up the stairs, and ran to the hall closet. I grabbed a flashlight and hurried back down. The beam of light bounced over the surfaces. It illuminated shadows and made lurching movements appear on the walls around me.

I shone my light into the corner. Water spewed from a pipe. I ran to the washing machine, reaching up over it to pull down on a lever, turning off the water. Water continued to drip from the washing machine and the small shelves that were under the pipe for several seconds, but at least the soaking deluge had stopped. My feet were icy in my boots, my pants halfway up my calves soaked. Water was everywhere. The floor was covered, the shelves drenched.

Cursing under my breath, I grabbed rags, old towels, and a bucket and started soaking up the water. I wrung the towels and rags out into a mop bucket. The wind had died down outside, and somewhere close by a branch scratched against the side of the house. When I was little, the noise always frightened me, like fingernails trying to pry open my bedroom window. I wrung out another towel. The dirty water formed bubbles in the pail when it hit the surface.

I heard a sound then, like the cry of a wounded bird. I stopped, listened.

Nothing.

A few minutes later, though, I heard it again. I put the towel down and moved toward the far wall, closest to the window. It was smeared and dirty, letting in just a thin slice of light from the outdoors. Yes, there it was again, the sound was faint but plaintive. An injured rodent maybe, or a bird close to the window that I couldn't see.

I sighed and returned to the water puddled on the basement floor.

* * *

When the floor was as dry as I could get it, I'd called the plumber for an emergency visit, then spent ten minutes hauling wood inside. It had taken another five to try and get the fire started. My fingers shook so much that I lost match after match on the hearth. Finally, the kindling caught. I sat back on my heels and watched the tiny flames for a few minutes. Chills racked my body. Gerda sat on the counter where she'd been this morning. I walked over to her and picked her up. She was surprisingly warm, probably because my fingers were numb.

"What is happening today?" I asked her, but she didn't have any answers. There was a warm tingle in my hands now, and I looked at her more carefully in the light. She appeared newer somehow. Her eyes were more blue than gray, and her hair was prettier, more glossy. Even her face and hands were less webbed and smoother. I shook my head and set her back in her place.

I slipped my coat back on, ready to continue the search for the cat when the phone rang. I picked it up just before the machine clicked on.

"Hello?"

"Isa, tell me that you've called the realtor and he just has his wires crossed." Nigel's voice was peckish on the other end.

I sighed. "No, I haven't called the realtor. I forgot—"

"That's convenient."

"Look, there's been a lot going on here and it slipped my mind."

Now it was my brother's turn to sigh, deeply and loudly.

"I'll call, okay? I said I would and I will. Just not at the moment. Sampson has been missing since this morning and there was a leak in the basement—"

"What kind of leak?" Nigel's voice was suspicious. I smacked a palm over my forehead, quietly, and closed my eyes.

"It's no big deal. The plumber is on his way. Look, I really have to—"

"Do you see? This proves my point, Isa. That house is a money pit. Didn't we just pay to have the roof repaired a few months ago? And now this. The bathrooms need to be updated and the wiring in the entire house really needs to be redone. It's probably a fire hazard." He sighed again. "How much is the plumber going to cost? Do they still charge extra for emergency visits? They do here."

"The roof was repaired last spring and pipes sometimes break. It's an old house, what do you expect?"

"I expect you to get your head out of the clouds and deal with reality for once," Nigel barked.

I was silent for a long moment. My heart hammered in my chest. Anger pricked the back of my throat.

"Sorry, but you know what I mean," Nigel said, his voice calmer. "It's not practical for you to live there anymore. I know you wanted to keep it in the family, but it's time to wake up and see what that dream is going to cost. It's only going to get worse. You really need to start thinking seriously about moving."

"I hate to cut you off when we're having such a lovely

conversation, but I really have to go. It's getting dark and I need to go out and look for the cat. Give my love to Lisa and the kids."

I hung up before he could respond.

* * *

"Sampson!" I yelled. My voice bounced off the nearest trees and twisted against low shrubbery. I yelled it over and over again until my throat was raw. The ground was soaked, and rainwater dripped from the branches and leaves overhead in big splashes when the wind shook them. Had he been able to find shelter in the storm? I'd already circled the house, checked the woodshed, and had walked partway into the trees and called for him. Still, there was no sign of him. I made kissing noises until my lips ached. But no flash of orange fur or a frustrated cry from a soggy kitty anywhere. I returned to the house. If I didn't get out of these wet clothes soon I'd end up with pneumonia.

The thought of a hot bath was like a physical craving, but there was no water. Besides, I needed to get back outside and look for the cat again, as soon as I changed. I left all my wet clothes in a pile in the bathroom, then toweled off hurriedly. I layered on long johns and a pair of jeans, thick woolen socks along with a long-sleeve shirt and old sweater, then went back downstairs. I'd just shoved my feet back into my mud boots when the phone rang.

The plumber, Mr. Sotta, asked a few questions and then told me he was on his way. The sky outside the windows had turned from slate gray to dark indigo by the time I'd made my way outdoors to look for Sampson again. My heartbeat fluttered in my wrists and my stomach was snarled with knots of anxiety. Where was that cat?

Chapter Sixteen

1944

"How's Sally?" Will asked. "I got here as soon as I could."

I turned from the counter and dusted my hands off. The numbness had finally subsided, but my mind still felt slow and dull. Will crossed the kitchen to me and took me in his arms. It felt wonderful. His strength seeped into me and covered me completely. It was like lowering myself into a steaming bath when every muscle in my body ached.

"She'll make it, though they aren't sure now how much damage there will be to her brain…." I sobbed then, great heaving, undignified gasps that shook my body.

"Shh," he murmured, "it's all right. I'm here now, and I'll stay as long as you need me to."

He rubbed my back and I let myself cry. All the fear and the guilt twisted in my gut loosened.

It was later, as we sat at the kitchen table, two mugs of coffee between us with a jigger of brandy in each, that I asked him about the doll.

"Where did you find her?" I kept my voice light.

"In a shop, near Berlin. I had a day of leave and when I saw her, I thought of you."

I smiled, but my hands shook on the mug. I couldn't very well ask Will if she was possessed, could I? But still, there was no denying the onslaught of disasters that had happened since she'd arrived in our house.

"Do you know anything about her?" I tried to keep my voice light, as though I were asking after his father's health. "Where the doll was made? How old she is?"

Will's face darkened.

"No," he said. "Geesh, what is this…. The Spanish Inquisition? Do you always ask so many questions when someone gives you a gift?"

Heat bloomed on my cheeks and I dropped my eyes to my coffee, stirred it needlessly. Will reached across the table and grabbed my fingers gently.

"You know that I don't like thinking about it, about when I was away. But that's no reason to take it out on you. Especially after—"

"Don't, please," I said. I didn't want to start crying again.

"I shouldn't have spoken to you like that," Will said. "Forgive me?"

I nodded, my fingers loosened on the coffee cup.

"I don't know much about the doll, though, just thought she was pretty. Like you." He smiled at me then and all the darkness around his eyes lifted.

I smiled back. "I hope I didn't get you in trouble, calling you at work."

He shook his head and looked away from me out of the dining room windows. The gray clouds were thick, the sky threatening rain.

"Doesn't matter," he said. "I'm not planning on staying there long."

"Oh?" I poured a little more coffee into each of our mugs and another splash of brandy. The heat of it had warmed me to my toes.

"Nah. It's a dead-end place. Guys have been working there for years, never moving up, never bettering themselves. The boss is a piece of work, too. Wants us to 'yes sir' him and hangs over our shoulders, making sure we do things just the way he wants them done. Even if his ways are outdated. Bad enough we've got the WPB to deal with, why not try to keep civilians' cars working the best they can while the ban is on?"

I nodded, but my concerns over the ban on cars and the War Production Board were far down on my list of worries. What about Will? Was he ever going to find a job that wasn't beneath him, one that he'd be satisfied with? As soon as the thought came, a wash of hot guilt flooded my chest. He was just having a hard time transitioning. Who wouldn't? So much change, so many things to worry about now, things about his future, our future, that he probably hadn't had time to work through what happened while he was overseas. There, it was all about staying alive, following orders. Here, now, it was different. Maybe in some ways that lack of direction was grating on him. Maybe it was causing him to doubt himself, doubt his abilities. Plus, there was the constant pain in his leg. He never complained about it, but I knew it must ache terribly and make work that much more of a challenge.

"...at work?"

"I'm sorry, Will. My mind was wandering."

"Ah, that's all right, sweetheart." He picked up my hand and kissed it. "It makes sense after the kind of day you've had."

I didn't correct him, just put my hand to his cheek.

"I love you, you know," I said.

His dark eyes locked onto mine, the pulse in his neck jumped.

"And I love you twice as much, Etta. I've been blabbing on and on about my small problems when you've got your hands full here. Is there anything you need help with? Anything I could do for your mother?"

My smile was tremulous and I shook my head, then nodded.

"If you don't mind, we could use a refill of firewood. I need to finish the biscuits and the stew before the boarders come looking for dinner."

Will kissed the top of my head as he stood, then drew me to my feet, both of his calloused hands holding mine.

"She's going to be fine. You're going to be fine, too. We're all going to be fine," he said this last part with a chuckle, low and deep in his chest.

"I know," I said. I put my arms around his waist and buried my face in his chest. "I know we will."

* * *

But everything was not fine.

The doctors said that, as was feared, Sally would likely have permanent brain damage. She would never again be the little girl we once knew, they warned. She might regain the use of her arms, but likely not her legs, and mentally would always be three years old.

"There are worse things," my mother said after we'd met with the doctors. "At least she's alive."

They'd tried to talk my mother into putting her in a home, a special hospital where she'd get care around the clock, but my mother shook her head before the doctors had even finished explaining. "No," she'd said. "My girl is coming home with me. Being in a familiar place, that's what she needs. That and her family. She won't be going to any home but ours."

Later though, when I was passing by her bedroom door at home, I heard my mother's muffled crying, and a whispered, "Why, why, why?" My heart clenched, and I hurried down the stairs as silently as I could.

* * *

Lily stopped over the night of the accident, a basket of fresh muffins still warm from the oven in her hands. She'd hugged me hard and we talked quietly as we washed the dishes that the guests had dirtied at dinner. My brothers and sister were nearly soundless as they did their chores. Mama was still at the hospital.

"Do you believe in spirits?" I blurted out during a lull in our conversation. My fingers slipped on the soapy platter. I nearly dropped it but got a tighter grip at the last second.

"You mean like ghosts?" she asked.

I shook my head. "Not ghosts really, but spirits. Good and evil, I don't know, beings, that float around where we can't see them and do mischief or good."

She was quiet for a moment and when I glanced over, her brow was furrowed. It was her pondering look. I kept quiet.

"My practical, no-nonsense side says no," Lily said finally.

"But?" I asked.

"But I have heard enough firsthand accounts from people who believe in spirits, ghosts, apparitions, what have you, that the rest of me says I'm not sure. Plus, I'm Catholic." She grinned. "It pretty much comes with the territory."

We were both quiet a moment. The kitchen was warm and cozy, the leftover heat from the stove filling the space that still smelled of stew and biscuits. There were footsteps overhead as guests returned to their rooms, some to change clothes before heading out to a pub, some to rest and relax for the night. The grandfather clock in the hall ticked loudly.

"Why do you ask?" Lily wondered aloud. I handed her the last dish and let the water out of the sink.

"You'll think I'm crazy," I said and swirled the dishrag through the gray water. I watched as the few bubbles that were left spun crazily toward the open drain.

"Me? Aren't I the most open-minded person you know?" Lily asked and laughed.

It was true. When I talked to Lily, she listened intently, as though she were making mental notes for later. I leaned with my back against the sink. My body and mind were exhausted. The lip of the ceramic sink dug into my back, but I didn't move. It had felt good to feel something, even if it was discomfort.

"When the…accident happened, I think Sally was playing with a doll. It was one that Will gave me. He brought it back from overseas and Sally fell in love with it. I caught her playing with it, and she made such a fuss that I let her take care of it while I was at work."

Lily nodded, her eyes pinned on my face.

"The doll is a little ugly—pale and plain. But when I was cleaning everything up, afterward…." I stumbled a little on that word but kept going. "When I was cleaning up, I found the doll partway under Sally's bed. It was pristine, not a drop of blood or smudge on her dress or hands or face. But more than that—she'd changed. Her body was shining white and her eyes a sparkling blue. Even her hair was pretty—shiny and real looking, not dull blonde. It was like she'd, I don't know, come to life in some way. And when I picked her up, she felt warm."

"Warm?"

I nodded. "At first, I thought it was just that I was cold from the shock, and I was. But she was radiating heat, like a fireplace."

Lily looked away for a moment and chewed her lip.

"And there's more," I said. "The mirror that fell from the wall has been there for years. It was nailed into the stud the way it's supposed to be. Even the officer that came over said he couldn't explain why it would have fallen that way. The nail itself was still intact, it hadn't broken. So, what made it come off the wall? Plus, the doll seems to just show up whenever anything bad happens. She was on the stairs after our boarder fell on them, she was in the kitchen when the fire started—"

"You think that the doll comes alive when bad things happen?" Lily interrupted.

I nodded, then shook my head, feeling frustrated. "Maybe. Or maybe it *makes* bad things happen. I don't know exactly. I just wish that you could have seen her, then you could convince me that I'm not crazy."

"Did you tell anyone else?"

That made me laugh, a quick bark of humor.

"No," I told her. "I didn't."

She chewed her lip again and stared out the window over the kitchen sink. "What about opening it up? Have you seen what she's made of? Or maybe bring her to Father O'Brien."

"Your priest?"

She nodded. "Maybe it's possessed. I read a story once about

121

a jack-in-the-box that was, once. It would start playing that tinkling music in the middle of the night. And it would move right up into someone's bed and pop out—"

"This isn't helping, Lily," I said, goosebumps running over my arms. I sighed. "I don't know. I'm likely being foolish. With all the stress…I'm sure I was just imagining it." I knew before the words were out that they were untrue. I hadn't imagined what I'd seen. It was too vivid, too real.

"Can I see her?" Lily asked.

"She's in my bureau. Come on." We left our aprons on hooks in the kitchen and Lily trailed me up the stairs. The light in the hallway was dim and the noises from upstairs had become even quieter. The door to my room was partially open. I pushed through and once Lily was inside, turned and closed it, then locked it with the key that stayed in the lock.

My bedroom was small, the bureau across from the door, my bed tucked under the eaves, and a small table with a lamp and a few of my most precious items perched on top. There was also a wardrobe, another hand-me-down from the people who lived here before us. We crouched in front of the bureau and I pulled open the drawer, dug through my wool socks and stockings to the bottom. My fingers felt the tightly wrapped package. I pulled the doll encased in tights out onto my lap. Lily looked on. I heard her breathing near my shoulder.

"You mummified it in your stockings?" she asked, and I couldn't help but laugh, though my hands trembled I unrolled the doll.

Gerda was lying face down when I uncovered her. I slowly flipped her over. I'd expected to see the pinkness of her cheeks, the blazing of her blue eyes. Expected to feel the heat radiating from her compact body. But there was nothing. She looked like her normal, pale, tidy self. Her hair was once again washed out, her skin the same milky white. Her body was no warmer than a doll's should be.

"She's changed back," I said, then felt stupid. "I mean, she just looks like she did before."

"May I?" Lily reached for the doll.

I nodded. "Please. I wish I could give her to you. I don't like dolls and this one gives me the creeps. If it wasn't from Will…."

Lily picked the doll up and turned it over again.

"She's heavy, isn't she? What do you think she's made of?"

"I don't know." I shivered. "Snakes and snails and puppy dogs' tails?"

"Or maybe the ashes of the dead?"

I looked over at my friend. Her dark eyes were serious and she was inspecting the doll intently, her fingers exploring the narrow seam that ran up Gerda's back.

"Lily!" I said. "You'll give me nightmares. Besides, ashes wouldn't weigh that much."

"They're actually very heavy. All of that bone, you know."

I shivered. "Do I dare ask how you know that?"

"I was on assignment, writing an article about cremation. For the school paper," she admitted. "But it was fascinating. Did you know that the furnace needs to be at least 1400 degrees for it to be hot enough to burn up everything? And the actual ritual of burning a corpse dates back to 3000 BC."

The front door opened and closed, then we heard slow footsteps in the hallway below.

"Claudette?" My mother's voice called softly from the bottom of the stairs.

"We'll have to figure out what to do later," I said, and buried the doll back in the drawer under the clothes then shoved it closed. Lily nodded, and together we went to greet my mother.

Chapter Seventeen

Present Day

"There's the problem. Right there," the man in front of me, slim in canvas work pants, said. His hair was salt and pepper and stood wiry around his skull. He pointed the wrench in his hand toward the spot where the water had gushed out.

"See that? That crack?" His voice was thick and nasally from a cold he was trying to recover from, he'd said.

I leaned closer, but in the dim light, it was hard to see anything at all. Though he'd reset the breaker box—something I hadn't had the sense to do—the light down here was still dim. He shone his powerful flashlight at the spot and then I could see what he meant. Clearly, there was a large crack, extending along the pipe from the top nearly to the bottom.

"That's called a fissure. It's like a hairline crack only, as you can see, this one is much larger."

"What causes that?"

He flicked off the flashlight. "Age, usually."

"But these pipes were replaced when the new washer was installed down here. That was only a few years ago."

He shrugged. "Bad pipe then. It happens."

I nodded. "Is it something you can fix now?"

"Yup."

Mr. Sotta was a man of few words. But he knew what he was doing, and he worked quickly. At that point, I would have paid him my life savings for a hot bath. I headed back up the stairs and he got to work. My thoughts strayed—what would it be like to work as a plumber or an electrician? Being invited into people's homes—into the places that guests don't see—imagine what you'd learn about people that way. What could he learn about me?

The basement was a mess of boxes filled with materials that I'd collected for my studio, but which hadn't yet made it there. There were also things from my parents: memorabilia from their trips tucked into plastic totes, piles of musty books that no one would want to reread, old chairs with broken legs and cracked seats, end tables that wobbled. All of it needed to be sorted, organized and cleaned out. This basement was like a graveyard of old memories. I wondered if Mr. Sotta would deduce the same thing.

I flicked on the radio; opera music filled the kitchen while leaves swirled past the windows. A storm was coming, the weatherman said, his pleasant baritone interrupted the music moments later. Maybe snow, maybe ice. There was a possibility of power outages.

Great.

"Mr. Sotta, I'm going outside for a bit," I yelled down the stairs. "I'll be back soon. Just holler out the door if you need anything." He grunted an affirmative response and I put my coat back on and grabbed a heavy-duty flashlight. Sampson was out there somewhere. At least, I had to assume that. I'd searched the whole house from top to bottom while I'd waited for Mr. Sotta.

I should have been in the studio. I wished I were, instead of trudging through the wet undergrowth. Rain-slicked tree branches deposited their bounty on my shoulders and head. My hat was soaked through and my pants were wet up to my knees.

"Sampson!" I called over and over, but there was no response. No flash of orange fur flew by my legs, no plaintive meows beckoned me further into the woods. I searched and called until well after dark. My flashlight beam bounced off trees and shrubs and rocks, making strange, grotesquely shaped patterns.

Where could he have gone? I pushed against the thoughts that came in droves: Sampson hit by a truck and lying in a ditch or chased by coyotes, only to be cornered and torn apart by their sharp teeth....

Finally, I returned home, dejected. I left my sodden outwear and boots in the entryway at the back of the house. Then I turned on the tea kettle and crossed to warm my frozen fingers and shivering body once again by the crackling fire. As I stood, I heard the sound from earlier once again, so faintly that I nearly missed it. A soft cry. A meow? I listened more closely, but the wind had picked up outside and whistled loudly around the windows. I moved closer to the windows, then bent low. The sound seemed to be coming from below me. The basement? But I'd already—

"Ms. Joven?"

I jerked upright and banged my head on the underside of the side table.

"Ow," I muttered, then backed myself out of the space and rubbed the spot. Mr. Sotta stood in the doorway of the living room, his form nothing more than a dark shadow in the dimness.

"I didn't realize how dark it had gotten," I said and flicked on a table lamp. A warm puddle of light dripped over the furniture and floor.

"You're all set, ma'am."

I nodded and smiled, the top of my head still throbbed.

"Great," I said and moved toward the door. "How much do I owe you?"

Five minutes later, and a few hundred dollars wealthier, Mr. Sotta backed his van out of the driveway. I stood on the porch for a moment and checked the sky. It was dark and thick clouds above drowned out any light from the stars. The wind blew through the tree branches and moaned around the corners of the house. I shivered and grabbed another armful of wood from the porch before I returned inside.

The second I opened the door, I smelled smoke. I ran to the woodstove, but it crackled cheerily. Then I remembered the tea kettle. I raced to the kitchen. Smoke billowed from the stovetop where a potholder had started burning. I grabbed an oven mitt from the drawer and pulled the pad away from the burner. It stunk and smoked. I opened the back door and heaved it out. It fell to the ground and sizzled in the mud. I left the door open, letting the cold, fresh air wash into the house.

What else was going to go wrong today? The radio suddenly turned to static. I glanced over and saw—no, that wasn't possible. Hadn't I left her sitting with the tiny tea set on the far edge of the counter this morning? I shook my head and my heart clanged in my chest.

Gerda lay on her side, close to the kitchen sink. Her little dress was spread out like a fan, her arms hung stiffly by her sides. A strange feeling invaded my chest and spread its way through my limbs. It was a heaviness, a sort of dread that I hadn't felt in a long, long time. There had been a lot going on these past several days, but there was no way that I was moving this doll around the house and not realizing it. I stared at her for several long minutes. My heartbeat increased as I finally moved to her, picked her up, and ran to my studio. I tossed her into an empty box under the worktable and then left, shutting the door firmly behind me. As I did, I heard it again. The same, small crying sound. Where was it coming from? I listened harder, closed my eyes, but heard nothing.

Then, there it was again. Had it come from the basement? I went back down the steep steps, my slippers clopping on each one. Mr. Sotta had cleaned the area up around where he'd worked, even going so far as to sweep the nearly dry floor. The broom's bristle marks were still on the cement.

"Sampson," I called out. My voice was loud in the enclosed space. "Sampson? Here kitty, kitty."

The only sound I heard was the tree branches that scratched again at the windows. I moved further toward the back wall. My slipper snagged on something, a rough piece of the concrete floor in the laundry room. There it was again—louder this time. It could definitely be a cat.

"Sampson!" I called, "Sampson, where are you boy?"

A gust of wind shook the house and it seemed to shake momentarily.

Ooooowwwwww, I heard and leaned closer to the back wall. It was fieldstone, like the rest of the basement walls, built when houses took years to build, not just months. I inspected every surface of the wall but saw nothing out of the ordinary. Just as I turned away to go back upstairs, I saw it. About three-quarters of the way up the wall was a hole, no bigger than the narrow side of a shoebox. Surely, he hadn't—I ran across the room and retrieved a chair with a cracked seat, then dragged it back to where the opening was.

I balanced on the chair, keeping my feet to the sides of the seat and away from the large crack down its center. "Sampson, are you in there?" I called. Another sound, more of a meow than the others. I jumped down from the chair and ran back upstairs, retrieved the flashlight, and ran back down. I nearly fell on the last stair as I tripped over my slipper, which had started to fall off. I climbed back onto the chair and shone the light into the space. It was nearly eye-level. At first, I saw only more stone and realized that depending on the angle from which you viewed it, the hole could look like an optical illusion.

There! A flash of orange. I put the flashlight into my left hand and stretched out my right.

"Sampson?"

There was a loud growl and then a flash of hot pain as something grabbed the back of my hand. Fiery heat ran down my right hand and I cried out and jerked it back out of the space. When I looked down, I saw three lines of blood across the back. But then I heard it. Sampson's purr. Seconds later, two orange triangles appeared at the bottom of the hole.

"Sampson? Sampson, it's okay, I'm going to get you out of there."

I rested the flashlight on the edge of the hole and plunged both hands into the hole. They connected simultaneously with the cat's warm, fluffy sides and I pulled upward. Sampson meowed three times and wriggled—either to get closer to me or to get down—but I held him tightly and climbed carefully down from the chair. Then he snuggled into my arms. His body shivered and his heartbeat near my chest raced.

"It's okay, buddy, I've got you," I said. "What in the world were you doing in there?"

His purr was loud, and he kneaded me with dirty paws. His tail sported a thick chunk of cobwebs and he smelled like old dust and closed-up places. I kissed the top of his head and carried him, still purring upstairs.

Chapter Eighteen

1944

"Are we really doing this?" I asked Lily and held tightly to her arm.

"We really are," she said. "Don't worry, Etta, it will be fine. Won't it feel good to get some answers?"

"Not if they are horrible and terrifying ones."

Lily patted my arm. Today was the day. Tucked into my bag and wrapped in an old baby blanket was the doll which we were going to dissect. We'd finished our shift for the day and hurried through our chores. I'd felt guilty leaving Mary in charge—Mama was back at the hospital—but needed to do this. The air was warm, and a breeze tugged at my hair.

Lily laughed suddenly and skipped for two paces, dragging me along with her.

"Don't worry so much, old thing," Lily said and grinned at me. "Smell the air." She filled her lungs. "Isn't it divine?"

I sniffed obediently and shifted the heavy purse to another spot on my arm. Lily was right. The air was tinged with lilacs, the smell of sprouting grass, and something else that I didn't recognize. Some newness, fresh and pure. I breathed deeper and smiled back at her. "It is."

"Are you okay?" Lily's voice was more serious. She slowed her gait and re-tucked my free arm into hers. "Are you worried about Will finding out?"

I nodded, then shook my head. Then nodded again. My stomach clenched when I thought about Will. What would he do if he knew? What if he came across us now? But that was ridiculous. He was at his father's house, looking at the classifieds for places to rent.

"I need to open my own place, Etta," he'd told me last night as we sat on the porch swing. The gentle rocking motion and Will's strong arm around my shoulders wiped away the heavy sadness that blanketed the house. It had helped me forget, at least for a few minutes, how different everything was.

"Your own garage?" I'd asked, surprised. He'd talked about this before but always said that it was years away. Once we were established, had our little house, a couple of kids, and a white, picket fence. But now?

"It will be difficult, getting the capital I need. My old man holds his purse strings too tight. But there are other ways." He'd paused then to light a cigarette. The smell was acrid and spoiled the sweetness of the nighttime air. He pulled a small silver flask from his coat pocket and took a swig. I didn't say anything.

"I need this, Etta. I can't keep on working for other men. Incompetent bas...well, men who can't see clearly how much better things could be. If they'd only give me a chance—"

"But where will we live?" I'd interrupted, my mind already racing. If Will used the money he'd earned while overseas—and there was likely precious little of it left between what he drank every night and his new wardrobe—our dreams of owning a small house in the country with a beautiful green yard would evaporate.

"I thought these plans—to own a garage of your own—I thought that was years down the road? I suppose we could stay here," I'd continued, answering my own question. "My mother could use my help."

"And another mouth to feed? More when the babies come? No, Etta. We can't ask her to do that."

"We'd pay her," I'd said.

He'd shaken his head stubbornly.

"But if not that, then how, Will? How can we find enough money to get a house and a garage for your business?"

"Don't worry," Will had said. He'd patted my arm and then squeezed me to his side. "I've thought it all out. See, I've got a little trust fund. Something I wasn't going to tap into until later, but I can use that for the house. And my earnings from the military for a down payment for the garage. Trust me, all right?"

Surprised, I'd nodded against his arm, the roughness of his jacket rubbing against my cheek. This was the first I'd ever heard of a trust fund.

"From your father? The trust fund, I mean."

I'd felt his body tense.

"Nah, not from him. Something else, something…from a distant relative." He'd paused to take a drag from his cigarette. The orange end glowed and cast strange shadows on the planes of his face. We rocked in silence a few minutes and my mind whirred.

"Hey, you haven't gotten rid of my gift, have you?" he'd asked lightly, pulling back a little to look at my face.

"The doll?"

He had nodded.

"No, of course not. She's upstairs in my room. Why would I get rid of her?"

Will had chuckled and tapped me once on the nose.

"Silly Etta. I'm just teasing you."

I'd relaxed against his side then and listened to the new leaves whisper in the dark.

* * *

Lily and I were nearly to the river, and I shivered even though the sun shone hot. The doll made the bag painfully heavy. Or maybe it was my imagination, or guilt, that made everything heavier. Will would never know. Absolutely not. That whisper of fear that had been preying on me would be silenced. After this was done, I'd know for certain.

"Let's sit by that little grove of trees," Lily called back to me. She'd been walking briskly, while I'd been dragging my feet.

"Etta?" She turned and realized how far behind I was. She walked toward me. "Are you feeling all right? You look pale."

My hands were clammy, and I tightened my grip on my bag. "Of course," I said, trying to inflect a cheerful note into my voice. "I'm fine. That spot will be perfect."

Lily drew close, her brows pulled down. She linked her arm through mine again and grabbed the bag with her free hand.

"You're a terrible liar. Come on," she said. "We likely won't find anything in this doll other than stuffing or horsehair."

I nodded. "I hope so."

We laid out a small blanket that Lily had brought and sat with the doll between us. Gerda lay on her back and stared up at the sky. Her porcelain skin looked much whiter in the sunlight. The river was quieter here than the spot where we sometimes took our lunch, more of a gurgle than a rush of water.

"Scalpel," Lily said, then laughed. The sound was bright and slightly lifted the sense of foreboding I'd felt since this morning. I pulled a pair of scissors from the bag, tiny silver things that my mother used when she did her embroidery. They were surprisingly heavy, with intricate scrollwork patterns over each finger hole. I slid my fingers into place and held the scissors over the doll.

"Turn her over, please," I said, and Lily did. She pulled back Gerda's dress. The seam was barely visible, and Lily had to pull firmly on either side. Between Lily's fingers marched a neat line of stitches.

"Ready?" I asked.

Lily nodded. "Ready."

Just then the sun was shouldered out of the way by a bank of clouds. The light dimmed and I shivered, then put the pointed end of the scissors against the doll's back and made the first snip. I worked slowly, being sure not to cut the cloth, just the threads holding it together. It was slow work, but finally, the cut was complete. The doll gaped slightly from waist to neck. I put the scissors down and took a deep breath. My fingers parted the fabric. I couldn't look at Lily, just slid my fingers into the opening and felt something silky and smooth underneath. I tugged gently and pulled the sides of the fabric open wider.

"Horsehair?" Lily breathed. She poked the hair with her fingers, rubbing strands of it between her fingers.

"Is it from a horse?" I asked. "It's so soft. It looks almost like…" My voice wobbled and then petered out.

"Etta," Lily breathed out, her forehead nearly touched mine.

136

"I think it's human hair." Her fingers poked gently into the hole we'd made. "Maybe it was a child with Scarlet Fever, and her mother kept locks of her hair as a memento. That's a beautiful thought, isn't it? I've heard of people doing that."

"I guess that could be," I said, but didn't find the thought particularly comforting. Besides, it didn't explain something else. "Hair wouldn't be that heavy, though," I said.

"Let's take it out and see what else is there."

"Will you do it?" I asked. "I can't." I shook my head, staring at the spill of fair hair coming out of her back.

"Of course," Lily said, but her hand remained immobile over the doll's back for several long seconds. The wind picked up and a few thin strands flew from the opening. Lily watched them go with her hand outstretched, as though to catch them.

"Please, Lily," I said through teeth that had started to chatter. The wind had turned cold and the clouds overhead had grown thicker. "Please, do it now." My stomach clenched as though an icy hand had grasped it and squeezed.

Lily knelt closer to the doll and gently pulled the hair free, smoothing it into a small pile beside the doll's stiff little arm.

"I feel something," she said, but then was quiet another minute. Her tongue poked out between her teeth as her fingers dug deeper.

"Here," she said and held up an object she'd extracted from the doll's back. She held her palm open to me. On it lay a small, golden object. A single beam of sunlight found Lily's hand at that moment, and the thing she held glittered in the light.

I moved closer, tried to understand what I was seeing. Then I gasped.

"It's a tooth. Oh my God, Lily, it's a gold tooth."

Lily grimaced in response, then plunked the golden nugget down on the little nest of hair.

"There's more in here," she said. I covered my eyes and sat back on my heels. Then I reopened my eyes. I needed to see this, needed to know what was here. This is what I wanted, wasn't it? Answers? Except now I wished I'd never asked for them to begin with.

"Look," Lily said, her voice a mixture of awe and disgust. She opened her fist. Inside lay a pile of other gold teeth.

I turned away suddenly and rushed from the blanket as the roiling in my stomach grew stronger. I ducked behind a bunch of bushes and retched. My temples pounded as I drew a handkerchief from the pocket of my skirt and wiped my mouth.

When I returned, Lily had extracted two piles of gold teeth. They lay on the pillow of hair. Human hair. Human teeth.

"Are you all right?" she asked.

I nodded and stared at the piles on the blanket. Some were bright and shiny, others dull. They were all different sizes and, most likely, ages.

"Where did they come from? Why would someone hide those in a doll?" I whispered. But I already knew. They were smuggled in the doll. Will's doll. My throat burned. My hands trembled as I looked at Lily. Her head was bent and then she sat back on her heels.

"I think you'd better ask Will that," Lily said gently, then turned to look at me. Her dark eyes studied mine.

"You think he knew?" I asked, my voice croaking. *Of course, he knew,* a hateful little voice said in the back of my brain. *The real question is, do you know him as well as you think?* Everything around me swayed and I thought for a moment I would be sick again. He couldn't have known. It was just a coincidence.

Could he? *Please, please no.* Not Will. He wouldn't keep something like this from me. He wouldn't do this, to begin with. It was grotesque. Horrific. Surely not my Will.... But then the mosquito of a thought that had been pestering me since last night landed, clear as crystal in my mind.

A trust fund.

A distant relative.

Will's interest in this doll.

Why else would he have given me a doll, when he knew I didn't like them? Why else would he have asked about it so frequently? Been so interested in where it was, that I kept it safe? He knew. He had to have. Anger filled my belly then, hot and white. It skittered around the edges of my ribs, pressed against my sternum.

"I have to go," I said suddenly. "My mother is going to need help getting dinner ready for the boarders, and I should have started peeling the potatoes before I left. I'll be rushing now to get it all done."

Lily continued to look at me for another long moment, her warm eyes filled with...what? Knowledge? Wisdom? I wanted to hit her or shake her. Why had I ever let her convince me that this was a good idea? I wanted to put everything back, to take everything back. This decision wasn't smart or wise, it was foolish. And it had created more questions than it answered.

"I need to know what this doll is, Lily," I had told her. "What she's hiding."

But now I wanted to wipe the knowledge out of my mind, to forget what I'd seen.

Oh God, help.

Lily looked at me with some emotion I couldn't place.

Sympathy? Then she nodded, started putting the gold pieces back into the doll, then covered them with the thick layer of hair.

"Are you going to sew it up again now?" she asked finally, once everything had been put back together.

I shook my head. "Later. I'll just wrap it tightly in this." I moved toward the doll with the baby blanket I'd borrowed from Sally's room, then pulled it over her snugly and tied the ends together.

* * *

Something had changed between us. When Lily and I parted ways in front of my house, she offered any help she could give, but I couldn't meet her eyes. I mumbled something else about my mother and then walked into the house and hurried upstairs. I hid the doll back in my stocking drawer, then rushed back downstairs to the kitchen. My mother would be home any minute from the hospital.

I scrubbed and peeled pounds of potatoes. I tried to tell myself that I was wrong. That he didn't know. That this was all just a huge mistake, a misunderstanding. I willed myself finally to stop thinking about it. To focus only on the gritty potato skins, removing the eyes with the sharp blade of the knife. But the images of the doll, of the pile of hair and gold, flashed in front of my eyes constantly.

I took a long pull off the bottle of cherry cordial that Mama kept in the high cupboard and used for special celebrations, or when one of the kids had a particularly bad cough. The sweet burn coated my empty stomach and relaxed my shoulders just a little. I practiced blocking the images in my mind. As soon as they appeared, I thought of something else. Of work at the mill, with the large, clanking machines. Of Lily's last birthday that we'd spent together at an impromptu tea party. Of my mother's face—expressionless and empty at my father's graveside. Anything to keep the other images at bay.

But when I lay on my bed that night, there was nothing else to think about. Nothing to shut out the thought of the doll filled with human hair and teeth that lay in my bureau drawer.

I got out of bed and retrieved the doll, along with my little sewing kit. Deftly I sewed her spine back together. The needle slipped and jabbed into my fingertip, and a big drop of blood appeared. I put my finger in my mouth as the tears came. Not for the pain—I welcomed that—but for what I'd discovered. And how it would change everything if it were true.

Chapter Nineteen

Present Day

I rolled over again and looked at the bedside clock. The red numbers assured me that only ten minutes had passed since last I'd looked. I grunted, turned the pillow vertically, and lay down again. I'd been tossing and turning for most of the night. Worries pressed against me in the dark and even limped their way into my dreams. I forced my body to relax. I evened my breathing and tried to think of nothing. But it was no use. Finally, I turned on the bedside lamp. Its yellow glow was eye-watering after the darkness.

Pulling on a robe, I walked quickly downstairs. The wind moaned around the corners of the house, like a mourning woman. I shivered and stood for a minute in front of the window in the living room. The firelight cast strange shadows that jumped on the walls and in the corners of the room.

I stoked the fire and added more logs, grateful I'd filled the wood stand before I'd turned in. I rubbed my hands over my face, feeling wired and bone-achingly tired at the same time. I went to the studio and turned on the light.

My hand flew to cover my mouth as I held in a scream. Inside the studio, boxes and bins had been overturned, cloth and ribbons and tools strewn everywhere. Clay had been emptied out of bags and lay drying in large clumps. I gasped when I saw the paint. The acrylics had been opened and squeezed, like giant tubes of toothpaste, onto my worktable, the shelves that hold my reference books, and even the light fixture on the ceiling was coated with paint. It dripped onto the walls and floors beneath. The paint was smeared over the white walls, too, and in some places looked like it had been thrown from the bottle. Splatters and whirls of it covered wide swatches of the wall. My brain felt fuzzy and dull. I couldn't quite take in what I was seeing. It's like I was still dreaming. I moved with wooden limbs to check the dolls that I'd made for the exhibit.

The inventory of dolls for the upcoming exhibit was carefully wrapped and labeled. Each in her own box, behind a flowered room screen. I took one deep, steadying breath before I looked behind it. Paper and boxes were strewn everywhere. Dolls had been upended, the boxes bent and torn. I clutched at the first doll I saw, a small winter fairy that I'd made two years ago. One leg was missing, and her head sported a huge crack directly down the center. I gasped, unable to stop the tears. A howl of rage scrabbled out of my throat. I sank back on my heels and buried my head in my hands. Sobs wrenched my chest until it felt like my ribs would crack open.

"Isabel?" I heard Marianne's voice in the living room. I tried to quiet myself, but the deep, gasping sobs wouldn't stop.

"Isabel, what…?"

Marianne stood at the door of the studio. Her hands had been pulling closed the ties of her robe but stopped mid-tie.

"Are you okay?" She rushed into the room and knelt beside me, then wrapped an arm around my shoulders. I turned toward her. Mews of pain still came from my throat. We sat like this for several minutes. Marianne rocked me gently and whispered "shhh" and "it will be all right" repeatedly until I finally stopped crying. She handed me a tissue from her pocket and I wiped my face and blew my nose.

"What happened?" she asked as she looked more closely at the room around us.

Then I sat bolt upright.

"They could still be here, in the house," I said. I stood up and pulled Marianne to her feet.

"I have mace in my purse," she said and started toward the door of the studio. "I'll check upstairs."

I nodded and walked quickly to the hall closet. I felt the silky smoothness of the old baseball bat my dad always kept there. A bubble of hysterical laughter gurgled in my throat. I'd gone from not locking the doors to preparing to crack someone's head open with a baseball bat in a matter of days.

The side door was locked. I remembered double-checking the locks on the front and back doors before bed, but maybe a window had been left unlatched. Had an intruder slipped in that way? The bat was cold and smooth in my hand and my breath was loud in my ears.

I crept down the hall, my feet noiseless on the wood floors, and avoided the spots that creaked. My pulse pounded in my throat. It was hard to hear over the rush of blood in my head and my own harsh breathing. I flicked on lights and checked windows as I passed by. They were all locked. There were no wet footprints, no man-shaped shadows. In fact, the rest of the first floor looked exactly as it had the night before. Nothing had been touched.

I heard Marianne's feet on the floors above, then, "Isabel?

There's nothing here. I'll make tea."

"Okay," I called back. "I'll call the police."

* * *

I sat with Marianne after calling the police and tried to be polite. My mind was a jumble of thoughts though, all related to the show and the dolls and supplies. What was I going to do? So much of the collection was ruined. I got up and paced, the jittery feeling in my legs making it uncomfortable to sit for another minute.

"Did you hear anything at all?" I asked again.

Marianne shook her head. "I sleep so heavily that I didn't hear a thing until…" She broke off. "Until I heard you cry out. It's strange though, isn't it? Why break into the house only to destroy your workspace? Was anything missing? Do you think they were looking for something?"

I shook my head. "It doesn't look like they took anything."

A knock sounded at the door and we both jumped.

"It must be the police," Marianne said and went to open the door while I stood and stared at the black leaves that whirled by the windowpanes.

Chapter Twenty

1944

I avoided Lily on the way to work that morning by slipping out earlier than usual and skipping breakfast. On lunch break, I managed to make it to the riverbank to eat without running into her, choosing a spot where we'd never sat before, hidden by a little grove of birch trees. But after work, I heard her voice as I waited to cross the street two away from home.

"Etta," Lily said breathlessly as she ran to catch up with me. "Wait, please." I wanted to keep walking, or better yet, to put my hands over my ears like Sally did when you told her something she didn't want to hear. I did neither.

"I'm sorry if I spoke out of turn," she said and put a hand on my shoulder. "I shouldn't have accused Will of knowing what's in the doll. He probably had no idea how it got there. It was just my writer's imagination getting the better of me again. Don't be mad, please?"

I looked at Lily. Her hat was askew, her eyes pleading, and the buttons on her light jacket were half-undone. I shoved away my anger at Lily. She hadn't meant any harm. *But what if she was right?* That little voice in my mind whispered. *What if Will knew all along?*

"No, I'm sorry," I said. "I didn't want to hear, because I don't want it to be true. Oh, Lily. What if you're right? What if he knew? What if…" A horrible thought occurred to me. "What if Will is the one who stole those teeth from dead soldiers? What if he cut them—"

"Stop," Lily said and took my arm. She checked for traffic and propelled us across the street, then turned me toward her. "I'm sure that Will didn't do that. He might not even have known, Etta. Don't let your imagination get away from you, too. I just meant, yesterday, that you should talk to him about it because then you'll know the truth and you won't wonder. He might have had something to do with it, or he might not know anything about it. But if you ask, you'll get the truth and then you'll have something to work from."

I nodded and we started walking again.

"I'll talk to him about it this evening. He's going to check out a property in Middlebury tomorrow, for his garage. He's stopping by to see me before he leaves tonight."

Lily squeezed my arm. "It's going to be fine," she said. Was it my imagination, or did her voice sound unconvinced?

* * *

"Claudette," my mother called up the stairs. I tried to pin the last curl, but my shaking fingers lost it again.

"Yes, I'm coming," I called down. I poked my head through the open bedroom door.

"Your young man is here," my mother said and dusted her floury hands off on her apron. Will stood beside her, cap scrunched into a ball in one hand, a bouquet of wildflowers in the other. He smiled up at me and for a minute, I couldn't breathe. I couldn't move. It was like all the oxygen had been sucked out of the house through a giant vacuum, and there was none left for my lungs.

"I'll be right down," I said finally. Did I sound normal despite the aching twist in my chest?

My mother smiled at Will and said something that I couldn't hear. She liked him. For the first time ever, she liked a boy who was interested in me.

I jammed the pin savagely at the curl and scratched my scalp in the process, then grabbed the doll, still wrapped tightly in her blanket. I stuffed it into the handbag on my arm. I didn't want to do this. For a wild moment, I thought I could get out of it. Pretend that none of what I'd discovered was real.

My mother needed help in the kitchen. That's where I should be, cutting vegetables and chatting with her and Will while I worked. But I couldn't go another night without knowing. At work, I'd made one careless mistake after another because of it. Mr. Johnson had threatened to send me home, telling me that unless I shaped up, I'd be out of a job soon.

"You look beautiful," Will said after I descended the staircase. My mother had returned to the kitchen.

"Thank you," I said, and he held out the big bouquet of flowers to me. They smelled sweet, almost overpowering, and I suddenly felt dizzy.

"Let me just put these in water and we can walk." I nodded toward the door then retreated before he could ask me anything.

He'd invited me to dinner when we'd spoken earlier, something special to celebrate the garage that he was soon to buy. If all went well tomorrow, he'd be the owner of an aging service station just outside of Middlebury. I'd asked if we could go another time, claiming fatigue. I knew that the conversation we needed to have shouldn't take place in a public spot, a crowded eatery filled with music and wine and happy diners who hadn't been lied to by the person whom they trusted most in the world.

I pulled a shawl over my shoulders and we stepped out onto the porch, then walked down the stairs in silence. The air was cool—unseasonably so—and I shivered underneath the shawl. It wasn't all due to the air, though.

Will slid his arm over my shoulders.

"Beautiful evening," he said. His words reflected my thoughts. I nodded, looking around. Stars were just appearing in the baby blue sky, a sliver of moon hanging like a delicate pendant between them. The sun hadn't yet gone down and it added a glow to everything.

"Will—"

"Etta—"

We both spoke at once, then laughed. The tension had broken somewhat, and for a few minutes, I basked in the comfort of it. Until I felt the weight of my bag on my arm. I stopped in the road and placed a hand on his arm.

"There's something important that I need to ask you. I don't want to—part of me wishes that I'd never found this out—but I did and now I can't stand not knowing if you know if you knew..." I lost my breath and tried to laugh again, but it sounded more like a sob.

"Sweetheart, what's this all about?"

Will tried to take my arm, but I increased the rate of my steps. I heard him sigh and glanced back. He shuffled forward, his cane keeping pace with his foot, and my heart fractured. I

149

slowed and slid my arm through his free one.

"I'm sorry," I said. "Let's walk by the river. Just a short stroll." It would be easier to ask these questions if I didn't have to look into his eyes.

"Etta, if you'd just tell me—"

"I will, soon," I said. I tried not to think about what it would be like after he knew what I'd discovered. What if there was no more "us"? A sharp, pointed blade jabbed my chest at the thought. But I had to do this, I had to know. If not only for myself and our relationship, then for Sally. Because if Will had done awful things, couldn't the doll that he'd given me be cursed?

In a house nearby, a baby cried, its wail starting slowly and then building in intensity. A few blocks away, a dog barked. Finally, we reached the river. Here the water was louder and angrier than where we usually sat. We strolled along the path for a few seconds in silence before I broke it.

"The doll you gave me, Will, where did you get it?" I blurted.

"The doll?" his voice was surprised, and then he chuckled. "Is that all this is about? I thought it was something serious from the way you've been acting. Now I can breathe easier." He chuckled again, patting my hand.

"Where did you get it?" I repeated. He glanced at me. I could see him from the corner of my eye, but I walked slowly forward and stared straight ahead. The road that ran parallel to the path was quiet. Only an occasional car passed by and made a strong breeze filled with the scent of exhaust and road dust.

"I got it from my sergeant. He found it somewhere in the city, a little shop. He was going to bring it home for his daughters, but he has two and thought they would fight over it. So he passed it along to me. Why, Etta?"

My hope that Will didn't know what was inside of it shriveled. I bit my lip and focused on my feet and the pebbles ahead of me at the roadside.

"I thought you said that you found it in a little shop. That you bought it for me."

Will stopped me by placing a hand on my arm, then turned me toward him.

"Does it really matter? Look, I did see one like it in a shop, but my sergeant gave me this one. I swear it. Etta." His voice sounded pinched to me, higher than usual. "What's all this about?"

It wasn't too late. I could pretend that his answer was the truth. Maybe it was—who was I to tell? I could leave this alone and go on with my life.

"Because I found something," I blurted out. "I found something inside of the doll and it scared the hell out of me."

Will stood in front of me with his mouth partially open. That strange, now-familiar darkness passed over his face. Something flickered in his eyes but was gone before I was able to identify what it was. He closed his mouth, sighed, and rubbed a hand over his face.

"And what did you find?" He dropped his hand and looked hard at the river. His face in profile was regal, so handsome that I wanted to weep. The sweep of dark hair, the straight, Romanesque nose, the full lips. I longed to throw my bag into the river and tell him that it was nothing, nothing. That I didn't know what I was talking about. That I'd never found anything and that all I wanted was for him to take me into his arms and kiss me.

But I didn't say any of that. I couldn't.

Instead, I opened my bag and took out the doll. Gerda was still bound in her shroud, and I pulled it off roughly. It fell to the ground along with my handbag. I'd thought about this all afternoon. A test for Will. But my hands shook, and my knees trembled. He glanced at me as I walked past him, close to the riverbank. The river was wild here, deep and wide across. The gray water churned and made white foam along the banks.

"Etta, what are you doing?" He limped toward me. I drew closer to the river. The mud sucked at my shoes.

"Do you know?" My voice was nearly a yell and the river tried to drown out the question. "Do you know what I found?"

Will shook his head, angrily.

"Move back away from the bank, Etta. You could fall in or lose her."

Anger filled me suddenly. It pressed hot inside my chest like vinegar.

"Why did you give me this, Will?" I shouted, my words tangling with the roar of the river. "Tell me now. Do you know what's inside of it?"

Will shook his head and tried to smile, but there was fear in his eyes.

"Etta—"

I held my arm out over the water. "I'll throw her in," I said. "Please, Will. Tell me."

He moved closer and I took a step back, then another.

"Don't!" I yelled.

Will stopped. He looked at me with an expression that I didn't recognize.

"Don't do that," he yelled. "We need her."

Chapter Twenty-One

Present Day

Officer Gentile didn't linger. He was moderately overweight, pale, had a face that could have been twenty-four or a decade older, and smelled of fresh coffee and aftershave. He made some notes on a pad and walked with me around the house. He inspected the outside entrances and asked questions about noises and the locks on the windows. The officer shook his head when Marianne offered him tea and left me his card. There was little he could do except encourage our double-checking the locks at night.

"Call me immediately if there are signs of anyone in the area that either of you don't recognize," he said. "Any unusual vehicles or things that look out of place when you're around the property. And if you hear anything else, don't hesitate to call it in. Better safe than sorry."

I thanked him as he headed back to his cruiser, then went to take a shower and tried to wash away the discouragement and the fear.

Marianne left around eleven for her volunteer shift at the hospital. "Are you sure you don't want me to call in? I could help you in the studio, get things put back in order."

"No, thank you," I said and smiled. "I'll be fine."

I worked in the studio for more than two hours. Mostly this involved throwing out paint, cloth, and tools that were no longer any good. I couldn't bear to sort through the dolls and survey all the damage at once, so I just pulled the screen back in place. I'd look later.

* * *

"No, of course. I understand," I said. My voice had a hollowness that I didn't recognize. Helen had called to ask where the images were that I was supposed to have sent her. I'd made excuses, knowing that I should have told her what had happened. But the words wouldn't come. At what point would she stop believing me? Already the centerpiece doll had been destroyed...would she think that I simply had cold feet? Couldn't take the pressure that this prestigious exhibit required?

"Couldn't I send measurements at this point, and leave the photos for later?" I asked. There was silence on the other end of the line for a long moment afterward.

"Isabel, is there something wrong?" Helen's voice had dropped an octave.

I wanted to tell her then. *Yes. Yes, something is wrong. Everything is wrong.*

"Surely your photographer can do a rush job for you," she said. "You've certainly worked together long enough to build a rapport."

"It's not that," I said without thinking, then caught myself. "I mean, it's fine. I understand. I'll get you the photos by Monday afternoon at the latest."

Helen sighed. "I guess that will have to do. If you're able to get them to me any earlier, please do."

* * *

I leaned over my worktable with my head in my hands. What was I going to do? I couldn't, wouldn't lose this opportunity. And yet, what exactly was I going to get photos of? A bunch of cracked and broken dolls missing appendages? I'm not sure how long I stood there. I alternately held my head in my hands, as though trying to squeeze a good idea out of it, and circled the studio. I paced and mumbled to myself. I arranged and rearranged paintbrushes and carving tools with jittery hands.

The thought came while I stood at the kitchen sink later that morning, eating a section of orange. The juice dripped down my chin and when I reached for a napkin in the cupboard, I could see them. A series of broken dolls. Each one bruised, battered by life in her own way, yet together they struggled up from the ashes, like phoenixes. My fingers tingled, and goosebumps ran up and down my arms like ants. Discarded dolls, dolls no one wants, the broken, the ugly. Remade. Reborn.

I'd never done anything like that before, but it could work. The dolls, already broken and cracked, would just need to be reworked, made into a cohesive display. I could age them, make them appear like fragile antiques that had already lived a life, and had a story to tell. Like Gerda. I glanced over to where the doll had previously sat with the tea set and felt suddenly fearful. I pushed the feelings away.

I should tell Helen of my plan, shouldn't I? The thought made my palms sweaty. No. Not yet. Not until I had something to prove to her that it would work.

I went back to the studio and got to work. It was late, past three o'clock in the morning, when I stumbled to bed.

* * *

The wind howled. Leaves whistled and snagged on tree limbs and branches. I was back in the meadow where I'd found the small gravestone. It was cold, and the wind blew through my clothes as though I wore nothing at all. I heard cracks and soft pops, like someone behind me had walked over brittle fallen branches. I turned in slow motion. I expected to see a hulking, dark figure in the trees, but there was nothing but shadows that danced and undulated. The moon above played peek-a-boo with thick, black clouds.

There! Again, the sound of branches snapping came, and then a shadowed figure emerged from the trees. Faint strains of music danced on the breeze. The man held something in his hands. And suddenly I knew who he was—the man from Church Street. The accordion player. His hands suddenly grew still. He grasped the big instrument but rather than playing music, he looked directly at me.

"Let the dead rest."

The words were low and grumbly in his throat, like quiet, far-away thunder. A crow cawed and flew around in two low circles before it settled on the gravestone. The man either didn't see it or ignored it, and continued to stare straight at me. I took a step toward the stone. I wanted to shoo the bird away. It glared at me with dark, shiny eyes and cawed again.

As I drew closer it flew away, screeched into the air above. The stone was darker than before. There were words on it. I leaned forward to read. Fingertips of fear danced up my spine and I realized my hands were trembling as I smoothed away the dead leaves. I tilted my head, trying to read the carved words on the cold stone.

"Gerda," I read. My heart fluttered wildly against my ribs and my knees grew weak simultaneously. Then Sampson was there and hissed at the stone, and made a strange yowling in the back of his throat. His bushy orange tail bloomed to twice its normal size. I turned back as though in slow motion. The soil around the stone was loose and looked freshly dug. I drew closer, my heart a jackhammer in my chest.

"You've gotta let the dead rest," the man said again, and I realized he stood directly beside me. I smelled the faint sweet smell of pipe tobacco and the stronger scent of dry leaves. Sampson yowled again.

I opened my eyes, blinking in the dim light of my bedroom. My heart pounded under the blankets and my throat felt sandblasted. It had felt so real. I turned toward Sampson, whose gaze was focused on the chair near the bed. His back was arched, his fur on end. Louder and louder his grumbles grew until he leaped from the bed and ran, feet skittering, out of the room.

"Sampson!" I called, throwing back the blankets. The air was like ice water outside of my cocoon. I reached for my robe which hung on the chair nearby.

Gerda sat on the edge of it and stared directly at me.

Chapter Twenty-Two

1944

K nowing a thing that you imagined is different than knowing it as truth. I'd thought about little else in the past twenty-four hours than this moment. My mind had gone back and forth and back again. Will either knew or he didn't know. Those were the two options, as I'd seen them. But this—understanding that he did know, and trying to make it stack up to my reality and everything I knew about Will—that was something very different.

My arms still held the doll up across my body, as though I was about to pitch her in the World Series game. They shook, and I lowered them back to my body. But when Will stepped toward me, I raised the doll back up and my chin, too, defiantly.

"I just wanted to have the best advantage. For us. A nest egg," Will said, his voice barely audible over the tumble of water. "I should have told you, but I knew that you'd, well, be like this." He waved a hand toward me.

The hot, angry heat that charred my chest leaked upward into my throat.

"Like this?" I laughed a choked sound. "Will, this doll is filled with people's teeth. *Human teeth!* How did you expect I would react?" I stopped and let my arm fall back to my side. It shook. "But you weren't going to tell me, were you?"

Will didn't respond. He stared at the ground.

"How did you get this doll, Will?" I asked, and this time my voice was quieter. I took a step toward him. "Please tell me. You owe me that much, don't you?"

Will's head jerked up and his face was flushed. His eyes were hard and shadowed.

"I owe you? This doll is our chance, Etta. I did this for you, for us." His voice was a low growl and when he stepped toward me again, I flinched. Then his face softened, and he put a hand out to me. I shrugged it off.

"Where did you get it?" I asked again, my voice dull in my own ears.

Will sighed, long and deep, and then turned slightly and looked out over the river.

"I did get it from my sergeant. But he didn't buy it. Look, I don't know everything about it, but he was...he was involved in...in something with a German officer."

"And he just gave it to you? For no reason?"

"No. He didn't just give it to me. He was killed. I took it from his things. No one else knew what was in it. The doll would have been lost. Such a waste, all that money...." Will shifted from one foot to the other. "Etta, I...." He sighed loudly and rubbed a hand over the back of his neck. His face looked old suddenly, old and tired.

"There are things that happen in war, horrible things, that we don't talk about. None of us talk about them. I can't tell you anything else about this doll, other than that the gold inside, it was payment for my sergeant to do what he felt he needed to do. And when he died, I took it. I took the doll because I

159

knew what was inside of it. And I knew that the money would be needed by us, to start our new life together."

I stood there, my body limp. It felt like all my strength, all the anger that was fueling me, was leaking slowly from my head downward, out of the soles of my feet and into the mud below.

"Was he a spy?" My voice was quiet. Will looked at me sharply, then away, toward the river. He nodded once. Reddish splotches had formed on his neck like dark pink flower petals had been pressed into his skin and left a stain.

"I guessed he was, but it's not like he came right out and told me. I found out about the doll after we'd played a game of cards and had a little too much to drink one night. He liked me, trusted me. But even so, he never would have trusted me with that. He was blind drunk and passed out soon after he showed me what was inside."

"And the teeth," I said, "they were from…from soldiers that you'd killed? Or prisoners of war?" My voice caught. The words made the thought more real and I choked on them.

Will didn't say anything. A moment later he shook his head.

"They were from the Jewish people. In the camps, I think. But they were already dead, Etta."

"My God, Will." My voice was barely a whisper. I doubted he could hear it over the roar of the water. I turned my head and stared into the muddy thrash of the river. Branches bobbed and tumbled in the eddy, white foam clung along the edges. The river was swollen; snow and ice had melted and gathered force as it flowed.

"We have to get rid of it," I said. My voice was stronger and louder. "It's the right thing to do. Using this," I motioned to the doll, "would be using blood money. You see that, don't you,

Will? Those poor, poor people." My voice broke and tears filled my eyes.

He looked at me as though I were a stranger.

"What are you talking about?" His voice was loud, and the red splotches that covered his neck rose toward his face. "They're dead now and they're not coming back. We need that money. That's our future, Etta. It doesn't matter how my sergeant got it or how I did. All that matters is that it's going to help us start our life together. Sweetheart," he said, moving toward me, his hand outstretched. He lowered his voice, then smiled. "Etta. Give me the doll."

I shook my head.

"We can't, Will. We can't start our life with this." I shook the doll. I wanted to throw it to the ground, stomp on it, rip it into pieces, scream. Will took another step toward me and instinctively, I took one away. I was close to the bank of the river now, where it fell down into the deep, roaring water below.

"We have to get rid of it," I yelled over the pulsing water.

"No," Will said and limped toward me quickly with his hand outstretched.

What happened next was a blur. It was as though time slowed to breaths and heartbeats, yet was covered in a cloudy, white fog. As Will moved toward me, I stepped away again without thinking. My right foot caught on an exposed tree root and I stumbled. Will reached for me—or for the doll? —and I moved automatically in the other direction, tried to right myself on the slick mud. I gasped as he lunged toward me.

And then I swung the doll as hard as I could toward the gray-brown, churning water. The doll sailed through the air like a

161

bird on a strong current, then started to tumble. I waited for it to cut through the surface of the water, but it didn't. Instead, the hem of Gerda's dress caught on a branch. It bobbed once, twice, three times on the branch. I stared in horror and willed it to fall into the water below.

Will yelled something at me and slipped and slid his way further down the bank. His cane fell, and he held onto a young tree. He put a hand out toward the doll, but couldn't reach it. The water roared in my head like a train.

"Will!" I screamed. "Will, don't!"

He stretched further. He reached and grasped. His fingertips missed the hem of the doll's dress by centimeters. His touch made her sway once again on the branch. He pulled back and then righted himself, tried to gain more solid footing. I moved toward him on wooden feet.

"Will, no!" I screamed.

When he leaned out again, his aim was off just slightly, but it was enough to pull him off balance. I stared in horror as his hand and then his arm flew through the empty air. His body followed. The graceful arc of his slim body lasted only seconds. Then he cut through the water's surface and was lost immediately in the swirling brown undulations.

Chapter Twenty-Three

I had to get Gerda out of the house. Something was wrong with her. There had to be...didn't there? Or was it me? I was under an incredible amount of stress. I could feel it inside, pressing against my nerves, jangling them. And in my thoughts, making everything appear scarier, more fearsome. Did I honestly believe that a doll could cause physical harm to my studio? But what about the ways in which she kept showing up places I'd never brought her?

It felt like I'd been inside of a kaleidoscope since she'd arrived, everything around me moving and readjusting itself over and over before I had a chance to figure out what was happening. I looked at her grayish face and sat back on the bed, drawing my knees up to my chest. The skin of my legs was icy against my soft stomach.

What if I tried to dispose of her? I thought about it for a moment. If it really was her causing all these awful things to happen, how angry would she be if I rejected her? Tried to get rid of her? Goosebumps ran up and down my arms and legs like an army of ants.

"What are you?" My voice was a loud whisper in the empty

room but seemed to reverberate off the walls. Her eyes, as ever, remained blank as a shark's.

A knock sounded at the door downstairs and I jumped. I pulled my robe on as I hurried down the hallway and then the stairs. As I passed the small window near the door, I saw two boys on the front step, one a foot taller than the other. They were bundled up in thick coats and wore dark dress pants.

"Good morning," the taller one said when I opened the door. I watched his eyes track over my face and neck, then down to my hands, following the red, scaly patches. He seemed to remember himself then and looked back up into my eyes and cleared his throat. "I'm Jameson Bartlett and this is Kyle." He nudged the second kid with an elbow to the side.

"Morning," the smaller kid said and stared at my skin. I tugged down the sleeves of my robe, pulled the "v" closer together around my neck.

"I'm sorry, I wasn't expecting anyone," I said. Both boys looked cold, with chapped, red cheeks and running noses.

"We're from down there," Jameson said, pointing diagonally across the back of my property.

"Did you walk all the way here?" I asked.

Jameson shook his head. "Nah. Our dad is in the pickup on the road. Our Boy Scout troop is doing a can drive. Do you have any you'd like to donate?"

"We'll take cold, hard cash, too," said Kyle with a snicker, and wiped his nose on the sleeve of his jacket. Jameson kicked the back of the younger boy's calf with his boot.

"No, we won't," Jameson said. "He was just kidding."

"I, uh, yes. I'm sure I have some in the closet. Do you want to come in and warm up while I get them?"

"Sure," Kyle said, and without waiting for me to move,

started to push the door wider.

"Kyle," Jameson hissed and grabbed a handful of Kyle's coat and pulled him back onto the step. "No, thanks. We'll wait out here," he said.

"Okay. I'll just be a minute." I closed the door and went to the hall closet. There were three empty wine bottles and about a hundred empty cans of flavored seltzer. Marianne drinks little else except tea. I lugged the bulging bag back to the front door.

"Thanks," Jameson said and reached for it. Then, "Come on, Kyle, grab the other end."

"You're welcome." The boys glanced back, balancing the bulky bag between them, and I waved halfheartedly and closed the door. Then a thought came to me and I jerked the door open.

"Boys?"

They stopped, turned.

I cleared my throat. "Do you know anything about the gravestone in your family's field? The one that's all by itself?"

"Oh, yeah. It's really old," Kyle said.

"It was a kid that died a long time ago," Jameson added. "My mom researched it once. Some girl—Mary? Lauren?—I don't remember, but you could ask my mom, she'd probably know."

"Do you know why it's all by itself? Where the girl's family went?"

"Yeah," said Jameson. "I guess the family that used to live where we do now, they had a lot of bad stuff happen to them. Their cows got sick and lots of them died. Then there was a fire and the house almost burned down. My mom said that after that, they just wanted to get out of that place. It's sort of sad that she was left behind. I don't think that the family

165

moved out of town, though, so they still probably came to visit her sometimes. I don't know." He shrugged.

"It's kind of creepy, isn't it?" Kyle asked. "She has a ghost, you know. Our older sister said she's seen it floating around out in the woods at night."

"Sarah never goes into the woods, you idiot," Jameson said with a disparaged look at his brother. "She's too scared," he added in a falsetto.

"You are too," Kyle retorted.

"Well, thanks," I broke in. "Is your mom home today?"

Jameson shrugged. "Yeah, she's baking stuff."

"Maybe I'll walk over in a little while. Thanks again."

Jameson grunted, and Kyle wiped his nose on his sleeve again. "Quit it," Jameson said as I closed the door. "That's so gross."

I pulled on a thick thermal shirt and overalls after the boys left. My thoughts re-picked at the thread that had started to unravel before the interruption. Something had to be done about the doll. Throwing her in the garbage seemed too big a risk, though. I wasn't sure that a doll could do things like those that had been happening here. But if so, I didn't want to risk making things worse.

With no better idea, I took Gerda down to the basement and wrapped her in an old, musty quilt. I felt a pang of guilt as I covered her face. Despite what she may have done, what she might be, I still felt a strange connection to her. An unexplainable protectiveness.

"I'm sorry," I whispered. Then I stuffed the swaddled doll into an empty plastic tote. The guilt in my chest grew stronger, but I dusted my hands off and walked back upstairs, closing the door firmly behind me.

I turned some music on and tried to think about other things. Maybe I would stop in and see Mrs. Bartlett a little later. Nancy? Nellie? I couldn't remember her first name but thought it started with an "N." It would be a relief to get out of the house for a while. Before I could do that though, my studio needed attention.

I felt nauseous as I looked at the broken dolls still laying in a heap behind the screen. I pulled them all out gently, dusted off their clothes, smoothed now-snarled hair, and cleaned away bits of broken clay and ephemera. Tears pricked my eyes and a hollowness pressed hard in my belly. All of my work! All of the hours and hours of time spent…. I wanted to shake my fists and stomp. And throw things. And wail.

Instead, I funneled the anger into action. I sat with a pad of paper and sketched one doll after another, not the way they were now, but the way that I envisioned them in the exhibit. A doll I'd nicknamed "Heathcliff"—because of his dour, sneering face—had been smashed on the right side. His arm dangled limply, and the right side of his face was torn open. Underneath lay the exposed clay.

I sketched out his metamorphosis: I'd paint the interior of his skull black and then carefully render a constellation of stars there. The stars could continue all along the right side of his body, dripping off his mangled arm. Another doll, a sort of Medusa figure, had lost most of her hair. I examined her body closely and found little damage, other than a few chips in her arms and legs. I closed my eyes, imagining her transformed. Several minutes later, I opened them and started to sketch again. This one needed hardness, something sharp to offset the now-gentle look she had with most of her spiky snake hair missing. Wire would be good. I rummaged in my materials and found what I was looking for—sharp, rusted-looking wire that I would tangle and place in spikes along her skull. It would be tricky to adhere, but a very heavy matte gel medium might work. If not, there were ways to remove the head entirely and replace it on her body. It was a long, tedious process, though, one I'd rather not undertake with the deadline I was working against, but I would do it. I had to do it.

I worked for another two and a half hours before standing up to stretch. I smiled as I looked over the dolls spread along the worktable. Each one had an "after" sketch neatly laid out underneath it. While there were still hours and hours of work to do, at least I now had a plan. I felt a little surge of hope for the first time in days.

One question looped itself around in my brain like an off-balance hula-hoop though: if it wasn't Gerda, then who had done that to my studio? I'd never been a paranoid person, but I couldn't help thinking that Marianne had the easiest access. The officer had said that it didn't look like the door had been forced or the lock tampered with. She could have easily slipped out of her room and down to the studio. But why? It made no sense. Marianne had never been anything but kind to me. Instantly, I felt a hot press of shame in my gut for even entertaining the thought.

But then…who?

Chapter Twenty-Four

1944

I heard a high-pitched scream. It took several long seconds before I realized it had come from me. The spot where he'd gone in was empty of everything except angry water. I rushed to the edge of the river.

"Will? Will!" I barely recognized my own voice, shrill, and anguished.

It was too steep in this spot to get closer to the water. I pulled my muck-covered feet out of the slippery goo and ran, stumbling, downstream.

"Will!" I screamed again.

I saw him surface then. For a second, his shoulders and arms and head were above the water. He was further out from the bank, headed toward the middle of the river. He was moving toward a rock, a big one toward the right side of the river. *Let him grab it. Let him get on it.*

I screamed again, "Will! Will! Get to the rock!" His arms flailed and then he disappeared for an instant, resurfacing further away from the large gray slab. He was pulled beneath the water again. I waded in, felt the strong current pulling at my dress, at my legs. I couldn't swim. I'd never felt so helpless.

Where was he? I searched the dirty water frantically. There! Will popped back up above the surface but his movements were slow and dulled. He threw his head back, sprayed water from his mouth, and took two gasping breaths before he disappeared below the surface again.

I looked around me wildly. I searched for something—anything—to help. A long branch, a length of rope. But the banks were swept clean, other than exposed roots and rocks.

"Help!" I yelled, running along the bank. I stumbled. "Please, someone!"

I looked back to where Will had emerged from the water seconds before, but couldn't see anything.

"Please, please, please," I moaned and searched for a bit of white or the dark black of his pants. "Oh, please."

I saw motion from the corner of my eye and looked further down the riverbank. Two men were standing, pointing toward the river. I followed the excited jabbing of their fingers and saw Will's white shirt bobbing in the water.

"Help him!" I yelled, scrambling along the bank toward the men. "Help!"

They didn't hear me at first, but then the man on the left, big and bulky, turned and looked toward me. He was the owner of the mill, my boss's boss, Mr. Sarducci.

"Please," I gasped. My foot caught on another root and I sprawled onto the bank. The mud oozed between my hands. I felt its cold wetness plaster the front of my dress to my chest. I tried to stand but the mud sucked at me, pulled me down. And then strong hands were on my arms and lifted me up. I heard something strange, a sort of howl. I didn't realize right away that it was coming from me.

Mr. Sarducci steadied me as I swayed on the riverbank.

170

"I'm sorry, miss," he said. "I'm afraid it's too late."

* * *

They held me back in a little circle when the emergency workers finally brought Will out of the river. Officer Shelton was there again. He reminded me of his name twice because I just stared at him. I heard words all around me, but none of them made sense.

"...saw him go under..."

"...current too strong...struck his head on that boulder..."

"...poor girl..."

"...Baxter boy, isn't it?"

And then, finally, my mother's voice. Her strong arms around me, her breath hot on my icy neck.

"Claudette, oh, Claudette. I'm here. I've got you." I could feel her heartbeat hammering through her dress, the smell of her—lavender and dust and the slight smell of sweat salty on her skin—breaking through the numbness. It was then that the tears finally came. A hot wash of pain down my face. How odd that pain you feel in your heart should end up on your face.

Someone—Mama?—pressed a handkerchief into my hand and led me further away from the bank to a little copse of trees. There, still hugging me tight, she rocked me and smoothed a hand over my hair like she had when I was a little girl.

"Poor girl," she said, her voice choked. "My poor, poor girl."

"I want to see him," I said moments later. My voice was a strangled whisper. "I want to see Will."

I looked at my mother and saw tears on her cheeks. She shook her head. "I don't think you should. It will be harder—"

171

"Please, Mama. Please. I need to."

She pulled away from me a little then. Her eyes searched my face. And then she nodded once and turned.

"Stay here." She walked back to the group of men, to the officers and the newspaperman and the googly-eyed onlookers just outside of the tight circle. She spoke softly to Officer Shelton. He frowned, glanced my way. I willed myself to hold my head high, clenching the handkerchief in my hands so tightly that my fists vibrated with every heartbeat.

Finally, he nodded. He spoke quietly to the others in the group and the circle dispersed, people moving in small clusters further away to talk and point at the river. My mother came back to me and led me toward the officer and the sheet on the ground.

"I've sent someone to his father," he said quietly as I approached, my mother leading me with a firm grip on my elbow. "He'll be here shortly."

I nodded, then looked down at the ground. The fabric of the sheet was pale. Soaked through in places, I could see the outline of body parts. A chest. Forearms crossed over it. The toe of one shoe. In these places, the sheet stuck wetly.

"Please," I said.

Officer Shelton squatted near the sheet, gave me a final look, and pulled it halfway down. Will's face and arms were white—as white as his shirt. His dark hair was soaked, and a bit of leaf or grass were tangled in the waves. Everything looked perfect otherwise, as though he were just napping. Except for a large, red abrasion on his right temple. Someone had said he'd hit a boulder—maybe there? I knelt beside Will, placed my hands over his. They were cold but still soft. He had dirt under two nails, I noticed and scratches over his knuckles.

I leaned my body over his, placed my head against his chest. I breathed in the scent of river water—fishy and earthy—and the fainter smell of Will: pine and cigarettes and the scent that was his alone. Will. My Will. I gripped his hands tighter. There was so much that I needed to say but I couldn't remember how to make words with my wooden lips, with my leaden tongue. Instead, a sound came from my lips—a howl.

My mother pulled me to my feet moments later, as the keening cries threatened to strangle me. They tangled around my throat and choked me. She led me away then. We stumbled away from Will. Away from the river that took him.

Chapter Twenty-Five

"Well my gosh, it's been a long time. Come in, come in!" Mrs. Bartlett—Nancy, she'd reminded me—held the door open. The warm scent of cinnamon and something sweet followed her out onto the front step.

"I'm sorry to just drop in like this, but your boys were at the house a little earlier and said you were home—"

She laughed, a pleasant guffaw. "I'm home most of the time. I feel like I spend my life in my kitchen. Or in the garden or barn. Come on in and sit down. Here, let me clear you a space."

Nancy moved to a large kitchen table overflowing with stuff. Paperwork was mixed with kids' craft projects—a leftover cereal bowl and a few crumbs were mixed in with file folders and about a dozen empty egg cartons.

"Don't mind the mess. We homeschool and it's a zoo in here most of the time." She shuffled things around on the table and created a rectangle of space in front of me. "I was just about to have a cup of coffee. Could I get you one?"

"That would be great, thank you."

"Mmmhmm," she murmured and turned back to the kitchen counter. She was plump but in a solid way, as though there was a lot of strength and muscle under the layer of softness. Her hair was blonde and her skin was smooth and seemed permanently tanned. As she moved around the kitchen, I studied the rest of the room. There were several long swags of ivy dotted around the ceiling and a big glass door looked out over the yard. There were no steps, I noticed, just a drop off a couple of feet to the weedy ground below. The house was large and rambling, and still in the state of being finished off, though I knew the Bartlett's had lived here for at least a few years.

"There," Nancy said and plunked a mug of coffee down in front of me. The mug showed a cartoon husband with his hands raised to the sky, yelling, "I don't work for the power company!" Behind the little man was a house with lights blazing from every window. "I thought you might like to try a cinnamon bun, too. We're having a coffee hour at church tomorrow, but I've got extras."

"Thank you," I said. "It looks delicious."

I'd worried that conversation would be awkward or stilted, but I needn't have. Nancy kept a running commentary on their "homestead," and told me about their layer hens and meat birds, the problems they'd been having with the coyotes lately, and the fact that her cold frames were still producing veggies this late in the season. "Can you believe it?" she asked, and then shook her head and smiled in amazement. "I mean, I would have installed them years ago if I'd known they were going to be so successful."

"Anyway," she said finally as I nibbled the last piece of my bun. "I'm sure you didn't walk over to hear all about my family

175

and farm. What brings you out this way?"

"Oh, I…." I paused to clear my throat. "I just wondered about that little grave near the tree line. I walk there a lot—"

"I know, Paul tells me that he sees you out there sometimes." She paused to take a sip of her coffee.

"Jameson mentioned that you knew a little of the history of who is buried there."

"A little bit, yes," she said and glanced out the window. "We were doing a unit on researching this part of the county, and I wanted to learn more about the people who lived on this property before we bought it. I like to work alongside the kids for the most part. I think it shows them that learning can be fun. I probably have a file around here somewhere—but have no idea where—about what I found. This area was one big farm at one point. Course, just about everyone in the area farmed back then. They owned something like a hundred and eighty acres. Can you imagine? We bought forty-five with the house, and that feels paltry in comparison.

"Anyway, the records were a little scant about the early history. But then a family moved here in the mid-1940s. Soon after they purchased it, a string of bad luck hit them. And I'm not talking like spilled milk sort of bad luck or a single crop that failed. They lost an entire crop one year, and after that, a lot of their cows got sick and died. Then their barn caught fire and part of the house burned with it. There was an accident soon after with a horse. They lost their little girl. She was only five when it happened. Poor little thing. I can't imagine it, can you? Losing a child—" Nancy's voice broke and then she smiled at me over the lip of the mug. Her eyes were shiny.

"Well, that was the last straw for the family, I guess. After she died, they left. Another family moved in some years later. Apparently, there was talk about the farm being cursed or haunted—it kept the place empty for a number of years. Eventually, a farmer and his wife bought it. Didn't stay long though. He got sick soon afterward and she ended up in a nursing home. After that, their kids hacked the land up into smaller parcels and sold it off, which is how we got this place.

"Anyway, that's why that little grave is all by itself out there." She paused for another sip of coffee. "It's the little girl's resting spot. Sad, isn't it? I try to go and clean it up now and then, put some flowers in the summer. Well, I have good intentions, but truth be told I forget all too often. I hate to think of her all alone, though. Poor little thing. Not that she knows it, but still."

We sat in silence for a few minutes.

I cleared my throat. "Do you know what her name was?"

"The girl?"

I nodded.

Nancy squinted and then nodded. "It was Amelia, Amelia Rose. I remember that because it was so beautiful. Plus, I always said if I'd had a little girl I wanted Rose to be her middle name. But I can't remember the family's last name. It might have started with a "P." Something like Peters...or Pelkey? I can't remember."

Tires crunched on the gravel driveway outside and when I glanced back, I saw Paul Bartlett's truck with two frozen-looking boys inside.

"There they are," Nancy said and stood. "The troops have returned. You're welcome to stay for dinner if you'd like. I don't know what we're having yet, but it would be nice to have company."

"Oh, thank you, but I've got to get back home. I appreciate

the offer and the delicious treat, though. It was nice visiting with you."

I stood and pulled my coat off the back of the chair.

"That's what neighbors are for," Nancy said and smiled wide. "Stop back any time. Course, if you're here during summer, I might put you to work in the garden."

I laughed. I'd just said hello and goodbye to Paul and the boys and started back across the field when I heard Nancy's voice call to me.

"Peterson!" she yelled. "That was the family's name."

I smiled and waved my arm and she waved back before following her family inside.

* * *

I thought about the little girl—Amelia Rose—and her family as I walked home. And how sad that she was all alone out there. What had ever happened to her family? I would clear the stone and plant flowers there this summer, for Amelia's grave. Maybe I could see about getting a new stone, if I could track down the dates of her birth and death, too. I had her name now, so she must be in the town records somewhere. It would feel good to do something nice for someone else. Maybe it would help me put my own situation in perspective.

I shivered. The sun was sinking along the edge of the horizon. I strode through the field and pictured letting myself into the house and going to stand by the fire…And then the thought snapped into my head like a camera shutter flicking. There was someone who had a key to my house. Julia. She'd taken care of Sampson ages ago—before Marianne moved in—when I'd gone to visit Nigel in California and as far as I knew, still had a copy. Had she used the key last night? I stood immobilized, leaned on the tree closest to me for support.

My legs suddenly felt limp. I replayed our conversation over our recent breakfast. There had been tension there, I knew it. But could she have been so jealous she would have done that? Images came to mind then, quickly merging one into another like a movie reel. The little barbs, the raised eyebrows and chuckles when I'd told her years ago my big dream of having a solo exhibit at a big-time gallery or museum, the look—disbelief?—quickly covered up when I'd finally told her about the Met. Her own struggles to sell enough of her artwork and gain a strong enough following to pay the bills every month. But this? Destruction of my studio...for what purpose? Revenge. It was the only motive, wasn't it?

My stomach felt filled with acid. I pushed away from the tree and stumbled back toward the road. Branches and roots grabbed at my boots, held me back. I pushed against them, struggled to walk normally, but the mud and wet leaves slipped and slid under my feet. I didn't realize until I'd reached the road and climbed back over the ditch that my hands were so tightly clenched, two of my nails had nearly cut into my palms. I headed toward home.

Chapter Twenty-Six

Will's funeral was held a week later. I went through the motions, but wondered, is this the way the left-behind fiancée is supposed to act? There was no book to read on the etiquette of grief. Inside, I felt hollow, like a tube. I had been carved out, emptied. Around me, people went on with their day-to-day lives—getting up and getting dressed, eating and talking, smoking, working, walking. But around me, people quieted. Their eyes looked away or became dewy. The latter patted my hand sympathetically and spoke meaningless words and phrases. "So sorry for your loss" and "he's in a better place now" but I felt only numbness.

At home, I moved through my chores automatically, like a robot might. Last night, Mama put a hand on my elbow. It took a few moments for me to register her touch. When I looked at her, I tried to smile, but the muscles of my mouth were paralyzed, like my insides.

"Claudette, why don't you sit on the porch and I'll bring you a cup of tea. Or go for a walk. It's a beautiful night. I'll take over the rest of the dinner preparations."

I looked down at the carrots that I'd been peeling. In the big sink, carrot ribbons lay in a pile. There was barely anything left to chop into chunks for the soup.

"I'm sorry," I said automatically, but Mama just pushed me gently away from the sink.

"No need to be," she'd said. "Just go and get a little fresh air."

I'd pulled a shawl over my shoulders and walked. The air was warm and balmy outside of the house. I didn't need the extra layer but kept it on anyway. It felt good to have over my shoulders, as though it was helping hold me together. I walked to the corner, looked at nothing except the road in front of me and the toes of my scuffed shoes. I knew that beyond my gaze, the world was exploding in color and fragrance, blooms heavy in the warm air, greenness everywhere. I didn't want to see any of it. I wanted only to close my eyes and sleep forever.

"Etta?" Feet sounded on the road behind me. "Etta!"

I stopped. My old-woman pace made it easy for Lily to catch up. She came up beside me, breathless. Her cheeks were flushed, her hat missing.

"I...." she stopped, as though forgetting what she was going to say, then started again. "How are you feeling?" She put a hand out, touched my arm. "Oh, that was stupid. Of course, you're miserable. I'm sorry. Can I walk with you?"

I nodded woodenly.

We turned, continuing the way that I had been going. Lily didn't say anything, just matched my steps. After several long moments of silence, Lily cleared her throat.

"This may not be the right time to tell you this, or ask you this, but I have to. Etta, I'm going to New York City." Lily stopped and grabbed my arm. I turned to her. Her face shone, and her eyes were bright. I could see now where the old cliché came from. She was full of life.

"I've been saving and have enough to last for two months, the way I've figured it. I'll find a job and there is a girl, Claire, that I went to school with. Anyway," Lily went on without waiting for a response. "She and I have been in touch. She's in theater and is losing one of her roommates, and invited me to move in. It's a small place, lots of roaches she said, but it's not far from the theater districts. And I'll get a job at a newspaper as a reporter. Well, maybe not as a reporter right away, but I could work as a secretary or typist or something until they promote me. Oh, Etta, it's going to be so exciting."

Lily stopped suddenly and put her hand out, touching me on the arm. "I'm sorry. I know I shouldn't be this happy when you're so miserable. I just, well…what I really wanted was to ask if you might like to come with me."

We stood motionless near the lookout over the river. Someone had built a small platform with rails, a place for tourists and locals to stand high above the water and look out over its churn. I turned my back to it.

"I—I don't think so, Lily," I said. "What could I do there? And what would my mother do without me here?"

"They have factories in New York, you know, or you could easily get a job in a kitchen. Just for a starting job, until you find something you like more. Or a hotel," she adds. "You have a lot of experience with guests already. Your mother would likely think that you need a break. A chance to just get away from," her voice stumbled, "everything. Just for a little while. A couple of months, Etta, would be wonderful for you, don't you think? Who knows what you might discover in the city."

I didn't want to discover anything. I didn't want Lily to encourage me, to try to lift me up. I just wanted to stay in my cocoon of sadness. But her enthusiasm affected me against my will. What if I did go with her? What would it be like to live and work in a huge, bustling city where no one knew me or about my tragedy? Wouldn't it be easier to heal if I wasn't faced every time I left the house with the river, reenacting Will's death over and over? If I could escape the house before Sally returned to stare listlessly at nothing for hours on end? But how could I leave my mother to deal with everything on her own? Still, something inside shifted, just the smallest centimeter. A tiny breath of fresh air going directly to that numb part of me. Was this how the Tin Man felt in the movie when he came back to life after so long lying rusted?

"My sister is looking for a job," Lily said, as though reading my thoughts. "She asked if your mother might need a little help. She's still in school, so it would just be in the evenings and early mornings, but she's good in the kitchen and wouldn't expect much pay. She said she's saving up till she can come and live with me."

A niggling feeling pressed at the back of my mind, that Lily and my mother had already discussed this idea, this plan.

"I can't, Lily," I said, and pushed the shifting feelings in my chest back into their box, closing the lid. "I just can't."

Lily sighed and linked her arm through mine.

"Maybe later," she said, but the hopefulness on her face was gone and her eyes were troubled. "Maybe in a month or two."

We both knew it wouldn't happen, but I felt my heart twist at her kindness.

"Yes, maybe later," I said and turned back toward home.

Chapter Twenty-Seven

Present Day

" **I** can't believe what you're saying. I think you need to
seek professional help, Isabel. Something is way out of
order in your mind for you to even consider this." The
words—Julia's words—bounced around in my brain as I drove
down the potholed road. I'd called her, my hesitant thoughts
becoming words that had become accusations. She'd never
raised her voice, even though I'd heard the rancor over the
phone line, thick as venom.

What had I done? What if I had been wrong? My heart
twisted in my chest at the thought. I should have waited.
I should have talked to someone, gotten another person's
feedback before I rushed in to hurl accusations at Julia. My
circle of friends was small, to begin with, and now.... Would
she ever speak to me again?

The car hit a particularly deep pothole and shuddered, the
wheel jerking under my hands. I relaxed my grip slightly.
No sooner had I hung up with Julia, before leaving the
house, than I'd received a call from Nigel. I'd stood, half-
listening—thinking still about my conversation with Julia—as
he reminded me of his impending visit.

"…early flight. Do you want me to rent a car?"

"What?" I said, snapping back to reality.

"My flight arrives early tomorrow," Nigel repeated, his voice patronizingly slow. "Are you still planning to pick me up or should I rent a car?"

"Oh, uh, no. I'll be there. Give me the flight information one more time."

Nigel sighed.

"I haven't given it to you for the first time yet, Isa. Are you all right? You sound…more distracted than usual."

"I'm fine," I said. "Just busy with the show. I have a pen and paper. Go ahead."

Thankfully, he hadn't quizzed me about the realtor that I had yet to call. The question was sure to come up when he got into town. I made a mental note to take care of it as soon as I got back from my errand.

* * *

I drove to the small library, just past the flashing caution light in the center of the village of Fairfield. Pulling into a spot, I left everything in the car except my keys.

"Do you have a public computer I can use?" I asked the pretty young woman behind the desk. I watched her take in my patchy skin before her gaze returned to my eyes.

"Sure, they're right over there." She pointed to a small bank of desktops. I thanked her and settled down in front of one, opening the web browser. My search for "possessed dolls" and "spirit possession inanimate objects" brought up lots and lots of videos, some of which looked more like horror movie sets than actual home footage.

185

While scrolling through the articles, though, I found one that looked promising. A priest and a psychologist worked as a team to treat patients with serious mental health issues in New York City. The psychologist did meticulous screenings and called the priest in when the situation deemed it necessary.

"People think that possession is something that went away in the 1800s, or that it can always be attributed to diseases like schizophrenia or other serious mental health issues," the psychologist explained. "But that's not true. Father Rourke has helped me on more than one occasion to do modern-day exorcisms."

I read further, my heart galloping in my chest. I looked closely to see if there were any mentions of objects being possessed, but found none. I went back to the search screen. There, toward the bottom of page two was an article titled, "Possessed Puppet?" I skimmed the article.

When Cindy Helms brought home a new marionette to add to her vintage collection, she had no idea the havoc it would wreak in her life. Helms, a former drama teacher, retired last year and has since traveled around the country. On one of her visits, she returned home to Ely, Minnesota, with a vintage marionette. Helms believed the doll was used in the infamous "Peter and the Wolf" marionette productions during the 1940s and 1950s. "It looked like a typical marionette," said Helms.

That is until Helms caught the puppet climbing the walls...literally.

"It was just a very unnerving experience," Helms said. During the six-month period in which she owned the marionette, strange occurrences happened in her family's home. The last straw, Helms stated, was when her six-year-old granddaughter was injured in

an accident while visiting from out of state. The puppet was in the room, Helms claimed, at the time of the accident.

"I'm not a believer in voodoo and spiritual things," Helms said. "At least, I wasn't until Peter came home with me." After the accident, Helms said that she disposed of the doll. "Ricki recovered, but I knew that there was something wrong with that marionette. I didn't want it here anymore. It gave me the creeps."

I closed the web browser, sat for a few minutes, and stared unseeingly at the blue screen. *This didn't prove anything*, my rational side reminded me. *People say they see ghosts, but you don't believe in that.*

But it's a possibility, another part of me responded. *And it's too much of a coincidence that so many bad things have happened since the doll showed up.*

I chewed on my nail and thought about options. And then I had an idea. Josef had an uncle that was a priest, didn't he? I retraced my steps to the librarian's desk and asked to borrow her phone.

"Josef, it's me," I said. I held the phone too tightly in my hand and my palm was sweaty against the plastic. "Listen, I'm sorry to bother you at work, but I wondered if you had the number for your uncle, the uh, priest." I turned my back to the librarian, who was pecking at a keyboard on the other side of the desk.

"Uncle Dick?" Josef's voice was cool. "Yes, of course. He's retired now. Has been for a few years, my mother said. I don't see him often... Why do you ask? I thought you didn't believe in spiritual stuff."

I twisted the phone cord in my fingers. "I, uh, don't. I need it for someone else. Please, do you have it?"

LET THE DEAD REST

"Hold on a moment. It's in my address book is in the back." He put me on hold; soft classical music filled the space between us.

My mind whirred over the articles I'd just read. I felt the old, familiar fear beneath my skin, the panic that skittered when first my mother and then—so quickly after—my father, lay dying. That sense of absolute helplessness. Yet at the same time, relief. Maybe this would give me an answer. Any answer had to be better than none. Didn't it?

"Are you still there?" Josef asked. His voice had taken on a more professional tone and I realized that a customer must have come in.

"Yes."

He rattled off Father Richard O'Malley's phone number, which I recorded on a scrap of paper. I thanked Josef and hung up, not bothering with a proper goodbye.

Chapter Twenty-Eight

1944

"Children, children come downstairs please!" Mama's voice rang out in the mostly empty house. The younger kids were doing their homework in their rooms. I was lying on my bed, tracing the cracks in the ceiling above my bed with my eyes.

"There's someone here to see you," her voice sang out. I started upright. Sally was coming home today, and I'd forgotten. My poor mother had had to drag her home all alone, in a taxi most likely, while I lay here uselessly. I stood up, smoothed a hand over my dress. Already the younger kids were banging down the stairs. Jimmy held an apple-head doll he'd made for Sally. He'd painted the face himself, carefully bending over the wrinkled apple face, his tongue sticking out a little in the left corner of his mouth. He'd grinned up at me when he'd finished. The doll's eyes were crooked, one larger than the other, and the cheeks—which he'd tried to color with tiny drops of beet juice—looked raw, as though someone had been slapping the poor thing.

"It's beautiful," Mama had announced, and we'd all solemnly agreed.

Mama had made the doll a pink dress and added fine yarn for hair. It was still ugly, but Jimmy held it as proudly as a new papa holding his firstborn.

"Do you think she'll like it, Etta?" he whispered, hanging back from the others as they pounded down the steep stairs.

"I'm sure she will," I said. My heart squeezed in my chest. How did you explain to a seven-year-old that his baby sister likely wouldn't even know his name or be able to speak, let alone appreciate a doll?

"Remember, Jimmy, Mama said that Sally will be different than…." My voice caught. "Than before. She won't be the same little girl. The accident hurt her brain and she…." But he just nodded and clambered down the stairs, holding the doll tightly to his chest. I followed slowly, every step weighted. I could see the kids' heads as they crowded in a circle around Sally and Mama. Tommy said something to Mama, and she threw her head back and laughed. Laughed! When was the last time she'd done that? Her eyes met mine and I stopped on the stairs, holding tightly to the railing.

"Come see, Claudette," she said, and her eyes sparkled. "Come see how beautiful our little Sally looks."

Sally sat on a suitcase that Mama had brought to the hospital. Her head was bent over the doll in her lap—Jimmy's gift—and her blonde curls tumbled down around her shoulders. Then she looked up and I gasped. She looked so, well, normal. Her face still bore long, pink scratches where the glass had cut her, and the side of her head where the mirror had hit the hardest had a small bandage. But her eyes were clear and focused.

"Etta," she crowed and lifted her arms up above her head. I stumbled forward and caught her up in a hug. She smelled of antiseptic and cookies and the sweet sweat of a child. I pressed her carefully to my chest. She held on tight, but something sharp poked my chest. I glanced down through teary eyes and saw her apple-head doll staring up at me. I laughed and swung her carefully around in one slow circle, then set her on the ground. She giggled and rocked her baby doll from side to side. "Rock-a-bye, li'l baby," she said, and everyone laughed. Sally grinned and held out her hand to Jimmy. "Time to play now?"

The kids moved from the room like a pack of puppies, Sally carefully wedged in the center and guarded by her two older brothers. "Let's play something gentle," I heard Tommy say. "How about jacks?"

I stared after them for several long moments before I felt my mother's hand on my arm.

"Isn't it a miracle?" she asked. "I didn't want to say anything at first, in case the doctors were wrong. They noticed that she was responding well after coming out of the coma, but still thought there was serious damage to her brain. It wasn't until just last week that she began to show real improvement. By then, I'd decided to just let things happen as they would and not tell any of you until you could see for yourselves. God answered our prayers. It's wonderful, isn't it?" My mother's eyes were shining with tears, her smile wide.

"It is wonderful," I said and grabbed her suddenly in an awkward hug. "I'm so glad, Mama," I said. "She's better," I said it out loud, testing the phrase's validity.

My mother laughed a little and pushed me gently away from her but kept her hands on my upper arms. "You never know what the future holds, Claudette," she said. "All may seem as black as night and then, suddenly, a bit of light breaks through. You just have to hold on long enough to see it."

I knew that she wasn't just talking about Sally anymore. Tears filled my eyes and I nodded. She kissed me on the cheek and followed the sound of the children upstairs.

* * *

"Oh Etta, come with me," Lily said. She grabbed my arm and held it tightly. We were sitting on the sun-warmed back steps, enjoying the breeze that wound its way around our calves and through our hair. Lily was leaving in six days. Six. "I wish you would. What's the worst that could happen? You won't like it and you can come back here. At least you'll have given it a try."

She paused and glanced at me. "You might fall in love," she said. "With the city, I mean. There is so much there. Enormous libraries and museums, art galleries and theaters and music halls. The respectable kind. It would be so wonderful, Etta."

Why not try it? The small voice in my head asked. Because I didn't have the proper wardrobe, I responded. I didn't have a job. I couldn't leave my mother and siblings. Because I was grieving, and starting a new life wouldn't help me forget Will, not really.

I had the money I'd been saving for when Will and I—well, the money that hadn't been given to Mama to help out. Maybe it would be a relief for her to have me out of her hair. Since Will's death—would it ever stop hurting to say those words together?—I hadn't been good for much. My boss had given me his sympathy and three days off work. I'd never gone back.

I closed my eyes and thought of Will. Not of his death. Not even of him as my fiancé, but as a person. He'd had so many dreams! Too many, it had seemed to me at times. But wasn't it better to live with big dreams and accomplish a few of them in your life, then not have any at all? To just accept the status quo and live day in and day out without a plan or a purpose? Wasn't Will's life fuller, richer, because of the dreams he'd had of the future?

What about me? My big dream had been to be Will's wife, and the mother of our children. To live in a perfect little house with a tidy little fence. That was fine as dreams go, but it wasn't going to happen. So, what other dreams lay buried inside? What other things might I become that I hadn't considered before?

The truth was that I didn't know. But for the first time in months—maybe even years—there was a curiosity deep inside that I wanted to explore. Who was I? Who was Claudette Hayes, really, and where did I fit in? Not in my family's life. Not in Will's life. But in my own life. Where did I want to go? Who did I want to be, really?

All of the excuses I'd given to Lily seemed at once slightly ridiculous. My wardrobe was plain but functional. If I were to seek out employment in a kitchen or even as a maid in a hotel, I'd likely wear a uniform. Sally was better, and my family was stronger than they had been in a long time. Mary had taken over most of my duties without being asked and Tommy—and even Jimmy—pitched in more than ever before. And my grief...it wasn't leaving, but I could mourn in the city as well as I could here, couldn't I? Maybe Lily was right, anyway. Maybe it would be easier to heal without the constant reminders, without seeing Will on every street corner, around every turn in the road, sitting on the porch swing.

"I think I might like that, Lily," I said, and linked my arm through hers. She grinned at me and talked excitedly. Her voice cut through some of the fog shrouding my brain as she discussed our future in the big city.

Something warm bloomed in my chest. Just a whisper, a tiny press of hope.

Chapter Twenty-Nine

Present Day

Father Richard O'Malley lived in a cabin tangled with ivy on a dirt road aptly called "No Man's Land." His was one of three houses, each separated by miles of forest. I drove slowly, my car riding into and out of the potholes carefully. I didn't want to get a flat tire or break anything important out here. The tires made a crunching sound as I turned into the gravel-lined driveway. Immediately, a medium-sized hound dog trotted to the car and barked his hello in loud bellows. I waited in the car until a gray-haired man, slight and gently stooped, emerged from the doorway.

"Mouse!" he called. The dog gave a final bark and then bounded toward the house. The man scratched the dog's ears and motioned to me that it was safe to get out. I opened the car door and was hit immediately with the strong fragrance of pine needles.

"Father O'Malley?" I asked. The man nodded and walked down the steps and toward me. He held out a hand that was rough and calloused.

"You must be Isabel," he said. "You're a friend of Josef's, is that right?"

I nodded, hoping no further explanation of our relationship would be required. The priest seemed to sense this. He smiled and released my hand.

"Would you like a hot drink? Come inside out of the wind."

It *was* windy. The strong breeze pushed and pulled at the nearby pine trees and sighed softly through the branches.

"Thanks," I said gratefully, grabbed my bag and followed him. "That sounds lovely."

"How long have you lived here?" I asked as he held the door open for me. I entered through the faded blue door and into a small, clean living room. To the right was an eat-in kitchen, to the left two closed doors—maybe a bedroom and bathroom. That was it. The whole house in one compact space. I liked it.

"About eight years now," said Father O'Malley. "Please, take a seat. Not you, Mouse," said the priest, and pointed the dog away from me and toward a large, scruffy-looking pillow in the corner. The dog sighed loudly and walked to the bed, nosed it a few times, then plopped down, his head on his paws. He stared at his master balefully.

"Mouse?" I asked.

Father O'Malley laughed, his cheeks scrunched up below his glasses.

"He was the runt of the litter. Had him since he was a puppy. I was looking for a good hunting dog, but he's a little slow on the uptake if you know what I mean. Now, would you like tea, coffee, or cocoa?"

I couldn't remember the last time I was offered cocoa and asked for that.

It was pleasant in the cozy cabin, and for a few minutes, I forgot the dark task that brought me here. I wanted to keep forgetting. After handing me a mug of steaming hot chocolate,

Father O'Malley sat beside me at the table, his hands wrapped around a mug of coffee. His right hand was scratched over the knuckles, and his nails were short and rounded.

"So, you mentioned on the phone that you have an object which may be possessed?"

He said it so matter-of-factly that I nearly choked on my cocoa. Were we really doing this? Sitting here in a kitchen, sipping hot drinks, and discussing possession? Part of me wanted to laugh, another to cry.

"Well, I'm not sure," I said, and put my mug on the table. It was old and oak, and there were rings and scratches left from many other mugs and dishes over the years. "To be honest, Father, I don't really believe in spirits or possession. At least, I didn't."

"Why?"

I told him then, about the article that I'd read about the possessed marionette and the priest/psychologist team. And about the bad things that had happened since Gerda's arrival. I told him about the way that she glowed during or after these things, and how I'd found her in places I'd never taken her.

"Hmm," he said. He was silent a long moment, then asked, "Were you religious growing up?"

I shook my head. "My grandmother used to take me to mass sometimes, but my parents never went. I have always felt like there is a…. I don't know, an entity or Great Spirit out there, but I've never thought much about the other side of things."

Father O'Malley nodded thoughtfully.

"When you think about it, it's like the plot of any good action movie. There's the good side and then there's the dark side. What do you do for work?" he asked abruptly.

"I'm an artist. I make, well, dolls. But not like this one." I motioned toward my bag. "Mine are more like sculptures."

"So, in your work, you must have to tap into your creativity quite a bit."

I nodded.

"And do you sometimes have off days? When things go wrong, you're not feeling inspired, or things don't work out the way you planned?"

I laughed dryly. "More often than I'd like."

"In the Christian tradition, we'd call that sin. Not your personal sin, but the sin of the world. It's the kind that started with Adam and Eve. It's what keeps people stuck in bad habits or mires us in hopelessness when we're faced with bad circumstances. Sin is like breathing—it's part of our nature."

"Okay," I said and sipped my drink.

"To make a long story short, if you think of sin as the dark side—for lack of a better term—and God as the light side, then it makes sense that there is this ongoing battle that none of us can see going on. And if there is a dark side, a dark presence in the world, then isn't it logical that it wants to wreak havoc in whatever way it can?"

"None of this seems logical," I said.

Father O'Malley chuckled. "Touché."

We were quiet for a few moments, the only sound the *tick-tick-tick* of a clock on the far wall and of Mouse breathing loudly on his pillow.

Then, "May I see the doll?"

I dug into my bag and extracted Gerda, then unwrapped her. The priest looked her over, then looked at me over the top of his gold-framed glasses. His eyes are so dark blue that they looked nearly gray.

"I'm retired, you know," the priest said and stood. "I haven't given mass for years now. Moved out here after retirement, to live a life of solitude. Normally I'd have to have the Vatican's approval to conduct an exorcism," he said and walked across the room. He returned with a battered book in his hands.

"But I think in this case we can make an exception. After all, you're not Catholic, I'm not officially a priest anymore, and this isn't a human being." He winked at me. Then he stood at the table, Gerda laid out before him like a placemat. He flipped through the tissue-paper pages until he found what he was looking for and with a soft grunt, started to read.

The words were surprisingly like poetry. I listened alternately to the passage, which was dotted with words and phrases about evil and darkness and goodness and light, the sound of Mouse's snores in the corner, and a woodpecker that hammered away at a tree near the cabin. I was lulled into a kind of dreamy state. The smell of the cocoa, the crackle of the fire, and the words all blended together and relaxed me.

Suddenly, the door to the cabin banged open. I jumped, nearly jerked out of my chair. Father O'Malley stopped reading and crossed the room. He closed it against a hard wind that had picked up outside.

"Sorry about that," he said. "The latch isn't working right."

He turned back toward me, and as he did, I saw something pass over his face. A sort of shadow. The temperature in the room felt colder all of a sudden. Mouse sat up on his pillow and whined.

Something on the table rattled. Quiet at first, like someone drumming their fingernails on the tabletop. Then louder, like hard rain that pounded against the wooden surface. The priest and I looked simultaneously. Gerda vibrated, her head, arms, and legs clacked against the surface of the table, as though an invisible hand alternately held her body down and shook her repeatedly against the tabletop.

Chapter Thirty

J ames looked surreptitiously around the branches of the small grove of trees where he was standing. His wife, Betty, stood further down on the bank by the Winooski River. He could see her lithe form and the basketball roundness of her belly where her best dress clung under the short jacket. He thought of the long ride ahead of them—back to Bakersfield, to the new farm they'd purchased. And what they might do after their daughter was safely tucked into bed that night.

"Golly, Betty, wouldn't rather live here in the city?" James frowned at the nasal voice of his mother-in-law. She could rankle him with only a look, a certain raise of her eyebrows. She couldn't accept it still—after six years of marriage—that her only daughter had married beneath the family. That out of all the young men she could have chosen, Betty had fallen in love with a commoner. A farmer.

James scrubbed a hand over the back of his neck. He could feel the heat of anger staining it red. He sighed and reached into the interior pocket of his best suitcoat—his only suitcoat, truth be told—and slipped a little flask out. He didn't drink much. But having his in-laws visiting had reunited him with his now good friend, Old Grand-Dad. The bourbon burned his esophagus and he welcomed the heat. One more quick slug, then he'd put it away.

He was about to tip his head back when something tugged at his free hand. Or rather, someone.

"Whatcha doing, Daddy?" his daughter asked. Amelia's eyes were dark and shining as she stared up at him. Her mother had braided her hair that morning, but it was coming loose. Dark wisps stuck to her neck and were shifted by the breeze coming off the river.

He screwed the cap back onto the flask and slipped it back into his pocket seamlessly, then rumpled her hair further with his other hand.

"Just enjoying the view," he said and turned her little body so that Amelia stood in front of him. He crossed his arms over her chest and leaned his head down low so that it touched the top of hers.

"You smell funny," she said.

"And you"—he stood up again and tugged on the end of her braid—"look as pretty as a princess this afternoon. Are you enjoying your grandparents' visit?"

"Yes. But sometimes Grandma is mean."

"She is?" James said with mock surprise. "What makes you say that?"

Amelia turned and looked up at him.

"She's mean to you and to Grandpa. She's too bossy and always wants to have her own way," Amelia said. "And she talks funny."

"Aw, you mean her accent?" James nodded when Amelia did

too. "That's just because she's from Jersey. They all talk like that there. Just like we probably sound funny to them. Anyway, sometimes your grandma can be bossy—that's true—but she really loves you a lot. And she loves your mom, too."

"What about you? Does she love you?" Amelia wrinkled up her nose, her freckles bunching over the bridge of crinkled skin.

"Well, ah, sure. In her own way. But let's go for a walk, huh? Want to go a little closer to the river and maybe get splashed a little?"

"Yes!" Amelia crowed and raced toward the water.

"Wait," James called. "Hold your horses, Amelia, and wait for your old man!" He jogged up behind her and she grasped his hand. It was small and soft in his. He was grateful, then, that they'd taken this Sunday drive. That the sun was shining and the air was cool and sweet, and that they were all together. He didn't get to spend enough time with his family. And with Amelia's baby brother or sister on the way, the time he spent with his firstborn would be even scarcer. It was good that they had today. Good that he'd taken the time to be here, even with so many other projects on the farm calling his name.

"Look at that, Daddy!" Amelia said, pointing excitedly toward the riverbank. He squinted but all he could see was the water, dull and brown, moving downstream.

"The water?"

"No. Look there"—Amelia jabbed a finger excitedly—"right there in that little tree. See that? It's a doll!"

"Where?" James asked, but before the word left his mouth he saw it. A tangle of blonde hair. A calico dress. A pale face and hands. It must have fallen from higher up, gotten snagged on the branch where it was hanging. He was already working out how he'd maneuver himself down the bank to the doll when Amelia pulled at his coat.

"Will you get her for me? Please, Daddy?"

James grinned and Amelia squealed with delight, jumping up and down.

"I'll try my best. But you stay right here. Don't go any further toward the river, all right?"

She nodded.

"You watch me and go fetch your mother if I fall in, huh?"

"Don't do that," Amelia said. "You'll get all wet!" She erupted into giggles as James slipped and slid his way down the damp bank.

It took longer than he thought it would. The doll's hair was snarled around the branches that held it in place. When he finally untangled it, he was sweating and breathing hard from trying to keep his balance. He collapsed near his daughter higher up on the bank and handed her the doll.

"Ooh, thank you, Daddy! Thank you!" She clutched the doll to her thin chest, then lunged toward him and planted a wet kiss on his cheek. "I'm going to go show Mommy."

He relaxed on the grassy slope, felt the sun filtering through the leaves above, and grinned. He might not be much according to his mother-in-law. But Amelia Rose thought he was the cat's meow.

Chapter Thirty-One

Present Day

"What's happening?" My voice sounded odd, highly pitched, and breathless.

Father O'Malley moved first. He jerked toward the table and outstretched his hand toward the doll. For a moment, I pictured him wrestling with Gerda, her jerking him like a ragdoll across the floor of the room. But she had stopped moving the instant his palm closed around her. I let out a breath. Was it over? We stood in silence for a moment. Mouse broke the quiet with a whine, then he began to pace from his bed to the door and back again.

"Can you let him out, please?" Father O'Malley said.

I opened the door with thick fingers and watched as Mouse hustled into the yard. He cast one worried look back at me before trotting toward a large weeping willow in the corner of the yard. I closed the door reluctantly and turned back to the priest.

"What now?" I asked. My voice sounded more normal, but I hid my shaking hands in the drape of my sweater.

"Now, I begin my work," he said.

I had questions suddenly that needed answers. I wanted

to ask him how many times he'd done this if he'd ever tried to exorcise an inanimate object before or only people, what happened if it didn't work, why he thought this had happened to the doll in the first place.... But the words were stuck, pinched closed in my esophagus.

He bent over the doll. Then he began to murmur words that I couldn't understand. Latin? I remembered the masses with my grandmother. These words had the same clipped syllables. The lights in the room dimmed, but I realized with a glance out of the window that it was the sun, swallowed up by dark clouds. It became so cold that it seemed as though I could see my breath in a white puff. I rubbed my hands up and down my arms. I stepped closer to the table and tried to see what Father O'Malley was doing.

Suddenly, the table started to shake and vibrate, like the doll had moments before. The feet *bang-bang-banged* against the old oak floors. I gasped and jumped back. Father O'Malley glanced at me, but I couldn't make out his expression. I moved closer, held my hands against the tabletop. It jerked and bucked underneath my palms, slapped into them again, and again until they stung.

Father O'Malley's voice was low, barely a whisper. But his tone was urgent, his lips moved to pronounce words I almost couldn't hear. Everything began to be muddled and I felt suddenly dizzy. I lost my grip on the table and sank into the chair that I'd left earlier. The coffee mug and cocoa cup were on their sides—liquid spilled out over the edge of the table and dripped to the floor underneath. I reached for them, dumbly, and then glanced at Gerda.

Her face was ugly, twisted, and rage-filled. Her faded blue eyes were bright and glowed with intensity, but her mouth was nothing more than a gash in the center of her face. Everything—her face, her tiny hands, and neat arms and legs—looked gray and crackled with age. And then I realized, horrified, that there was a noise coming from her. I wanted to clap my hands over my ears to drown it out. It started as a thin sound, raspy, like a single fingernail being drawn over a chalkboard. Soon, though, it turned into a loud drone. A buzzing filled the air next, like a million honeybees. I moved to cover my ears, but my hands were still full of the mugs. Without thinking, I let go. Both crashed to the floor, the remainder of coffee and cocoa pooled in puddles under the table.

The noise grew louder and louder. Father O'Malley continued to speak but I couldn't hear anything over the drone. He glanced at me. Then he motioned for me to hold the doll down. I stood, unable to move.

"Isabel!" he yelled. I woodenly extended my arms. My hands covered the doll's body. It was like holding onto a block of ice covered in cloth. I stared in horror, unable to look away from her face. Her eyes had become black holes, sunk into her head. Her nose had fallen away and there was only a dent where it used to be. Black smoke wafted from her mouth in a tiny tendril of frigid air. The scent of sulfur and burning hair filled the air. I wanted to scream, to run, but instead, I closed my eyes and held on. Father O'Malley touched my shoulder a second later. I jumped and nearly lost my hold on the doll. He motioned for me to let go, to move back. In his hand was a crucifix, long and silver with an image of a tortured Christ embedded on the front.

He put one hand on the doll and it bucked and jerked as he moved the other hand, the one holding the crucifix, over the doll's head. His words were louder now, nearly a shout. The droning sound turned into a scream. It was the worst sound I'd ever heard, like a woman being cut open, like a wolf being razed, a soul screaming its way to hell. My hands shot up to my ears and I cowered beside the table, my eyes fixed on Gerda. She continued to writhe and buck, but slowly, slowly her motions became less frantic. The priest continued reciting the ancient words. I couldn't hear anything over the sound that was coming from the doll.

And then, suddenly, everything stopped. The quiet was deafening in its wake. Gerda lay still. Her feet and hands and arms and legs returned to pale white. Her face—I glanced quickly—was coming back together, the way that it was before. The black holes began to turn white and fill back in, her blue eyes bright and her tiny button nose reappeared. Her mouth was once again drawn up into a pink bow.

Father O'Malley collapsed into the chair I'd vacated. He stared at the doll. His hair was mussed, his glasses crooked. His hands, I noticed as I reached for one of them, were shaking.

"Are you all right?" I asked, my voice barely more than a frog's croak.

He nodded but said nothing. He breathed heavily through his nose. His eyes looked from the doll to the crucifix, still in his free hand, and then back again. We sat like this for several long minutes, the warmth of his calloused hand melded with the iciness of my own. The only sound in the room was our breath and the *tick-tock, tick-tock* of the big clock.

Then the outside door jiggled. Claws scratched against the wood and a low whine sounded. I moved to open it and stood back as Mouse plowed through and rushed to his master. Father O'Malley pet the hound dog absently. After a few long seconds, the priest seemed to finally take in his surroundings. Mouse put his front feet on the chair and leveraged himself into Father O'Malley's face, licking his chin and cheek. Father O'Malley chuckled and ran a hand along the dog's side, then pushed him gently from the chair. The spell was broken and the heaviness of the air itself started to dissipate.

Father O'Malley looked at me.

"Well, that was something," he said. I laughed, a choking, dry sound. But then my shoulders started to shake, and tears came from the corners of my eyes. I crossed back to the table and sat next to him, wiped at my eyes with my sweater's sleeve. He patted me once on the shoulder, the same way he'd patted Mouse, then gave it a warm squeeze.

"Is it really over?" I asked, embarrassed by the wobble in my voice.

He nodded.

"I don't know what just happened, but thank you for whatever it was," I said.

Father O'Malley looked at me tiredly and smiled. "I didn't do anything, really. Just acted as a sort of conduit."

"Well, it worked," I said, and looked down at Gerda. Her face and arms were smooth, with no sign of the capillary cracks, and her cheeks just a bit pink.

"She looks like new," Father O'Malley said.

"Yes," I shivered. "But I still don't want to keep her."

Father O'Malley laughed again. It was a wonderful laugh—fresh and wholehearted and rich.

"I don't blame you," he said. "We're trained in this. In exorcism," Father O'Malley said, "but it never gets easier. I've done my fair share over the years, but I've never actually performed one on an inanimate object before." He stood, and

209

gave Mouse another scratch behind the ears. "We're supposed to dispose of them. Any icon or object that has been part of an exorcism. Unless you want to do the honors?"

I hesitated, started to shake my head. But suddenly, I knew exactly where the doll was needed. Where she could finally, hopefully, find rest. A place where she wouldn't be lonely.

* * *

I left twenty minutes later. Father O'Malley wouldn't accept any payment for services rendered, but I did talk him into taking a donation for the church where he'd acted as priest for so many years. I turned my car toward home, Gerda wrapped once again in the bottom of my bag. As I drove, the words of the accordion player kept coming back to me. "Let the dead rest." Finally, I thought I knew what he meant.

Chapter Thirty-Two

I t was just after five-thirty in the morning. I had gathered a heavy flashlight, a shovel, and tucked Gerda into the pocket of my father's old barn coat which I pulled on over a sweater. I wished Marianne were here, to do this with me. Her sister had a stroke, though, and Marianne had gone to stay with her family in New Hampshire for the week.

I walked into the woods, the air around me filled with sounds of early morning. Dry leaves scratched against tree trunks and each other. Branches creaked and groaned in the wind. Far away, I heard the high keening of a single coyote and then the yipping reply of another. The air was cold, my breath rose in filmy white clouds before my face. I'd left Gerda in the garage the night before while I'd taken a hot bath, then had gotten up and moved her to the car. Then later, I'd put her in the back shed. It hadn't mattered. I'd still felt her presence, like a heavy lead blanket that made breathing hard. I'd slept poorly, tangled in my sheets with her small body filling my dreams.

I pulled the coat closer, a hard part of her—head or foot or hand—dug into my thigh through the pocket. I used the shovel like a walking stick, the dull *thud-thud-thud* made a rhythm with my breath and footsteps.

My world had turned inside out in the past few weeks.

Everything I knew and believed had been stretched thin and taut, like a piano wire over-stretched. And one question kept circling: who had sent me the doll? And why? They had to have known of its power. But who wanted to destroy me? Who would gain by taking more from me than I'd already lost? A hot flush of shame pressed in my chest as I thought of the accusations I'd hurled toward Julia. But who else...?

My foot caught on a tree root and I stumbled. The flashlight slipped from my fingers. It blinked out, back on, and then out again. I reached for it in the leaves, the warmth of the barrel comforted in my hand. The path to the clearing opened before me. Clouds moved over the moon and blocked out the sliver of brightness momentarily. The coyotes keened again, farther away, and the sound echoed against tree trunks and bounced upward toward what was left of the stars.

And then, finally, there I was. I walked to the side of the clearing, staying near the tree line until I found what I was searching for. The white gravestone was dull in the pale morning light. I shut the flashlight off and moved toward the stone with purposeful steps. It was hard and cold under my hands as I smoothed away a tangle of grapevine and dried leaves.

"All I know is your name," I said aloud, my voice loud in the crisp early-morning air. "Amelia Rose Peterson. It's a beautiful name. But I'm sorry that you're all alone. I hope that you were loved in this life and that you've found peace." I imagined what the little girl had looked like—long, dark hair and a mischievous smile. I pictured her on a swing made from an old board, barefoot in a white summer dress, freckles across her nose. And I pictured Gerda, too, an unloved doll, one that was owned by a wealthy little girl who'd had too many toys and cast this doll into the back of a closet. I hoped that bringing together the child and the doll would fulfill a need for each of them that had gone unrealized in this world.

I moved to the left of the stone, placed the shovel tip into the ground, and jumped on the edges. It didn't cut through the sod at first. The earth here was wild and untamed; tall dried grasses covered every inch of the meadow. It made it hard for the shovel to make progress. But finally, it did and broke through the thick, heavy soil. Shovelful after shovelful was dumped onto the meadow grass, while my breath and the shovel made a kind of rhythm. I dug and dug under the lightening sky.

When the jagged hole was about two feet deep, I stopped. Pulling the shovel upward, I tossed it to the ground alongside the newly dug grave and sank to my knees. My heart thrummed. I could feel it under my ribs, but also in my wrists and along my neck, pulsing hard. I needed to say something and searched my mind for wise words, but none came. I pulled the doll from the deep pocket of my coat.

"I'm sorry," I said finally, and placed the doll, still wrapped in cloth, into the hole. "I'm sorry for whatever happened to you to make you this way. And I hope that you'll find peace now. Both of you."

Iciness trailed up my backbone as I bent to shovel in the first soil. I glanced over my shoulder as the earth crumbled over the cloth. I half expected to see someone—a person or a ghostly figure outlined against the expanse of trees—but no one was there. There was no sound, except for the branches that clicked together, leaves that rattled against the bark.

Chapter Thirty-Three

The next morning, I woke suddenly, the sheet twisted up around my neck. I'd heard something, but what? A bang. Or a loud click? Sampson stirred beside me and then meowed.

"It's okay," I said, not believing it myself. "Everything's fine."

I pushed myself up then pulled the sheet away and swung my legs over the side of the bed. My toes groped for slippers, avoiding the icy floor. Sampson wriggled on the bed, but I put a hand out to pet him.

"Stay here," I said, and surprisingly, he listened. He turned himself around one more time, then tucked himself into a ball near my pillow. I walked to the top of the stairs. What time was it? The sky outside was still tinged with gray and the clock I passed in the hallway said it was just after six.

A knock sounded at the door downstairs and my heart stumbled in my chest. Who would be knocking so early in the morning? I lurched back to my bedroom and pulled on my robe, belting it as I walked down the stairs and to the hallway closet. There I grabbed the now-familiar baseball bat. Its handle was smooth and silken in my hand. My heart pounded, and my eyes were wide as I passed the mirror in the hallway. I ducked into the living room and walked to the front door. I waited. Another knock.

"Who is it?" I asked, my voice a high whine in my own ears. My hands around the bat trembled.

"Isabel? It's me. Let me in, it's freezing out here."

"Nigel?" My brain whirred, trying to process this information. Not a psychotic housebreaker but my own brother. Nigel.... Here? And then I remembered. "I'm so sorry," I said through the door as I fumbled with the lock. I swung it open. Nigel stood on the porch, hair windswept, a frown deepening the lines around his mouth. "I've been so busy, I'm afraid I got my days mixed up. Come in, come in."

"Thanks for picking me up at the airport." Sarcasm was laced through Nigel's voice as he pushed through the door. He was slender, tall, and would have been handsome had it not been for his too-high forehead and too-close-together eyes. I kissed his cheek, which was icy cold, and closed the door behind him. A waft of frigid air had followed him in.

"We're having a cold snap," I said dumbly.

He shivered. "You're telling me. It was eighty-five when I left Long Beach."

"Let me get you something to drink. Have you had breakfast?"

"No." He slung his bag on the chair nearest the door and followed me into the kitchen. I felt, rather than saw, him taking in my living quarters with disapproval. Books lay scattered in various states of reading in the living room. A bunch of dead flowers in a vase sat precariously close to the edge of the mantle, and two baskets of unfolded clothes were hunkered near the couch. I'd been lax in my housekeeping since Marianne had left. And occupied with other things.

"Taking up a new hobby?"

"What?" I turned, then realized I still clutched the bat in my hand.

"Oh," I tried unsuccessfully for a laugh and propped the bat in the corner. "No, I'm just not used to getting visitors this early in the morning."

"Everything all right? You look skinny and tired."

"Never one to mince words," I said lightly and rummaged around in the cupboard. I avoided his gaze and pulled out two mugs and the coffee filters. Sampson strolled into the room and rubbed against Nigel's legs with a meow. Nigel patted his head twice and edged him away with his foot.

"What?" he said when he caught me looking at him. "He'll get hair all over my pants."

I rolled my eyes. "Heaven forbid. Anyway, it's just the stress from the show, I think, that's made me lose a little weight. And a bit of sleep." *Oh, and a psychotic, possessed doll that I've been dealing with.* I scooped coffee into the pot. "I've been putting in some extra hours to get everything ready."

"The show?"

I turned to look at him. I must have looked like a fish, mouth agape. He couldn't really have forgotten the most important event of my career, could he?

"The Met?" I said the words slowly, as though he were hard of hearing.

"Oh, right. The museum thing. That hasn't happened yet?"

I turned back to start the coffee pot, my jaws clenched together. "No, not yet," I said. "But it's coming up soon. You know it's just the biggest event of my life. I thought you might remember it."

"Right, right," Nigel said. "Slipped my mind. Work's been crazy. So, how's the prep going?"

216

"Not well," I said and turned back to him, leaned against the counter, and crossed my arms. "My studio got trashed, the cat went missing for a couple of days, there was that, uh, leak in the basement and—"

"Your studio? What happened?"

"I'm not sure," I lied and felt the now-familiar weight of dread along my shoulders like a physical force pushing me down. "At first, I thought it was an intruder, but the police—"

"The police came?" his voice went up an octave.

"It's all fine now. There wasn't anyone, or at least, we saw no signs of one. It was likely the cat. Listen, I'm sorry that I forgot it was today you were coming in." I had to get him off the subject of my studio and the police. "I feel terrible. Why didn't you call?"

Nigel shook his head. "I did. You didn't answer. Really, Isabel, isn't it time you got a cell phone like the rest of the modernized world?"

I finished adding the grounds to the pot and flipped the button on. "They don't work out here. Plus, I'm rarely away from home, so it's just easier to have the landline. I turned the ringer off last night when I was doing some work for the exhibit and must have forgotten to turn it back on. How'd you get here anyway?"

"Rental."

"Ah," I said and turned back to face him. My arms were still wrapped around my waist. A defensive posture, I remembered suddenly from a workshop I'd been forced to take on public speaking in college. I let them hang at my sides instead, but that felt strange, so I stuffed both into the pockets of my robe.

"How long are you here for?"

"Two days."

"Anything special you want to do while you're visiting?"

"It's not really a pleasure visit, Isa. I'm meeting with one of our firm's clients tomorrow morning...and we need time to talk. You know, about things."

My stomach clenched, and I had to force myself to relax my shoulders.

"And then tomorrow afternoon," my brother said and glanced out the kitchen window, "I need to meet with the attorney one more time, to sign some final paperwork for the estate."

"Again? I thought your last meeting was the final one?"

"Just some last paperwork," Nigel says again. Then, "Look, Isa. You know the real reason that I came here. I'm worried about your safety. And now that you've told me the police were here, that someone broke in..."

The coffee maker beeped, and I turned gratefully to pour us mugs. "We don't know that anyone broke in and I don't want to have this conversation right now, okay?" I said and turned back toward him. "Please, can't we just have a normal visit like regular siblings do?"

"But that's just it. This isn't normal." He waved his hand around my kitchen. "You're not normal." He sighed heavily through his nose. "I didn't mean that the way it sounded. I just mean that I don't think it's safe for you, living out here like a hermit. Why not move to Long Beach with me? Lisa would love to have you close by, and it would be great to see the kids grow up, wouldn't it?"

I snorted. "Long Beach is safer than Bakersfield?" I didn't wait for him to answer. "I can't."

"Why? There is nothing holding you here anymore. Bring your cat and rent this place out for the first few months if you're not sure. Lisa has been looking at properties close by, and there are some really good deals on condos and apartments in the area. Plus, the kids would love to spend more time with you. There are a lot of artist groups that you could join." He held his hands up as I shook my head. "Look, you're my responsibility and—"

"No," I said the word quietly, but inside it sparked anger that rose in my chest. "I'm not a child, Nigel, and I'm not some spinster aunt from the nineteenth century that needs to be taken in and looked after. I love it here. This is home. Besides, I have a roommate now, Marianne."

Nigel sighed again and reached for the outstretched mug of coffee. Then he continued the conversation as though I'd never spoken.

"So, rent this place out to her. There are great cultural venues—museums and galleries—just a short drive from the house. The winters are mild; you wouldn't have to shovel or wait for the plow guy to fit you into his schedule. And there are lots of outdoor things to do—hiking and biking and camping…"

His voice drifted off and I finally met his gaze.

"You never called the realtor, did you?"

I shook my head. "It's been so crazy around here that it completely slipped my mind. But the truth is that I'm not interested. Why waste his time and raise his hopes on something that isn't going to happen? Look," I said and took two steps across the kitchen. In an uncharacteristic show of affection, I lay my hand over his, squeezed his fingers. "I'm not moving. Not to Long Beach or anywhere else. This is home. Thanks for the offer, but"—I patted his hand and withdrew mine—"no, thank you."

Nigel shook his head.

"I don't understand you."

"I know that," I said. I sipped my coffee. He never had. Unlike him, I never wanted the thirty-year mortgage and two-point-five kids and regular job, and the ever-increasing raises that went along with it.

He sipped from his mug, walked over, and stared out the window over the sink.

"So, how's the doll?" he asked. I knew he wasn't admitting defeat, that this branch in the conversation would somehow circle back to moving to California. Or, at the very least, giving up this house and moving into a condo somewhere nearby. But I played along.

"Which one?"

"You know, the vintage one."

I studied his profile. A muscle twitched in his right temple, just above his eyebrow.

"How'd you know about that?" I said and took another sip of coffee. Its bitter, hot warmth traveled like lava down my esophagus.

"What?" Nigel asked, still looking out the window. He glanced over at me. "You told me. On the phone."

Had I? I didn't remember doing that, but maybe I had in passing on one of our recent, perfunctory chats. I thought back, tried to organize all the events of the past couple of weeks, but the fragments lay jumbled.

The muscle was still twitching in Nigel's forehead. I heard my mother's voice in my mind and closed my eyes for a minute.

"Nigel Robert, did you do this?" she asked, pointing to a broken *pot of flowers and a shattered glass figurine that used to sit on the shelf above it. Nigel was eight or nine and shaking his head*

furiously.

"No, Mom, I didn't do it. It must have been Bertie."

Our mother sighed.

"Nigel, look at me, please."

Her voice was quiet but stern. Nigel shuffled his feet around on the floor. One of his socks made small puffs in the soil that had spilled out of the pot. Finally, he turned toward her. She placed a hand on each side of his face, cradling it. And then, with her thumb, smoothed back the hair on the right side of his forehead.

"The dog didn't do this, Nigel," she said, her voice just as quiet, but not tinged with sadness. "This spot"—she tapped gently on his forehead—"gives you away every time you lie."

"Do you?"

I opened my eyes.

"What's that?" I asked and cleared my throat.

"I said, you don't feed the birds this early, do you?"

"What? Oh, no, not until late November or early December. Nigel," I said before I could talk myself out of it, "did you send me that old doll?"

"No. Why would I do that?"

"Just asking." I shrugged. "She was very old, an antique from Europe. And I know that you and Lisa love your antiques."

"Was? Did something happen to her?"

"Yes. She…. I had to get rid of her. She didn't seem right for me. It was strange when she arrived; the package was unmarked. I'm not even sure who delivered it, to be honest."

"That is strange," Nigel said. And the muscle in his forehead jumped and jumped again. "How old was she?"

"I tried to find out through a local historian. She narrowed down the time period—probably the early 1940s. She thought it might have been made in Germany or France."

Nigel glanced at me from his spot by the window. "You gave her the doll to research?"

"Mmm, yes. For a day or two. But then there was an accident and she fell—the woman at the historical society, I mean—so she didn't get to finish researching it. It was just the oddest thing, that this doll just arrived one day out of the blue. I mean, who could have sent it? I've been asking myself that for two weeks now."

Twitch went the muscle in Nigel's forehead. I moved closer to my brother. "You're sure you didn't send her to me?"

He glanced at me, then back out the window.

"No," he said. "You know I'm not interested in that sort of thing, Isa. If you didn't like the doll, then of course it's within your right to get rid of her. I just hope that you had her evaluated for financial purposes before you did that."

He sipped his coffee, then glanced from me to the window again. "It would be foolish to give away an antique-like Gerda without having her valued first. She could be worth a lot of money, you never know."

My heart stopped beating for an instant when he said her name, then galloped hard under my ribs.

"What did you say?" I asked, my voice quiet and much calmer than I imagined possible.

"What, about having her valued? It's a fairly simple process really, you just need—"

"No. You said her name. You called her Gerda." I felt dizzy suddenly, the walls around me wobbled around the edges. "How did you know that?"

"You told me. Earlier, when you were talking about her, you called her Gerda."

"No, I didn't. I didn't tell you her name. You sent her, didn't you?" I said, my voice half-whispering.

Nigel sighed and rubbed a hand tiredly over his face. Then he looked at me, turned his body only halfway toward mine. I knew by his expression that I was right.

"Why, Nigel? Did you know what she was? What she might do to me?"

My fingers were clenched around the coffee mug so hard that they'd turned white.

"Look, Isa. Try for a minute to look at things from my point of view. I've tried and tried to get you out of this place," he paused, "but you insist on staying. I don't know why you can't see how much easier life will be once you listen to me. You cling to this place so stubbornly, but there's nothing here for you. Mom and Dad are gone. Don't waste the rest of your life here when there is so—"

I gaped. "I can't believe you. You sent me this, this thing—this possessed doll—to try to force me out of the house?" My voice had grown louder. I banged the mug down so hard on the counter that it cracked in my hand. Hot liquid scalded my palm and ran in rivulets over the counter and dripped down the cupboards below.

"You know that I don't believe in all of that stuff. But the old man was persuasive, and Lisa said that it wouldn't hurt to try. She really feels it would be best if you were closer."

"Lisa was involved in this, too?" I cried.

Nigel nodded and had the decency to at least look chagrined. "We picked it up at the auction they had down there"—he pointed kitty-corner from the house, straight in the direction of the Bartlett's—"when we were visiting one of those last times before Dad.... The auctioneer was an old man who liked to tell tales. At first, we thought he was just lonely, wanting to gain our sympathies, maybe. So he wouldn't have to dicker on the prices of the few pieces we were interested in.

"He told us that the doll was hexed or cursed or something. Bad things had happened to the last people that owned it. In fact, the last owner had given it to him years before—not taken any money for it—just to get it out of his house. Then, apparently, the auctioneer had bad things start happening in his business. He blamed the doll. He told us he'd brought it back after the old farmer had died, and put it back in the house for a while until the auction took place.

"I don't believe in all that stuff—spiritual mumbo jumbo—but Lisa talked to him longer than I did. She thought it was real and that the doll really might have some sort of, I don't know, abilities." He said the word with a half-laugh, as though embarrassed. "We had it in the storage unit—had forgotten all about it—but Lisa was looking for some old tax paperwork in there recently and…well, I admit that it was a foolish move on our part. The doll was expensive too—"

"She was expensive?" I spat the word out like it was gravel. "That's what you're thinking about right now, how much she set you back? Nigel, do you understand what you've done? What happened to me these past couple of weeks? And you—you don't get to choose what's right for me, not now or ever. I'm not your child." My voice was tinged with hysteria, the edges of the room turning gray.

"Isa, you're being a little overdramatic don't you think? Be reasonable. There—"

"You aren't responsible for me," I said, and my voice had raised a full octave. "I am. Now get out of my house."

Nigel sighed through his nose and pinched the bridge of it between his long, slender fingers. "Isa, listen. Once you've calmed down, you'll be able to see this ration—"

"Did you hear me? I said get out."

My chest heaved but my voice was calmer.

"But—"

"Now." My finger shook as I pointed toward the door.

He looked at me, stared incredulously. Was he waiting for me to break like I had so many times before? Because he was always right. Always logical. The man who always had everyone's best interests at heart. Unless they didn't mirror his.

He sighed, loudly, and moved toward the door.

"I'll stop back over tonight after you've calmed down. We'll go to dinner and discuss this like—"

"No," I said. "Don't stop back. Just go home, Nigel." I said, and my voice was calm despite the tumult inside my body. "Please, just leave."

He looked at me one more long moment, then shook his head. He picked up his bag and let himself out. I shut the door hard behind him and leaned on it, pressing my forehead against its cold smoothness.

Memories of the past several months slid over me like a scratchy and uncomfortable blanket. Terse phone calls and irritated, infrequent emails from my brother. Reminders that his family wanted me closer, even though I doubted my preteen niece and nephew ever thought about me other than at Christmas and birthdays.

And while Lisa and I had never been exactly chummy, I never would have thought that she'd instigate a plan like this. That either of them would. Nigel was the most inside-the-box thinking person that I knew. It was staggering to believe that he wanted his way so badly that he'd resorted to this trick to get it.

I turned and slid down the door, letting it absorb my weight. Then I sat with feet outstretched, my arms wrapped around my middle. I felt as brittle as a bone inside and as hollowed out as a tunnel. No tears came, but inside I felt a deep, hot, and very old rage.

Chapter Thirty-Four

A Week Later

I surveyed the wooden crate in the studio. The last of the dolls for the exhibit at the Met had been packaged. Each had been carefully labeled for the Lila Acheson Wallace Wing, the gallery space set aside for contemporary artists. Each piece had been laboriously packaged: first with acid-free tissue paper, then polyethylene foam for protection, and lastly placed in the wooden boxes that were specially made for each of the doll's measurements.

Sighing, I stood and stretched my back. I leafed through the binder one more time. It was filled with images of the dolls, the exhibit layout, the measurements—down to the centimeter—for the placement of each one of the dolls. Rather than my original concept of a complex background, I'd instead gone with something very simple. I'd hand-dyed cheesecloth in large batches—black, shades of gray, and pale yellow. The backdrop would graduate in color with the darker, grimmer colors at the bottom, rising to lighter shades of gray, and finally the buttercream yellow at the top. It signified the dolls rising from the ashes to the light. Kind of like me. I'd named the series "Battered Not Broken."

Nigel had left a day and a half after he'd arrived. He'd called more than once, but I just let the phone ring and ring. I did meet him at the airport at his request for a cup of coffee. He didn't apologize but hugged me awkwardly. My back was as straight and stiff as an arrow. He whispered in my ear, "I was just trying to help," before gathering his carry-on and walking to the security checkpoint. I found a note he'd tucked into my coat pocket when I reached in to extract my keys in the parking garage.

"If you really want to stay, I can make it work with the attorney," it said, and was signed simply, "N."

With the crate packed and the courier due later this afternoon, the only thing left for me to do was pack. Helen had suggested a new dress for the opening gala, but I'd opted for a simple black pantsuit. I'd lost weight these past few weeks and had easily slipped into a size below my normal. I chewed on my lip as I surveyed the bed. On it lay clothes, shoes, the jewelry that I hadn't worn since my mother's funeral, and an open suitcase. Inside the case was one item: a furry, orange cat.

"Sampson!" I scooped him up in my arms. "Are you planning to come with me?" I kissed the top of his head. "Don't worry, I won't be gone long, and Julia is going to take good care of you. She even bought you some special treats that I'm not supposed to know about."

I'd met with Julia and apologized for the accusations about my studio. I didn't know if things would ever be the same between us again, but at least she'd accepted my apology. Her offer to watch Sampson for me had to be a good sign, didn't it? Sampson butted the top of his head into my chin and I scratched under his. I walked to the window across the room and stared out.

The sun was just peeking around the edge of a massive wall of gray clouds. Its light cast beams into the room, lit up certain spots while it left others in darkness. Funny how that worked. Areas of my life I'd never expected to be illuminated had been, while others, places deep down, still lay in darkness. Maybe they always would, and I'd learn how to better live alongside them. Or maybe, with time, all those dark places would come into the light. The question was—would I be brave enough to explore them?

Epilogue

Eastern Germany, 1942

General Hans Dietrich clasped his wife's hand. Ana's was cool and dry in his. She glanced at him briefly. Her eyes had once sparkled, but now they were dull and flat. Her skin had turned a faint gray since he'd been home last, and around her eyes were whispers of wrinkles. He squeezed her hand, but she only lowered her head back down and closed her eyes.

He swallowed and felt the same stiffness in his spine and along his shoulders that always accompanied nervousness. It was ridiculous, really. That he could face men in battle, deal with the blasts and bullets and hatred of the enemy, yet sitting here in the library in his own home feel so much dread.

He knew this wasn't right—what they were doing—but how could he deny Ana? She'd been through so much, too much, and if this brought her a modicum of peace, then who was he to deny her that?

Ana's birdlike hand twitched in his then and he lowered his own head and grasped the hand of the woman to his left. She was wild-haired and dark, smelled of French cigarettes, and the faint scent of bourbon at ten o'clock in the morning.

Still, she was Ana's guest. They all were. Together, there were nine people around the table. All friends of Ana's, except for the woman whose hand he held. Madame Genevieve was a transplant to the area, so she'd said, vague on where her roots were. But all of them were here to help Ana and Hans grieve. And maybe to speak to Regine again.

Regine. He hadn't uttered her name once since his arrival. She'd been buried already by the time he'd made it home. Ana had been here to carry that weight all alone. It was unforgivable on his part, but due to the war, also unavoidable.

He could still see their little girl everywhere he looked. When he sat in this room, he expected her to bounce through the door as she often did with a mischievous smile. He'd played his part as the stern general, folded down his newspaper, or closed his book with a snap, but she knew as well as he that it was a game with her. That as soon as she giggled and held up her hands, he'd swing her up into his arms, and watch her fair, long hair and her half-open, laughing mouth chortle. Hans still waited before they started eating a meal, looking every so often out of the corner of his eye at the place she'd sat, trying to convince himself that it was empty and would remain so.

He couldn't speak her name. If he did, he would surely crumble. His darling, beautiful little girl.

"You should speak to her now, Frau Dietrich," Madame Genevieve said, her voice raspy and dry in the dimly lit room. The curtains had all been shut, the lamps turned off. A single taper candle flickered in the center of the wide, wooden table. Nearby, one of the guests shifted in their chair and it creaked slightly. There was no other sound except their breathing.

"Regine?" Ana's voice wobbled, then cracked. He wanted to look at her then, to tell her that this was all a mistake. That it wouldn't help. But he didn't. He was too much of a coward. If he looked at her now, at the hungry longing on her face for their little girl, he wouldn't be able to take it. Instead, he stiffened his spine and clenched his teeth together. It would be over soon, this little charade. And perhaps Madame Genevieve had a parlor trick that would bring Ana a bit of comfort.

"Regine?" Ana said again, her voice slightly stronger. "Darling, are you there? I miss you so much. We all do. If you are there, please let us know."

Silence.

"Regine, it's *Mutter*. Please, darling, please...." Her voice broke again, and Hans heard a sob behind the last word. He moved to stand, but Madame Genevieve gripped his hand more tightly. He glanced at her in anger, but she looked back at him and shook her head, then nodded toward the candle. It flickered as it had before, but then the flame turned a greenish hue. He blinked, and it was yellow once again. The woman beside him smiled grimly.

"Try once more, Frau Dietrich," the woman said.

Ana cleared her throat quietly. "Regine, please let us know if you're here. I brought your dolly, you see?" Ana was smiling, her lips pulled gently against her too-thin cheeks. The candlelight made her face look even thinner, skeletal. He closed his eyes, not wanting to see the dark holes the shadows cast where her eyes were or the smudges of sadness that lay across the planes of her face.

"Regine—"

"Shh," hissed Madame Genevieve suddenly. The room, which had been quiet before, was silent as a tomb. "I sense something."

Hans opened his eyes again. Everyone in the group had

232

opened theirs as well, and all stared at the candle in the center of the table. Except it wasn't in the center anymore, but two feet to the right. It stood tall in its silver holder, very close to Regine's doll. A cloth doll with a porcelain head and hands and feet that she'd named Gerda. The doll's coloring matched Regine's perfectly. He'd bought it for her soon after he'd been called up, told her that she should care for it and that he would ask for a full report when he returned.

"I promise I will, *Vater*," she'd said, her eyes shining as she'd stroked the little doll's back and cradled her head with her small hand. "I'll take good care of Gerda."

"I know you will," he'd said and ruffled her hair.

Now the doll lay flat on its back, its eyes wide open and staring blankly at the ceiling above.

"I feel her presence here," Madame Genevieve said. "I can hear her voice too, but faintly, oh, so faintly."

"You can?" Ana said, her voice raised in a panicked whisper. "What's she saying?"

"She says...wait, it's hard to make out the words." The old woman was silent. All eyes stared at her. Ana was half out of her seat, leaning across the table toward the older woman. Her grip on Hans's hand was so tight that he could feel her rings leaving impressions deep in his flesh.

"She says that she loves you. And that she is happy where she is."

"What else?" Ana's voice was raised now, louder and more fevered. "Why can't I hear her? Regine? Regine?" She gasped out a sob and stood, then grabbed for the doll. She held it in her hands so tightly that her knuckles were white. "Regine, can you hear me, darling? It's *Mutter*. I miss you so much. *Vater* does, too, and Gerda. Please, please let me hear your voice. Let me—"

"I'm sorry," Madame Genevieve said. Her voice cut through Ana's words like a dull knife. "I'm sorry, Frau Dietrich, but she's gone. I'm afraid we won't hear more from her today. But perhaps tomorrow, we can try again—"

"No." Ana's voice was little more than a growl. She clutched the doll to her chest and looked wildly around the room, as though she expected to see Regine hiding in the shadows or playing hide-and-seek in the drapes.

"Ana," Hans said and stood. As he reached for his wife, she lashed out. Her left arm flailed and struck him hard in the chest. The movement surprised him, and he took a step back to gain his footing. "Ana, please—"

"No," Ana said again. "She's still here. I can feel her. Can't you feel her, Hans?" She focused on him then. Her eyes were wild and in the dim light, her chest heaved. Her hands clenched the little doll so tightly that Hans feared its head or arms might shatter in her grip.

"Bring her back," she snarled at Madame Genevieve. "You bring her back to me, you old witch!"

Madame Genevieve looked startled. "I'm sorry, there is nothing more I can do. I do not control the spirits, madam, I am only a conduit for—"

"Shut up! Don't say another word unless it's about Regine. Not unless you are speaking on her behalf. I need to talk with her. I need to speak to my daughter!"

She sat then, abruptly, and placed the doll back on the table, close to her. "Take my hands," she commanded. The woman on the other side of Ana grasped her hand and around the table the link was reformed.

"Hans?" Ana asked and held her hand out to him. "Please."

He sat and took her hand again. Then she bent her head low over the doll and touched it with her forehead.

"I call on the spirit of Regine Dietrich to enter this room. I open the doors that were closed to us since her death and command that her spirit returns to us now."

Silence.

No one moved. No one, Hans thought, even dared to breathe. They waited, motionless, for something to happen. But nothing did.

Then he heard a sound, a mewling, like a lost kitten or a newborn lamb. He glanced up and saw Ana's face, contorted with grief, her pain as palpable as the chair under his legs or the table that he rested his arms on.

"Please, please," she moaned, and he moved to stand up. But then her voice changed. It became a low, guttural sob. "I call on any spirit from the other world to enter this room. Let me know that you exist. Help me to believe."

Madame Genevieve gasped quietly. "No, you mustn't, Frau Dietrich. That is very dangerous—opening the door for all the spirits—you must nev—"

"Quiet," Hans said sternly.

The room was silent for another few seconds. But then there came a soft rattling. A gentle *tap-tap-tap-tap-tap* against the tabletop. Hans watched in fascinated horror as Regine's doll began to move. It vibrated lightly at first, then harder and harder until it nearly bounced off the table. Ana gasped, and he looked at her, expected to see fright marring her features. Instead, he saw pure joy. She took the doll in her hands.

"There you are. I knew you'd come." She cradled the doll in her hands and brought it close to her chest.

Madame Genevieve stood suddenly. "This is not good. This

is a dangerous game you are playing, m‍ḍ‍m. Very dangerous. No good will come of this, I swear it to you."

Ana laughed then, and the sound glittered like crystal.

"They are real after all," she said and smiled a watery smile. Ana clutched the doll, Gerda, to her chest just under her chin. "There is a spirit world, don't you understand? This is a messenger. And now I'll be able to speak to my Regine. You'll see."

She stood and murmured words to the doll that Hans could not hear. He stood and put a hand out to stop her as she moved from the room.

"Ana, wait. Please—"

She looked back at him over her shoulder. Her smile was full and deep. "You'll see," she said again.

BONUS

Start reading the first book in the "Monsters in the Green Mountains," series, *Silence in the Woods*. In 1917, four friends and photojournalists set out in the woods looking for answers. Why have so many hikers and hunters gone missing in the area of Shiny Creek Trail?

The two couples anticipate a great adventure, one they'll tell their kids about someday. No one imagines the evil lurking in a remote cave. A horrifying discovery leaves one person dead and two others missing.

Two months later, Paul, one of the four, returns to the forest to find his wife. But will he find her before someone—or something—finds him?

Chapter One

Paul Rogers
Friday, November 2, 1917
Vermont State Hospital for the Insane

He should be used to the screams by now. Paul tilted his head, pulling the wool blanket over it and tried to muffle the sound. The shriek rose like a wave—growing sharper and more hysterical before falling away again. Then a pause. It gave false hope: one would believe it was over. But then the high-pitched wail would begin again.

Nearby, Timmy shifted on his bed, his breath a soft whistle through his nose. Ward III was full tonight, the overflow of men spilled out into the large room next door, a hastily created Ward IV, still filled with half-cartons of supplies and stacks of old paperwork. The hospital was grossly overcrowded and Paul was lucky to have a bed at all. Many other inmates—because in Paul's mind they were all inmates and not patients—were stuck in hallways.

Footsteps sounded in the hallway, a heavy tread. Even though Paul wanted the screaming to stop, his stomach turned. He knew who was coming.

Seconds later the man's scream ended abruptly in a bark of pain. Paul uncovered his head and lifted it gingerly in the low-lit room. A large, dark shape loomed over the bed by the far wall.

"Other people are trying to sleep, you filthy mongrel," the aide said in a raspy voice, not bothering to whisper. The man's scream had turned to a whimper.

"Quit your snottin' and shut your fat mouth," the aide said. He lifted his arm and the thump of something hard against flesh turned Paul's stomach. The whimpering died to a litany of gasping breaths.

"If I have to come in here again, I'll take you to isolation. You don't want that, do you?"

More quiet gasps. Apparently, the aide must have seen the head shaking no because he retraced his path to the ward's doorway.

Paul sank back onto his bed, stared up at the spiderweb cracks in the high ceiling above. Many of the aides and nurses were kind at the hospital. But a handful was not and the night monitor for Ward III was one of these. Truthfully, it made no difference to Paul whether the other man screamed the night away or not. He hadn't slept a full night in weeks. When he'd first arrived he'd been in so much pain he hadn't been lucid. Later, after the medicines were decreased, he was able to get his bearings…and almost wished for the sweet oblivion the tiny pills had offered.

But he couldn't—wouldn't—allow himself the luxury. Whenever he closed his eyes he saw the horror he'd witnessed deep in the woods again and again. The same images would flicker, an endless loop. The two couples—he and Jane, Allan and Deidre—and the woods, always dark and twisted, like ghostly photographs from long ago. Then the blood on the ground, a body swinging and stiff at the end of the makeshift noose—

No.

Paul sat up, putting his feet on the bare, cold floor underneath him. Timmy let out a partial giggle and Paul glanced over. The big man was so large his bulk didn't fit on the bed. A roll of flesh, soft and white like dough, flopped over the side of his cot. His face was serene, full-mooned, with his lips parted in a smile. Even in sleep, Timmy was happy and blessedly oblivious. Paul envied the big man. His childlike mind meant that he never fully grasped the harsh realities of life.

Timmy had been here for a long time. Paul wasn't sure how long, but years, decades maybe. The other inmates were a mixture of long and short-term stays. Some were here because of their penchant for masturbation, others because of devious behavior with matches or knives. Some because of melancholia or delusions. That was why Paul was here. "Delusional imaginings," were the words the psychiatrist, Dr. Hastings used. But Paul knew what they really were: memories. The mere word brought more to life: Jane's face, streaked with tears; his voice and hers screaming Deidre's name; the wild, whipping wind of the storm; the pain in his leg after he fell...

What if we'd never gone in? The question had spun incessantly in his mind over the past two months, like a record tirelessly turning on a Victrola. What if they hadn't though? Would he be safe at home rolling onto his side in his own bed and pulling Jane close? She would nestle into him, her hair smelling like sandalwood and her skin soft and creamy. He'd been a fool to bring her on that trip. To agree to go at all. If only...

There was the second thought that never stopped rotating through Paul's mind. *If only.* If only they hadn't gone. If only Allan and Deidre hadn't been so excited about the trip into the middle of nowhere. If only Jane had caught a cold and they'd

241

stayed home, or Paul had been called away. Instead, they had agreed with very little convincing on their friends' part.

"It will be an adventure like none you've ever had," Deidre had said. "One you'll tuck away to tell your children about." She'd painted a picture—she was a writer by trade—of an adventure so mystical and exciting that first Paul and then Jane had agreed to it wholeheartedly. If Deidre hadn't become a writer, she would have done just as well as an actress. He could see her even now, her auburn curls jiggling as she'd thrummed with excitement. It had started with the mystery of that particular piece of woods. Missing people. An unidentified animal.

Had there been misgivings on Jane's part that he'd missed? Had his own excitement clouded his vision? Had it made him see only what he wanted—a grand escapade and a chance to write the story of the decade—missing entirely the doubts of his wife?

"Of course we must go," Jane had said that blurry night when they'd been preparing for bed. Paul had overindulged in the fine whiskey that Allan had insisted on purchasing. "Only I wonder…" Her voice had trailed away.

"Yes? What do you wonder, lovely Mrs. Rogers?"

She'd stood before the dressing table, brushing her long, blonde hair. Her eyes had been far away, focused on something in the distance.

Paul had rolled off the bed where he'd been laying on his side and come up behind her. He stared at their reflection in the mirror and rested his hands on her shoulders. She wasn't delicate, his Jane, but neither was she large. Just sturdy, well-built. Her shoulders were warm and smooth beneath his hands and he'd felt a sudden surge of warmth between his legs.

"Nothing," she'd said finally. She'd smiled, put the brush to one side, and stood. She'd turned in his arms then, kissed him deeply. She had a little hitching breath that escaped her when he held her like this and he'd come to know and love it. He'd wrapped his arms around her and forgotten everything else.

Until now.

Paul stood to his feet. His right leg was healing nicely the doctor said. He pulled up his pajama pant leg now to inspect the skin in the milky light. Where the skin had been sheared off, new, pink tender skin had grown. His ankle was where the near-break had happened. When Paul had been sitting or lying down too long it still ached.

He shuffled to the open door. Here, an aide slept, slumped to one side in a straight-back chair. He was snoring softly. It wasn't the same one who'd been in Ward III earlier. Paul passed by him lightly and went out into the hallway.

The hallway was wide and long. Paul started down it toward the washroom. Moonlight streamed through the large windows, making a thick grid of squares on the floor. The iron bars in every window casting their shadows onto the floor beneath his feet. Paul thought again about Jane's unasked question that night.

What had she wondered? Had there been a premonition of what would happen in those dark, tangled woods? Had she felt a shiver of fear and chalked it up to nervousness at being out in the wild? Or had she somehow known then that not all of them would make the return trip home?

* * *

"Ah, Paul, good to see you," Dr. Hastings said, his voice low and deep. He got up when Paul entered the office, made a show of shaking Paul's hand, and then indicating which seat Paul should sit in. As though they didn't do this exact routine twice weekly.

Dr. Hastings was a thin, tall man who looked more like an accountant than the director of the state's largest mental asylum. He wore small glasses on his hook nose. The sunlight pouring into the room made it overly warm and a gleam of sweat shone on the man's high forehead.

"And so, how are you, Paul?" Dr. Hastings took up his normal posture behind the large desk that separated them. One leg was propped on the other, creating a writing surface for his small notebook and a perfectly sharpened pencil.

Paul nodded. "Very well, Dr. Hastings."

"Good, good. Glad to hear it. And how have the visions been?"

"Nonexistent, sir." Paul purposely kept his face neutral.

"Wonderful! That is indeed good news, young man." Dr. Hastings moved as though to jot a note on the writing pad, but then stopped. He surveyed Paul over the top of his glasses. "Now, Paul, I hate to ask you this—you strike me as an honest-type," he smiled a small, tight smile. "But you wouldn't simply be telling me what I want to hear so that you'll be released early, would you?"

Paul's shoulders tensed but he made a point to relax them. He looked Dr. Hastings straight in his watery, pale-blue eyes. "No, sir. I really am making good progress."

Dr. Hastings regarded him shrewdly for a moment before murmuring a, "Hmm," and scratching a note onto his pad. "And the nightmares?"

"They don't happen when I don't sleep, sir," Paul wanted to

say. But that would mean explaining the trick he'd been using for the past several weeks to regurgitate his nightly sleeping tablet and all the other medications that Dr. Hastings had prescribed him.

"I still have them at times," Paul shrugged. Did it look nonchalant? "But much less frequently than I used to."

"Very good, very good." Dr. Hastings had the habit of repeating his phrases, a habit Paul found mildly annoying on a good day and teeth-clenching on a bad one.

"Sir, I believe I am well enough to be put to work. My leg has healed well and I would like to do something to pass the time. The days are long—"

"Well, we can certainly address that. Certainly address it," Dr. Hastings interrupted, peering again at Paul over his glasses. "I know they've been overworked in the laundry." His voice faded as he looked at the wall behind Paul. "Hmm, yes, that might be a possibility."

Paul's heart fell. The laundry? It would be impossible to carry out his plan from there. He needed to get into the workroom. There, the male inmates built basic furniture like chairs and small end tables. And once a week a gentleman who owned a furniture store in Brattleboro sent a truck to collect the pieces the inmates had made. Paul intended to get onto that truck, one way or another.

"That would be fine, sir," Paul said, his voice as resigned as his face felt. "Though I had hoped to be given a task in the workroom. You know, growing up my father owned a carpentry shop. I spent years assisting him and—"

"Yes, you've mentioned that before," Dr. Hastings interjected, his fingers sifting through the file of notes on the large desk. In fact, Paul's father had been a farmer but Paul had believed creating a background in woodworking would be beneficial. Apparently, not.

"Now tell me, Paul, before we get off track here—there are no more thoughts of the man-beast you saw in the woods?" The older man's voice bordered on incredulous. "It was all you'd speak of when you arrived. And yet now you say that your mental status is much improved. So improved that these delusions you had are now suddenly—" Dr. Hastings snapped his fingers together. "Poof. Vanished."

Paul tried and failed to force a smile onto his face. He wanted it to be true. Wasn't that enough? Even the mention of the thing he'd seen in the forest brought back other memories: the blood on the ground, the body swinging…the hot breath of it—that thing—on his neck. But really, what did Paul remember? That time was full of shadows, of glimpses that he wasn't sure were true. Had he seen the beast or just imagined it in his fevered state?

"No, sir. When I came here I was sick with fever and infection. The beast I claimed to have seen was just a—what did you call it, Dr. Hastings?" Paul frowned as though trying to remember. "A delusion. An apparition created by my overwrought mind."

Dr. Hastings nodded once, slowly. "And so, Paul, even if you see images of it—this apparition—you would no longer hold onto the belief that it is real?"

Paul shook his head. "No, sir."

"Hmm," Dr. Hastings said, and flipped through more of the papers, eventually he stopped and drew one from the pack. He turned it so that Paul could see it clearly on the desk.

There, scribbled in a trembling hand, was an image that Paul had tried very hard to forget. A dark figure covered the page, all the way to the edges. It had the figure of a man but was covered in a thick mat of blackish-brown fur. It was a simple drawing—like one created by a child's hand—but there were enough details to make out what the creature looked like. And one feature, in particular, was disturbingly accurate: its golden eyes searching for Paul's own from the page.

He wanted to shiver, to shake, to snatch the paper up and crumple it into a ball and throw it across the office. But he did none of those things. Instead, he simply shook his head at Dr. Hastings, holding his gaze.

"Just a fevered vision of a sick man, doctor," Paul said. "Perhaps my illness affected the part of my brain which had seen something like this long ago. Some mishmash of a creature from childhood nightmares." And yet, Paul remembered its smell. Gamey and strong. He remembered the feel of its fur under his hands, surprisingly soft. And he remembered those eyes...

The doctor was silent a moment. Then, "Perhaps," said Dr. Hastings slowly. He slid four more drawings similar to the first across the desk. "And yet. I ask you to look more closely, Paul. Are you certain that your belief is truly gone? Or is it instead that you want to tell your doctor what he wants to hear?"

Paul forced himself to study each of the pictures. He saw the creature, the Bigfoot, hunched near a small grove of bushes; another where he was mid-stride, his great, shaggy head turned toward Paul, its big arms hanging loosely by its sides, fingers nearly touching its knees, and then two more pages covered in drawings of the beast's face and those strange eyes like gold coins gleaming from its face. Paul looked at the drawings and kept his face expressionless. He'd learned in his work at the newspaper to create a blank slate of his features. Any expression when he was interviewing a source could lead their account in another direction. He'd trained himself to keep his face empty of emotion, keep himself neutral.

"They aren't very good," Paul said finally with a half-smile, and Dr. Hastings chuckled as he gathered them back into a pile.

"Never mind that. They were real. Well, real to you anyway, in that moment of time." Dr. Hastings leaned his arms on his desk and made a teepee with his fingers. He placed his chin directly in the center. "Paul, you've made good progress here. I'd like to see you gain your strength more fully and put on a little more weight. You're still sleeping well you say?"

"Yes, sir," Paul lied. "I am."

"Well, that is good. That is good. Sleep is restorative to the body and all of its systems. Never skimp on sleep, Paul." He actually wagged a paternal finger toward Paul's face. Paul clenched his teeth, forced his head to nod in agreement.

"Of course, sir."

"I see no reason, young man, why you shouldn't be back home for the New Year." Dr. Hastings smiled and began to gather his papers together.

"The New Year?" Paul spluttered. "But that's two months away! Surely I could be discharged before then?"

With the overcrowding, Paul was surprised that his release hadn't already been planned. But then, his family was paying privately. At five dollars a week, Dr. Hastings had little incentive to see him leave.

Perhaps he'd played his cards all wrong, Paul thought, anger jabbing into his chest. Rather than pretending to be fully healed, he should have been a troublesome patient. One who caused ruckuses and stirred up the other inmates. Then the good doctor might be more willing to let him go.

"No. No, Paul, I believe this is in your best interest," Dr. Hastings said. "Your very best interest. I will talk with the head of the workroom, young man, and let you know what I discover. I tend to believe, however, that you will be better utilized in the laundry at present. But we shall see. We shall see."

Chapter Two

Jane Rogers
Friday, September 7, 1917
Start of Shiny Creek Trail

They'd been walking only twenty minutes and already Jane could feel the city sliding off of her. It wasn't an unwelcome feeling. She enjoyed living in the city—restaurants, the theater, book readings, and other events—it was what she'd become used to. In the city, something was always happening. Out here though...Jane paused, watching her husband's back as he rounded a bend in the trail ahead of her. Out here there was only quiet. It was peaceful, but also unnerving. The constant sound of wheels, machinery clanking, people talking, the hum of life was missing. The noises made up the background of Jane's days. She'd grown used to them.

The air here was different too: thick with the scent of pine needles and the earthy, sweet smell of decaying leaves underfoot. Above, tree branches danced in golden light, lit like candles by the sun. The leaves had just started to change. Green had turned to shades of yellow. Red and orange would come later in the season. For the most part, though, the forest looked like it did during the other times they'd hiked in summer.

Except, Jane couldn't shake the feeling that someone was

watching them. She glanced over her shoulder for the tenth time and quickened her pace.

Silly.

Of course, she felt unnerved. The setting was completely at odds with normal daily life in Burlington. Why wouldn't she feel peculiar?

"Everything all right?" Paul asked. He'd stopped on the trail and Jane, lost in thought, had nearly bumped into him.

"Yes, sorry," she said, her breath already coming a little harder in her chest. "Just thinking how beautiful it is here."

"It is that, isn't it?" Paul smiled as he tilted his head upward, taking in the leaves and branches and sunlight that formed the canopy above them. He turned back to her.

"Jane, I meant to ask you if this trip was really something you wanted to do." Paul returned his gaze to her, his eyes searching her face. "I mean, Allan and Deidre can be persuasive, you know that. But if you were uncomfortable, we could have bowed out. I suppose it's a little late to tell you this now, but—"

"I wouldn't have missed it," Janes said, forcing her tone to be cheerful. "Go, Paul, or we'll fall far behind the others."

Paul nodded. "If you're sure."

"Yes. Yes, I'm very sure."

He smiled at her and stuck his hands under his pack's straps to alleviate some of the pressure. He started walking again. Jane followed but her eyes smarted. Why did Paul automatically assume Jane would be uninterested or unwilling to go on an adventure like this? It was true she wasn't the most fearless in their little foursome, but she was hardly a wilting violet.

The two couples had been friends for so long she sometimes

forgot that originally it had been Deidre, Allan, and Paul—the Three Musketeers—who'd met in college. Paul's comment unintentionally hurt. It reminded Jane again that she was the outsider. Paul and their friends were photojournalists, while Jane was a mere secretary. She was the only one in the group who had grown up in the country, too, not Burlington where Paul was from, or Boston where Allan and Deidre were originally from.

What Paul said was true though: Deidre and Allan were always trying new things, going on new adventures. Jane wondered meanly sometimes if it wasn't only so that they could recount their harrowing tales to everyone.

Jane took a big breath and drew her shoulders back. Already an ache had formed between them from the heavy pack. While her work wasn't as exciting as the others, it was steady and reliable. Indeed, she's surprised her parents and Paul's by bringing her own savings account to their marriage, something that was unheard of a generation ago.

Paul had big dreams. His work at the newspaper was solid and steady but what he really wanted was to become a photojournalist for a big-name magazine like *National Geographic*. And why shouldn't he? Allan told him constantly that he could do it if only he'd set his mind to it. But there was something in Paul, some unnamed fear that Jane had come to recognize was pulling him back from his dream.

That's why this trip was so important. Shiny Creek Trail, deep in the Green Mountains of Vermont, was where eighteen-year-old James Smithfield had gone missing in 1897. It was also the location where several other people had been lost—some returned, some not—and the spot where a decade ago, three hunters had spotted the man-beast.

Jane shivered. The image in the newspaper that she'd found was still fresh in her mind. The monster, the Bigfoot—tall and shaggy—had filled her dreams for the past weeks since she'd found the article. But was it real? Or had the men taken a photograph of a friend dressed in a costume? It wasn't unheard of, the pranks that people devised to gain publicity and capitalize on it.

Her foot caught on a root and she let out a small grunt before catching herself on a nearby sapling. Hunched over, she felt it again. That feeling that someone's eyes were on her. She righted herself slowly, straightening her pack on her shoulders. Jane looked around. All along the path were trees, trees, and more trees. Bushes and other low-lying shrubs clambered over the forest floor, half-dead ferns and tilted stumps filled in otherwise bare areas.

Jane turned to the right and then the left. But there was nothing out of the ordinary. No one out there: no heads peeking around tree trunks or faces camouflaged in the shrubbery. Still, she couldn't deny the feeling. She smoothed her hands over her front. She felt naked hiking in only bloomers. Perhaps it was simply that discomfort which made her feel conspicuous. Deidre seemed to enjoy it, had laughed gleefully as she'd tossed her skirt back into Allan's shiny new Peerless.

"Now we'll be as free as the birds," she'd said to Jane with a grin. Jane, always practical, had folded her skirt neatly and deposited it into her knapsack. If they met another group on the trail, she wanted to be ready to put it back on at a moment's notice. Paul, anticipating her discomfort, had told Deidre and Allan to start without them, that they'd be along momentarily. They would eventually see Jane in just the bloomers of course, but there was something mortifying about removing her skirt in front of the others. She'd felt a wave of love toward Paul at his suggestion the others go on ahead. He was like that: always considerate, always thinking of her feelings.

Jane readjusted the bloomers' waistband and hitched her pack up higher. She tried to shake off the feeling of being watched and quickened her pace to catch up to Paul.

* * *

"Darling, don't you want to snap a picture of me?" Deidre's voice, teasing, called to Allan across the campsite. Jane paused in hammering the tent peg to glance at her friend. Deidre, in true form, had applied a fresh coat of lipstick and plucked a handful of ferns that she used as a feather fan behind her head. With her auburn hair loose around her face and her body twisted into a sultry pose, she looked like a pinup girl in one of the magazines Jane's boss hid in his bottom desk drawer.

Jane shook her head, smiling, as she went back to pounding the peg. It had gone in easily at first but now vibrated in her hand under the mallet. Paul squatted beside her and grinned. He smelled good: pine and the faint trace of aftershave mixed with sweat.

"You might have hit a rock," he said. "Want me to give it a crack?"

"Yes, please," Jane said gratefully. She stood. Her legs and back ached a bit. She felt tired but exhilarated. They'd hiked deep into the forest, at least six miles from the pull-off where they'd left Allan's car. The ascent hadn't been overly steep—not yet—but Deidre had looked grateful when Paul had suggested they stop and make camp in the late afternoon. Allan, in contrast, had been disappointed. Jane could tell by the tight line of his mouth, but he hadn't said anything. As for herself, Jane could have kept going at least another hour or two. Her body was tired but not fatigued.

She'd always had great stamina. "My little mule," her mother had often referred to Jane as growing up. Not the most flattering comparison, but it was true. In Jane's family, being strong and able to weather storms was a given, so "mule" in her mother's mind had likely been a fine compliment.

"Mule?" Paul had said incredulously when she'd told him once. "No. No, that's not right at all." He'd frowned. "There are many other "m" words to describe you. Marvelous, minx, magnanimous, miraculous—"

"Stop!" Jane had laughed then as Paul had pulled her over on top of him on the picnic blanket. He'd tickled her face with his scratchy jaw, then pulled back and looked at her, the laughter faded from his eyes.

"And the most important m-word of all." He'd said and his voice had grown deeper.

"What's that?" Jane had asked. Her hands on his chest, she'd propped herself up to look at him more easily.

"Mine."

She'd felt a thrill as his lips had covered hers gently at first, then more urgently. His hands had caressed her arms gently, then moved to her sides. Then they were traveling over her entire body until she was warm and breathless, her skin pink, her eyes closed. Waiting for—

"…did you, Jane?"

Jane opened her eyes, her cheeks hot with embarrassment. "Pardon?"

"I just asked if you'd brought any of the articles along with you, other than the two we'd talked about this morning," Deidre said, walking over. She'd discarded her ferns and was pinning the front of her hair up out of her face. She'd knotted her shirt up in the front, showing a pale swath of flat belly between her blouse and bloomers.

"Oh, no, I'm sorry," Jane said. "I brought just the article about James Smithfield and the one about the hunters."

"Oh, don't give it another thought," Deidre said, waving a hand through the air. "I just wondered, that's all. My, your tent looks inviting," she said, peering at the perfectly taut sides of the Rogers' tent. "Would you like to switch?" Deidre cast a disparaging look at the tent Allan was still erecting. It hung droopily from the poles, its sides wrinkled.

"I'm sure he'll have it looking just as good in no time," Jane said, brushing her hands together. "I was going to start a fire. Would you like to help me gather wood?"

"Oh," Deidre said, wrinkling her nose. "I suppose so."

"Did you have something else you wanted to do instead?" Jane asked.

"No, not really. Well, to be honest, put my feet up and read a book but I suppose that would be bad form considering my husband is sweating and swearing at the moment."

As if on cue, Allan muttered something under his breath, the cigarette in his lips wobbling.

Deidre grinned at Jane. "Yes, let's go collect sticks, shall we?"

"I'll put on a pot of coffee when we get back," Jane promised.

"And I'll pull out the whiskey for a little extra boost," Deidre said.

Jane laughed. The women linked arms and headed into the woods.

It took no time at all to find enough dry branches to build a roaring fire. They were about to head back to camp when Jane paused. Deidre was a few feet away. She'd abandoned her own pile of sticks and was picking wide leaves from a plant which she wove into a crown.

"It's for Allan," Deidre said in a conspiratorial whisper. "King of the tentmakers." She laughed. Jane smiled. She was about to look away when something moved behind Deidre. A few tree branches nearby shook and then were still. The wind? But there wasn't any, not even a slight breeze. Deidre caught Jane's eye.

"What is it?" she asked, her hands growing still.

Jane motioned at her to be quiet, her eyes still searching the branches near her friend. There was nothing though, no movement, no sound.

Everything was still.

Jane let out her breath and smiled.

Then the leaves nearest Deidre moved again. Deidre whirled around. The leaf crown flew from her hands. She stumbled backward, toward Jane who met Deidre halfway and pulled her back. Faster, faster from the thing that was rattling the branches and shaking the leaves.

Was it a bobcat? A bear? Jane searched her memory for predatory wild animals in the state. Panthers. Did they still have panthers here or had they all been hunted out? She searched the trees and low-growing shrubs nearby, looking for any movement. For the flash of tan or brown fur. She expected any minute to see a large, furry body hurl itself toward them, roaring. But there was nothing.

"Maybe just a raccoon or some other animal walking past," she whispered finally to Deidre. "We should get back to camp though. Can you manage your branches? If not, I can—"

"Look!" Deidre's voice hissed hot against her ear. "Something is there." She pointed her finger shaking.

Jane felt an icy trickle of fear fall down her backbone. She looked. Where Deidre had been standing moments before, the branches were settled back into place. Nothing was amiss. Jane saw only the same dull, tired leaves of autumn and the tangled undergrowth. She was about to turn to her friend, ask what she meant.

Then she saw it.

In a crack between two large trees, hidden was a dark shape. More shadow than hard lines. A man? But no. Much too large. It was hunched over, as though looking for something on the ground.

"Bear," Deidre's whisper was barely audible. "What do we do?"

Jane shook her head. Everything felt slowed down, the air molasses-thick. The animal raised itself slightly higher. It was massively tall. Jane swallowed hard. Branches undulated around the animal's shape. It was hard to make out in the thick undergrowth.

Jane stood, mesmerized. In the dim light of the woods, the dark shadow against dark branches was nearly impossible to see. Then, for one instant, Jane saw its head in profile. Shaggy. Large—larger than any animal she'd ever seen. Huge, in fact. But there was something else. Something that her brain was trying to process but failing to. She realized suddenly what it was: the animal's profile was all wrong. Flat where its snout should have stuck out. Like a bear missing its nose or a panther standing upright—but neither of those images made any sense.

"Run!" Deidre hissed again. She grabbed Jane's hand and

pulled her back toward the trail.

Chapter Three

Paul Rogers
Monday, November 5, 1917
Vermont State Hospital for the Insane

He must be absolutely crazy. Paul clenched his fists and forced himself to breathe. The silly girl in front of him—Martha, the young kitchen helper—was yammering on and on about her desire to be an author.

"...don't you think so?"

He smiled and gave her a wink. "I think you can do anything you set your mind to, Miss Shirley. Now, about that favor?"

Her face—open, smooth, and honest—grew shadows around the edges. "Oh, I'm just not sure. I don't think my fiancé would approve."

Paul felt his breath tighten, then stop in his chest. This had to work. It had to. He couldn't wait until January for his release. Jane could still be alive out there. Wandering around, cold and afraid. Hungry. He'd left her to fend for herself. His wife, his love. His Jane.

Paul dug deep and plastered a big smile on his face. "Miss Shirley, do you know what makes one a good writer? What separates the average pack from the elite? What sets apart your..." He searched his mind frantically for the name of the

British mystery author Martha loved. "May Edginton from the rest?"

She shook her head slowly.

"It's courage, Miss Shirley. Courage that these writers experienced in their real life and which later shows up on the page. Now, you could argue that breaking a rule here or there isn't courageous. You might even think it foolish. But I ask you, Miss Shirley, what adventure hasn't included a few broken rules? Did Lewis and Clark follow the rules perfectly to explore new territories? Did President Washington follow the rules of war when he attacked the Hessians on Christmas Day?"

Martha's face was rapt, her eyes focused completely on Paul. Let this work. It *must* work.

"There can be no fulfillment of dreams if there is no courage, Miss Shirley," Paul said. His voice trembled slightly. Martha no doubt believed it to be from conviction. Truthfully, it was desperation.

"Yes," Martha said, her voice less timid. "Yes, I see your point." She took a deep breath and let it out, her shoulders straightening as she did so. Paul could almost see the gears spinning in her mind as she debated with her conscience.

"All right then. I will help you. I'll tell Jacques that it is for love. That, he will understand." Her cheeks bloomed pink and Paul wanted to rush forward and grab the girl in his arms, leap about the room with her crowing.

Instead, he smiled in what he hoped was a benign manner. "You'll make a fine author someday," he said. "Of that, I have no doubt."

* * *

His escape was arranged for that Wednesday. The truck from the Brattleboro furniture shop arrived at the asylum at nine o'clock. Then the driver—a silly-looking old codger with a wild beard and nearly bald head—would go directly to the kitchen for breakfast. He was completely smitten with one of the cooks, Martha had told Paul, and would dally as long as possible over his meal. Jacques usually waited until the driver returned to load up the truck with the new chairs and other small wooden furniture that had been produced. This time though, Martha had convinced her fiancé to get the furniture on straightaway, allowing Paul a precious minute to stow away in the deepest, darkest spot in the truck and hide there.

Paul had no money at the asylum. He had, however, promised Martha that when he returned home, he'd send her five dollars. "A nuptial gift for you and Jacques," he'd said with a wink. Martha had blushed red and thanked him. The two planned to elope later that month, a secret that Martha had confided when Paul told her of his desire to get out of the asylum and back to his wife.

Now, Paul stood at the corner of the building in the shadows. He'd crept out of the hallway when the aide's back was turned, a surprisingly easy feat in the steamy bowels of the asylum's laundry rooms. He'd begun working in the massive laundry room three days ago, quickly learning the job and all it entailed. It was hard, hot work that left his mind lots and lots of time to roam. He'd used it to plan out every step of his escape and the journey beyond. Because of his current mental stability—along with the unknown talent of regurgitating his pills—Paul was given more freedom within the building by Dr. Hastings. In fact, the good doctor had himself introduced Paul to Mr. Connolly, the head of the laundry. "You're doing well,

Paul. Doing well," Dr. Hastings had said with a half-hearted slap on the back.

The smell of soap and bleach still filled his nose now as Paul watched the furniture truck intently. He saw a young, slim man emerge from the building. He was dressed in work clothes, with a woolen cap jauntily set on his dark, curled hair. This was Jacques, Martha's fiancé, a transplant from Quebec.

Jacques greeted the driver whose bushy beard stuck out a foot from his face and covered his chest and belly. The spindly man waved his arm toward the building as he talked to Jacques. The Frenchman shook his head in response, then listened another moment and nodded before replying.

What was happening? Was this a normal conversation or was Jacques telling the driver of his fiancée's plan to help a crazy man? Paul's fingernails dug into his damp palms. A single word spun around in his head in short, jerky circles: Jane.

Jane. Jane. Jane. Jane. Jane.

Then, finally, the bearded man nodded and ambled off toward the door of the building. Minutes later, Jacques gave a short, low whistle. That was the signal. Paul crouched and ran to the side of the truck furthest from the building.

"You go here," a voice said by Paul's ear. He hadn't even heard the younger man approach. "Stay down. No see, eh? No see you." Paul climbed up the side of the tarp-covered truck and burrowed into the corner. An old horse blanket that smelled of mildew and something even worse was lying in a heap nearby. He quickly swept it over him, making himself as small as possible.

"Remember, eh?" Jacques spoke from the side of the truck, tightening the ropes. "No noise. You make go before truck

263

stop."

Paul nodded, then realized Jacques couldn't see him through the truck's tarp. "Yes. I will."

It seemed hours before Jacques finished loading the chairs and small tables into the truck and longer still until the driver re-emerged from the building, smelling of bacon grease and coffee. Paul's stomach grumbled. He'd had nothing to eat since last night's dinner.

The men talked briefly.

"What, you loaded it all up did you?"

"Ah, yes. Simple today. Easy go."

"Well, thank you. Thank you kindly. You have yourself a good week now."

"*Oui*. You do same."

And they were off. The truck rumbled to life and Paul bounced back and forth like a tennis ball between the pieces of furniture closest to him before the truck pulled onto the main road. Then the ride smoothed with only an occasional jostle or teeth-snapping bounce.

Paul stretched his legs out and threw the blanket to the side. Before it hit the floor of the truck he saw a gray knapsack. It was the type used by the asylum when inmates had day trips. Each was labeled clearly with a label that shouted, "Vermont State Hospital for the Insane." He pulled it toward him eagerly and opened it. At the top was a piece of paper folded in two. Opening it, Paul saw the neat, curly script of a woman's hand.

For Romeo as he seeks his Juliet. Nourishment for the journey. May true love always win!

Yours in admiration,
Miss Martha Shirley

Paul's smile broadened as he dug into the pack. Inside was a canteen full of water, a dented flashlight, a small, empty pot, matches, a loaf of bread, a chunk of cheese, three apples, and another, smaller bag filled with ginger cookies. God bless Martha Shirley.

* * *

It took Paul nearly two days to reach the small town of Glaston. It was just outside of the tiny town that Shiny Creek Trail began. The town featured two rows of tidy but plain houses, one church, a general store which boasted both an apothecary and post office inside and a small bakery. He could smell the leftover scent of cinnamon and warm bread in the air as he passed behind the building.

The night had been growing dark when he arrived. Paul had been let out by one of the many motorists he'd gotten rides from since jumping from the furniture truck outside of Brattleboro. The leap into the undergrowth had hurt. His leg, which always ached, had felt fiery that night as he'd sat by the small fire in the woods. Paul worried that he'd done serious damage, but the next morning after he'd walked off the stiffness in his limbs, it hadn't felt any worse than usual.

Now, he passed by the last of the small houses. Dinner smells edged out from under the doorframe and around the windows. The smell of something meaty and warm made his mouth fill with saliva. Hunger had plagued him since leaving the asylum. His belly pinched and grumbled but he rationed the food in small allotments. If he found Jane—no when he found Jane—he wanted to give the food to her. She'd be so hungry.

An image came to mind, one he continually tried to block out but that crept in anyway. Jane, half-naked in the chill November air, dirty and bedraggled. Jane, bruised, with cuts and scrapes bleeding. Her former luscious curves and sturdy planes replaced with protruding bones and sagging skin. Jane, with haunted eyes filled with fear...

Paul shook his head, trying to clear it. As though the thoughts were a spider's web that could be torn down. Jane was resourceful and strong. She was still alive, still intact. She'd have sought solace in the forest. Solace from that thing...

Other images came then.

No.

He couldn't indulge himself in regret over what had happened. Not now. All his energy, his focus had to go into getting to the trail and finding Jane. Shivering—whether from fear or the cold, he wasn't sure—Paul crept alongside the last house in front of him. This one stood off a ways from the others on the street. From the slightly neglected look of it, Paul guessed it had been the first one built. He took a chance and peeked into a window. A family was just preparing for dinner. Two little girls set the table and a tiny boy, crying, clung to his mother's skirt as she stood at the stove. Paul edged away from the window. More smells of cooking food emanated from the little house and flowed by him in the cold night air. His stomach growled.

He moved stealthily toward the small chicken coop. Stealing one of the birds was tempting but too much of a risk. Chickens had a tendency to squawk and make other loud noises. Instead, Paul had decided to go after the eggs.

Propping open the door of the coop, he was hit with the ammonia smell of chicken droppings and the more pleasant scent of hay. He couldn't see anything in the dim room but felt his way around the corners and shapes. First, a pitchfork that he nearly knocked over, then a barrel. He found the first nesting box and scrabbled around it with his hands. It was empty, save for the hay. He made his way around the tiny room, feeling first in one box and then another. A few had chickens in them, but most sat along the top, roosting for the night. They were quiet, other than an occasional murmur when he thumped one with his hand.

Finally, the fifth and seventh boxes had what he was looking for. Paul scooped the three eggs into his pockets and retraced his steps in the dark, finding his way out of the coop. From there, he made his way to the dirt road that led further into the woods. He walked for a long time, trying to pick out landmarks from when they'd driven through here in Allan's big Peerless. He recognized the covered bridge but little else in the dim light. About twenty minutes later, Paul found the grassy pull off across from Shiny Creek Trail. Paul had been half-worried he wouldn't be able to find it again. He could see the spot where they'd left Allan's car that day, and when he closed his eyes momentarily, he could hear the voices of Jane and his friends as they'd called to each other, excitedly loading packs onto their backs.

Now, Paul gently laid his own smaller pack down. The air was brisk and the moon was half full, helping him to get his bearings as he gathered sticks. After he'd gotten a small pile, he moved to the edge of the clearing with a clear line to the road and squatted to start layering the sticks and branches. Tonight, he'd dine like a king.

Later, after the fire had died down and Paul had wrapped himself and his knapsack up with the horse blanket, he again went over his next steps. He'd been able to refill the canteen and take a long, satisfying drink from a well in town. That would keep him at least a couple of days if he were careful with it. It would be a two-day hike at least to the cave.

The cave.

More images flooded into Paul's mind at the word. Dark, dank walls. The smell of mustiness and earthy decomposition. The light bouncing from their nickel-plated flashlights on the cave walls. And then, later...

He'd need to get an early start, Paul reminded himself and turned on his side. He drew his knapsack tight to his belly. He shouldn't keep it with him. It could attract any bears who weren't yet in hibernation or other animals to him. But he was too tired to try to hang it from a nearby tree. And anyway, he didn't have any rope. He'd hoped to find some—a laundry line in town—but hadn't had any success.

It would be all right. He was only going to sleep for a couple of hours. He wanted to get an early start.

He was just drifting off, the firm tug of sleep pulling him under when he heard it. A small cry—a mewl really—that snapped his eyes open.

His thoughts instantly went to Jane. He pushed the blanket away, let the knapsack tumble to the ground.

"Jane?" he whispered loudly. "Jane, is that you?"

There was silence for a moment. Then a single branch snapped loudly across the clearing. It sounded like a gunshot in the quiet meadow. Paul swung his head wildly in that direction. His heartbeat crashed in his eardrums. Without moving his eyes from the tree line where the noise had come from, Paul scrabbled a hand over his pack, searching for his flashlight.

He needn't have bothered. At that moment, Paul's eyes connected with the light eyes staring back at him. Paul stared dumbly at the animal. Its fur was golden and even in the dim light of the quarter moon, Paul could see the sharp, yellowed teeth of the catamount. They were latched around the body of a limp rabbit. The small gray creature's head hung loose. Its dead eyes stared as though looking directly at Paul with a warning.

Go back.

Purchase *Silence in the Woods* at your favorite bookshop or online digital retailer.

Also by J.P. Choquette

"Monsters in the Green Mountains" series:
  Silence in the Woods
  Shadow in the Woods
  Under the Mountain

Stand Alone Novels:
  Dark Circle
  Epidemic
  Subversion
  Restitution

About the Author

J.P. Choquette is the author of thriller novels set in Vermont. Her books, "turn pages, not stomachs," and frequently tie in the themes of art, nature, folklore, and psychology. She is a member of International Thriller Writers.

A lover of Gothic books and movies, J.P. enjoys being in nature with her family, spending time in old cemeteries, reading in the garden, and visiting junk shops.

Learn more about the author at her website, www.jpcho-quette.me, where you can grab a free short story.

You can connect with me on:

- http://www.jpchoquette.me
- https://twitter.com/jpchoquett
- https://www.instagram.com/jpchoquette_author

Subscribe to my newsletter:

- http://jpchoquette.me/free-story-newsletter